TWO CITIES

WILLIAM J. PALMER

ANAPHORA LITERARY PRESS

BROWNSVILLE, TEXAS

ANAPHORA LITERARY PRESS
1898 Athens Street
Brownsville, TX 78520
https://anaphoraliterary.com

Book design by Anna Faktorovich, Ph.D.

Published in 2017 by Anaphora Literary Press

Two Cities
William J. Palmer—1st edition.

Library of Congress Control Number: 2017946908

Library Cataloging Information
Palmer, William J., 1943-, author.
    Two cities / William J. Palmer
    256 p. ; 9 in.
    ISBN 978-1-68114-364-4 (softcover : alk. paper)
    ISBN 978-1-68114-365-1 (hardcover : alk. paper)
    ISBN 978-1-68114-366-8 (e-book)
1. Fiction—Thrillers—Political. 2. Nature—Ecology.
3. Political Science—Public Policy—Environmental Policy.
PN3311-3503: Literature: Prose fiction
813: American fiction in English

TWO CITIES

WILLIAM J. PALMER

Other Works by William J. Palmer

Fiction—Novels:

The Detective and Mr. Dickens
The Highwayman and Mr. Dickens
The Hoydens and Mr. Dickens
The Dons and Mr. Dickens
The Wabash Trilogy:
> *The Wabash Baseball Blues*
> *The Redneck Mafia*
> *Civic Theater*

The Uses of Money

Non-Fiction—Books:

The Fiction of John Fowles
Dickens and New Historicism
The Films of the Seventies: A Social History
The Films of the Eighties
The Films of the Nineties: The Decade of Spin

PART ONE

Oil and Water

Chapter One

The Times

*I*t was the most screwed up of times. Not necessarily the best or the worst but definitely dangerous. Terrorism was organized and ruled. Peoples across the Middle East were either rising up against their brutal governments or fleeing them. Refugees slogged their ways westward. In America, the cities were torn apart by crime, ingrown racial hatreds, gangs, homelessness and gunfire in the streets. All the social evils that were supposed to be kept penned up in the cities, especially drugs, were spreading out of their urban ratholes and infecting suburbia like a twenty-first century plague. And the country world of farms and fields and families was the training ground for guerilla militias. Division moved across the country like a growing shadow darkening the national dreams of equality, diversity, and opportunity.

The President and the hapless Congress sat on the thrones of America unable to agree on anything. The doors to the throne rooms were closed to almost everyone, except for the heads of the largest corporations and their representatives who financed election campaigns. In the gathering darkness, the people were marching in the streets and the media were wailing and gnashing their pens and videocams.

In Washington, the Congress was confused, as usual. They believed that the wars and taxes were the issues. But the wars were only to distract the people from the oil scam that the banks and the corporations were running on the country.

In L.A. the people were more angry than anyone else about the country's insatiable desire for more oil. All the bought and paid for pols in Congress had their sights set and all their forces locked and loaded on the potential for Pacific Ocean oil. All that was needed was the go-ahead from Washington, passage of the new offshore drilling bill. But the people were no longer asleep. They sensed how fragile the California ecology had become. They lived their lives on the edge of the earthquake after all. Like the terrorists, they too were beginning to get organized. The eco-troops were forming up, ready to build a line of defense all along the California beaches.

But no one in London or Paris or Washington paid much attention to any of these things because terrorism ruled and gas prices were coming down to spectacularly high lows even though the poles were melting and the oceans warming and the forests dying (or being raped). As the poet said at the beginning of the previous century, things were falling apart and the center could not hold. It was, indeed, the most screwed up of times.

Chapter Two

Two Brothers

*I*t is the last week of April in O'Hare Airport in the heart of the heart of the country and looking out of his airplane window at six AM the runways are dark and slick under a cold and steady rain. Sidney Castle of Tellson, Castle and Hong, Los Angeles, is on the red-eye to Washington, D.C. to get his brother Charlie out of jail. Charlie Castle with his long, blonde surfer hair, his movie-star smile and his creative, metaphorical political rhetoric goes to jail quite often. He is the up-front, on-camera, in-your-face voice of OceanSave, the most activist of all the west coast ecopolitics (some, especially the loggers and the nuclear power plant people, say 'eco-terrorist') groups. At a march, on a picket line, at a protest meeting, or blocking a power plant gate, Charlie is always the one who attracts the cameras and the microphones.

Sidney and Charlie look much alike. In fact, standing beside each other at the defense table in a courtroom, they could easily be mistaken for twins. Sidney's hair is styled and elegant, darker and starting to gray at the temples. Sid is the older brother and it shows around his eyes. At 32, Charlie's eyes are deep set and burning with the intensity of conviction. At 37, Sid's eyes are tired, wise to the world, cold with calculation and sending out tiny wrinkles of worry.

Though they look alike, though both have prestigious law degrees—Charlie's from Georgetown, Sid's from Stanford—the Castle brothers are as different as sandals and Florsheims. While Charlie walks at the front of those who are trying to save the world, Sid spends his life defending those who have made themselves stains on society's surface. While Charlie marches with the young and the hopeful and the involved, Sid defends the rich and famous, the perverse and murderous, the addicted and venal and powerful. While Charlie is the voice of the environment, Sid is the mouthpiece to the damaged stars. Yet when

Charlie goes to jail, Sid is always the first one he calls.

This time it was an Earth Day Rally on the Mall in front of the Lincoln Memorial. Sid saw it all on the network news, though they had to bleep out parts of what Charlie was shouting to the crowd once he got his beloved microphone. This time he called the President a "lying asshole" on national TV, and the crowd went wild, literally. A couple of police cars got tipped over and set on fire. The tear gas floated over Foggy Bottom like the clouds of confused hot air that floated in the Senate and the House of Representatives. The DC police waded into the crowd with nightsticks and flashlights as if they were in Afghanistan or Iraq or Libya or Yemen or Egypt or anywhere else around the world where protest against an unjust government was an issue. They arrested Charlie on an arm-long list of charges ranging from inciting to riot to threatening the President, none of which intimidated Sidney in the least. He'd defended Charlie on all of them or versions of them many times before and the first amendment had not yet failed to win out (and get Charlie out).

Six AM in O'Hare in a bleak spring rain and Sidney's cell phone, only momentarily liberated from "airplane mode" beeps its text-message alert. CALL NOW. JERRY. It is from Jerry Creogan, Sid's limo driver and personal bodyguard. Everyone who is anyone in LA has one, but Sid actually needs one since he deals so intimately with murder, drugs and the animosities of power that stain the LA landscape like dog shit on the beach. Sid marvels that Jerry can even operate a cell phone because his hands are so big and he uses them like sledgehammers to open paths through crowds. Jerry's message is a not uncommon one but its "NOW" command signals a bit more urgency than usual. Without hesitation, Sid returns Jerry Creogan's message.

It rings three times because it is only four AM in LA, and a sleepy Jerry Creogan answers:

"Hullo,"

"Jerry, what?"

"He's out on bail already."

"How? Who?" Sid is genuinely surprised.

"You're not going to believe *this*."

"Try me."

"Congress. Congress bailed him out. He's going to appear before a Congressional committee this afternoon."

"No shit?"

"No shit."

"Why?" Sid is already processing this surprising turn to his brother's political celebrity, but he wants to hear Jerry's version, acquired he presumes straight from Charlie, anyway.

"Charlie thinks they're just doing it to piss off the President."

"Yeah, they're giving him a forum, a bully pulpit."

"You can come home then. That is why I tried to catch you halfway."

"Are you kidding?" It is the first time Sidney has really been amused by anything in weeks. "I wouldn't miss this for the world."

Chapter Three

The Walls of Power

Sid Castle sits in the gallery of the House of Representatives listening to his brother Charlie tear the reigning administration a new one.

"Mr. Castle, just exactly why did you hold your massive rally on the Mall and why is your organization, what is it (turning for help to his young blonde female aide, then consulting his notes), oh yes, OceanSave, why is your organization so terribly hostile toward the present administration?" the questionably Honorable Senator from Massachusetts (and the most vocal critic of the administration no matter what the issue) starts off the whole circus with a question so vague and wide and suggestive that it allows Charlie all the latitude and invitation to say anything he wants. The overly Honorable Senator is laying in a belt-high hanger that has "Hit me out of the park" written all over it.

"Congressman, (then directly to the TV camera) and everyone else around the world who has been watching this administration lay waste to everything that stands in its way," Charlie has no problem hitting the ground running, "Sunday was Earth Day. Three hundred thousand of us marched on the Mall to protest what the President and his oil company cronies are doing to our world."

Sid loves to listen to Charlie talk to crowds. Charlie sculpted his arguments out of all the crimes and cover-ups and corruption in the con games of money and power that the politicians were always playing. Charlie painted the landscapes of his indictments with images of American nature that would give Wordsworth, Edward Abbey and Ansel Adams wet dreams. His best-selling book, *The Death of the Ocean*, had made him enough money to indulge his eco-politics and his surfing to his heart's content. Sid had helped him proofread it because he was the one in the family who could spell. After the book, OceanSave had pursued Charlie like a gigolo on the scent of a rich, beautiful, and wild debutante. They seduced him into being their spokesperson, their talking head. For Charlie it was just too good to be true. He could talk to the world anytime he wanted. The royalties from his book kept rolling in. It had gone global thanks in no small way to his visibility with OceanSave. Sid suspected that his brother was not only speaking out for OceanSave but was also bankrolling some of their projects.

And OceanSave had become a lobby to be reckoned with thanks to more than twenty million dollars in political action money raised in the last year alone. It had more than 200,000 members ready to flood their congressmen and women with emails, texts and personal letters, not to mention being ready to march on Washington or LA or anywhere else at the drop of one of Charlie Castle's rabble-rousing speeches. OceanSave was no small potatoes and they had certainly caught Sid Castle's attention and triggered within him a still imperfectly formed fear that his younger brother was getting in over his idealistic blond head.

As Sid sits high in the gallery listening to Charlie's recitation of the Administration's sins against the environment, the world and the American people, he remembers how he and Charlie used to go surfing together at the Wedge and off the Huntington pier when Charlie was a teenager. He'd taught Charlie to surf and summer afternoons they'd take off by themselves in Sid's pick-up and go look for waves. Strangely enough, they'd never really been competitive. Sid was so much older. There wasn't any macho point really. They'd surf side by side, and when the waves subsided or they'd had enough, sometimes they'd just sit on the beach and talk. About all kinds of things. About where Sid was and where Charlie wanted to go. About California and the ocean and what was happening to it. About books and movies and girls and cars and going to college. Charlie loved to talk. It wasn't so much that Sid was the big brother or the mentor or somebody more powerful than Charlie, but that Sid listened and asked questions (like a good lawyer) that Sid already knew the answers to. But Sid's questions were what gave Charlie a chance to work things out on his own, and they both knew it.

"This President, this sorry excuse for a leader, wants to start tearing the heart out of and draining the life from those natural blessings, those gifts of nature, that give our country all of its meaning and beauty and spiritual value." Charlie is getting to the meat of his subject now and the Congressional committee is just letting him go and the TV cameras are eating it up.

"It's not bad enough that he's laid waste to most of the Middle East in his wars for oil, but now he wants to turn the whole west coast of our own country into a huge oil field." That was what Charlie had come to talk about and that was why his Congressional audience had bailed him out of jail and given him his national podium. Charlie gave them exactly the kind of show they wanted. He delivered his message alright, about the ocean and the environment, but none of them cared about that. What they got out of Charlie was anti-spin against a President that half of them despised. What they got out of Charlie was credibility from an author and leader of the environmental conscience of the country. At their cocktail parties and state dinners and lobbyist lunches, they all called Charlie a tree hugger, an eco-nazi, a Pollyanna, whatever, but they liked his looks and his bad mouth and the fact that he drove the President of the United States crazy. Charlie sure had a way with words alright.

"Like every other generation of Americans, we have to continue to look to the west," Charlie is winding down because he always ended with California and the west coast. "The old monied East of F. Scott Fitzgerald, the blind beltway of all you politicians, the geriatric Florida coast where a wall of high-rise condos blocks everyone off from the ocean, the east has failed America and now Washington is trying to screw up the west too. You can't let it happen. You have to take the west seriously. There's a reason everybody in America, except of course New Yorkers (that drew an embarrassed laugh), wants to live in California. There's all kinds of reasons. Here they are."

As Sid listened to Charlie talk right in the middle of the House of Representatives of the United States of America, the feeling moved through his body like a heat making his face burn with how fiercely proud of his little brother he truly was and of how not so proud of himself he felt.

Chapter Four

Death Threats

Afterwards, outside on the front steps of the Capitol, Sid waits for Charlie to clear the cameras and the questions and the groupies. As he watches Charlie weave through this part of his performance, Sid realizes that his brother is getting to be like some rock star or celebrity gangster constantly dogged by both the legitimate and the illegitimate press, and loving every minute of it, manipulating it to his own uses, spinning the fabric of it out of his own words, ideas, eco-political agendas, a comfortable denizen of the spin generation.

"Get me out of this wasteland," Charlie cries, laughing as he skips down America's steps in flight from the reporters. He grabs Sid by the elbow and propels him downwards. "God, get me out of here. Oh brother, where art thou?"

Sid has to laugh. Charlie loves to talk in movie lines. Others speak English and Spanish, but Charlie opts for what since they were kids they had always called 'Movish.'

"Of all the gin joints in all the yada, yada," Sid laughs in reply as they cut through a small grove of trees and come out on a city street. Sid hails a passing cab and within moments they have made their get-away.

"Who were those guys?" Charlie couldn't resist once they were safely inside the cab.

"Okay Sundance, you can come down off your eco, or should I say 'ego,' horse now. It's just me, your boring brother."

"I know. I know. But somebody's got to say all that stuff to all those people because it's all true. They'll get about half of what I said right when they write it up or cut it for TV. But, hey, half isn't that bad. Maybe a couple of those Congressmen will hear me and vote against the administration's environmental policies. Who knows? Somebody might teach pigs to fly!"

They both cracked up. Sid suddenly felt how good it was to be sequestered in a cab driving across Washington with his brother. Charlie could make anyone feel better no matter what their malaise.

"Seriously Sid, you gotta get me outta here. This place got scary this weekend."

"What happened? Did they rough you up in jail? I can..."

"No. No. They know better by now. They know I've got the best lawyer in America for a brother. Hell, nobody messes with me. No, it was in the streets where it got ugly. Sixty-eight Democratic Convention ugly. Civil Rights Marches ugly. Egypt and Syria ugly. The cops came after us with nightsticks and flashlights and dogs and tear gas. Who knows, I think they're just looking for an excuse to make it Kent State ugly. And if they start shooting I'm gonna go down because I'm the one marching in the front row."

"You really think it's that bad?" Sid had trouble, as did a lot of other uninvolved or disconnected Americans, putting the burgeoning ecology movement on the same plane with the Civil Rights Marches or the Vietnam War Protests of a half-century past.

"It was this weekend. Washington was like a powder keg. We've never had numbers like this for a march before. There must have been four hundred thousand on the Mall on Sunday."

"That oughta sell a lot of books."

"Screw you. The eco groups are finally starting to get organized, to work together. There were so many people I think the cops panicked. That's why it got ugly."

"So what's the big deal. The cops have broken up your rallies before. Hell, it's not the first tear gas you've run into."

"I know. I know. But this time it felt different. Like they were really out to hurt us, to scare us off. I could see people dying out there. Luckily, no one did this time. But it's gonna happen. I think somebody's trying to kill me, Sid."

"Whoa now, whoa down little brother, we talking generically as in cops in crowds or are you saying someone's trying to kill you, you personally."

"I don't know." Charlie is uncharacteristically serious for this moment. "I don't know whether to take this stuff seriously or not."

"What stuff?"

"Last Friday I got this, and then Saturday, the day before the rally, I got this one." Charlie pulls two envelopes out of his back jeans pocket and passes them to Sid. "Read them in order. I thing they're from the same guy."

ECONAZI, YOU LAUGH AT OUR PRESIDENT NOW, BUT HE GETS THE LAST LAUGH WHEN YOU DIE. This first note was crafted out of the usual assortment of mismatched letters clipped from a glossy magazine.

TOMORROW AT THE RALLY WE'LL COME FOR YOU. SAY GOODBYE, the second wolfish note read.

"Looks like pretty run-of-the-mill crazy script to me," Sid tries to talk the threatening letters away. "You've gotten crap like this from nut-cases before."

"Yeah, I know. You're right. But this time it just doesn't feel right. That's why I want out of here now. I need some time to chill, to get out of the public eye for a while. This place is like that circle in Dante's hell where they punish you for all your sins of pride."

Sid had to give his little brother credit for seeing things clearly. Charlie knew that if he hadn't made himself so visible, hadn't put himself out front with all the cameras and the reporters, hadn't said the rabble-rousing things he always said, that assassins wouldn't be stalking him now, that he wouldn't be getting death threats in the mail, that he wouldn't be on the 'ten most hated' list of Right Wing talk radio. For some reason Sid thinks suddenly of John Lennon, and that's when he starts taking Charlie seriously.

"Okay, what if I get Jerry Creogan to bodyguard you for a few weeks. He's the best. Nobody will get to you with him on your side."

"No, no, you need Jerry. Probably more people want to kill you than me. I just want to drop outa sight for awhile."

The taxi pulls up at the Belle Terre, the tiny, elegant European bed-and-breakfast hotel with the hanging garden, buried in the back streets off of Dupont Circle. Charlie wasn't so dumb. He always stayed there because it was virtually unfindable, so far off the beaten track that neither paparazzi nor hit men could find it and ambush him. Sid approved. Not much that Charlie did was low profile, but this hotel was. Sid had been staying there for over fifteen years and his fast-talking had convinced the Italian owners that Charlie, long hair, media bad boy image, and all, was an acceptable guest.

They keep talking as they enter the hotel and go straight through the tiny lobby to the garden.

"Jerry can take care of that. He can find you a safe house and staff it around the clock."

"No, not Jerry, not yet, maybe if this death threat shit gets deeper. I had something else in mind."

They sit at a small table by the grape arbor in the garden. Mrs. Angeletti takes their order for two bottled beers.

"What?" Sid asked.

"Let's rent a car and drive back to LA together."

"Are you nuts? You can't jump bail. I don't care if the Congress of the United States did bail you out."

"Screw them. The DC cops will drop the charges. You'll see to that. You're the best lawyer in America. Thank god I've got you or none of the stuff I've got to do would ever get done. You're why I don't care if I get arrested once a month."

"You jump bail, it'll make you a fugitive."

"It's not as if I haven't been a fugitive all my life."

"Yeah, you have jumped bail before."

"See. Now you're feeling it. Let's rent a car and drive."

"Car? I've got clients."

"They can wait. It's only four or five days."

"I can't drive to LA with you. It would take a week. I've got other clients."

"C'mon. Do it, Sid. You haven't taken a vacation in years. Turn off the cell phone. Put a 'Gone Fishin' sign on the Century City office door. Go for a ride with your brother."

"Drive all the way from here to LA. I just can't go off the map like that."

"Sure you can, and besides, I need you to drive so I can run the camera."

"Camera? What the hell are you talking about?"

"Look. Think about it. The cross country trip. We'll talk more about it tomorrow. I'll let you keep your cell phone on, okay."

"It's crazy."

"No. It'll be cool. Trust me. Just you and me again, Butch and Sundance, making a run for the coast. Now go get out of that suit. Try to look like a normal person. We've got a big night ahead of us."

"Fasten your seat belt. We're in for a bumpy ride?" Sid smiles as he mimics Bette Davis.

"Naw, just some good country rock and you get to meet the twosome in my life."

"Two?"

"That's what I said, Sidney my boy. Man, you need to get out more."

Chapter Five

Alison in Wonderland

As fast as Charlie can change into a less raggedy pair of designer jeans and Sid can swap his dark suit for a silk button-down shirt the color of glossy rust, they are in another cab, on the go across Washington again.

"We're hitting *Elmo's* in Georgetown. There's a country rock band playing there tonight that will knock your California socks off."

"Country rock? What's that all about?"

"May the force be with you," Charlie smiles and winks. "Washington is a country kind of town these days since this administration has been in office. But that's not why this band is cool."

"I give. Why is this band so cool?"

"Because of their politics, Sid, their politics."

"What politics? I thought all country music cared about was pickup trucks and dogs."

"Forget it, Sid, its Washington," Charlie mocks his older brother in Movish. "You ever hear of the Dixie Chicks?"

"We're going to see the Dixie Chicks?"

"Nope, but the next best thing, even more radical chic."

"Very funny," Sid resigned himself to Charlie's whimsy. "But why a country rock club? Why not dinner in a nice Georgetown restaurant like *Avondale* or *Ruggierio's*."

"Because we're meeting Alison there and I want you to meet the band. We're all working together."

Sid has to laugh. "Working together. You have all the musical talent of a chainsaw. I remember when you tried to learn the guitar. It sounded like bad bagpipes!"

"There's good bagpipes?"

"Who is Alison?"

"You'll like her. She's a lawyer too, like us."

"You're not a lawyer. You're some kind of media eco-freak."

"Wait 'til you meet the Headhunters if you think I'm an eco-freak." Charlie is having a good old time with his up-tight, legal eagle older brother. He's managed in the brief passing of their cross-town cab ride to pretty thoroughly confuse Sidney. Only when they pull up in front of the rock club does the web of gibberish that Charlie has been spinning start to make any sense.

"M.D. Farrow and the Headhunters

Live Nightly"

the neon lights of *Elmo*'s marquee trumpets to the streets. A stunning tall girl with dark auburn hair, broad athlete's shoulders, clear green eyes and a radiant smile stands at the curb well away from the line-up of wannabe clubbers at *Elmo*'s door.

"There she is," Charlie points.

Usually when Sid first looked at any pretty girl his guy eyes naturally focused on her physical attractions: her breasts, her legs, her figure in that order. But this woman is different. Her smile when she sees Charlie waving to her from the window of the cab is like the sun coming out at night. Her smile makes Sid sit up and pay attention.

He has to hand it to his younger brother. Charlie knows a pretty girl when he sees one.

"That has to be Alison, right," Sid grumbles at Charlie who is already out of the cab and wrapping his arms around her, leaving Sid to pay. "And the Headhunters are the band," Sid grumbles to the cabbie as he counts out the money. "And I always get stuck with the check," Sid grumbles to himself as he climbs out of the backseat and steps over the curb to meet Charlie's latest love.

The two of them are beaming at Sid as if just seeing each other had switched on the moon and the stars in their young faces.

"Alison, this is my big brother."

"Mister Castle, it's a..."

"Sidney, no Sid, please," he interrupts her.

"It's great to meet you. Charlie has told me all about you, and I've followed your trials just like everyone else in America."

"Ah, Charlie tells me you're a lawyer too."

"And an accountant," Charlie cuts in before she can answer.

"Ah, three lawyers and an accountant out on the town," Sid tries to make a joke of it, "we'll be lucky if nobody takes a shot at us tonight."

"In Washington there are so many lawyers," Alison laughs, "that we've got all the people who think we're sleazeballs and shysters outnumbered."

"Even if they do have us outgunned," Charlie puts in his two cents of social commentary.

"Boy, look at that line to get in," Sid, who really didn't have much interest in spending the night in a country rock club, tries to hide the hopefulness in his voice that their plans might change.

Alison smiles knowingly, but Charlie just laughs at Sid's naiveté: "Give me some credit, brother. You think you're out with a couple of wannabes? C'mon, no problem."

Taking both Alison and Sid by the arm, he waltzes them up to the huge bouncer dressed all in black: black turtleneck to black slacks to dark sunglasses right down to his skin. The man looks like the incarnation of midnight. But as soon as this towering, scowling prince of darkness sees Charlie, he bursts into a sparkling toothy grin and leaps to detach the velvet rope so that Charlie and his guests can pass directly through.

"Good evening Mister Castle, go right on in. They're expecting you. Way to give them hell this afternoon." The demonic gatekeeper is evidently a political observer.

"Thanks Terry. This is my brother Sid. He's got the twenty dollars I owe you. If he doesn't give it to you right away, I'd like you to break his thumbs."

With that Charlie and Alison disappear into the club leaving Sid fumbling in his pocket under the bemused eye of the hulking bouncer.

"He doesn't really owe you twenty bucks, does he Terry?"

"Nah, not really."

"Does he do this to everybody he brings here?"

"Yeah, pretty much."

"Why do you let him in?"

"Because he's a good tipper."

"Yeah, right," Sid has to laugh as he hands over the twenty.

"And he knows the band," Terry grins at Sid as he pockets the twenty.

Just for a split second Sid indulges himself with speculation on what Jerry Creogan would do to this Washington bouncer in a fight.

Inside, Sid catches up with Charlie and Alison at the bar. To his surprise, it is actually quiet though crowded in the club. The bar is three deep and most of the tables around the dance floor are filled, but the lights are low and the usual writhing chaos of a city dance club hasn't kicked in yet. But it is early and the band isn't due for another fifteen minutes.

"You still drinking beer?" Charlie asks, and when Sid nods yes, Charlie orders him two Coronas. He and the girl are drinking Vodka and something light orange.

"Over here," Charlie steers Sid by the elbow through the tables on the edge of the dance floor to one right next to the stage with a "Reserved" card on it. "I know the band," Charlie winks, as they sit down.

"So Alison," Sid makes the first polite foray into conversation, "what do you do here in Washington? What kind of law do you practice?"

"She's a whistle-blower," Charlie answers for her gleefully. "She is a fugitive from the oil barons, from Amerigas."

"Are you about finished?" she slashes the words at him, clearly not amused.

This one seems like something more than the eye-candy Charlie has dated in the past, the sharp tone of her voice shoots that flash intuition across Sid's mind.

Charlie shuts up and an awkward silence falls over the table.

"I take it you don't work for Amerigas anymore," Sid breaks it.

"No. Now I work for OceanSave and I must say the money was a lot better with Amerigas."

"She's a rising star. She really is," Charlie isn't being flip this time, is probably trying to placate her so that he can get her into his bed later in the night. "She pulled the plug on the shady accounting practices at Amerigas. She's why the Amerigas CEO is appearing before a federal grand jury this week."

Sid ignores Charlie. He wants to hear the girl tell it. He really wants to see what she is made of. "Did you blow this whistle as an accountant or as a lawyer?" It isn't a true lawyer's question because he only suspects the answer, doesn't know it.

"As a lawyer," Alison answers before Charlie can butt in again.

"And an accountant," Charlie butts in despite her efforts (and Sid realizes that maybe for the first time in his life his brother is actually impressed by a woman rather than simply desirous of her).

"How did it happen?" Sid coaxes her. "How did you become an accountant, a lawyer and a Washington whistle-blower so young?" He can see in her face that she likes the way he has posed the question.

"I started out as an accountant, right out of Notre Dame. Worked as an auditor for a big six firm in New York for almost five years. But I was going to law school at night at NYU. When I graduated I got a job with Amerigas here in Washington, in their legal department, not as an accountant. But I hung out with some of the accountants. We were in the same building in Arlington, played tennis together, coed softball. Then one night, late, in a bar, one of the girls, an auditor like I had been, broke down and started crying. She said her boss was asking her to do stuff she didn't want to do."

She stops to take a sip of her drink

"Sexual harassment?" Sid states the obvious.

"That's the first thing I thought too," Alison talks around her straw, "but no, that wasn't it. She said that her boss, the head of the accounting department, was asking her to violate legal accounting procedures. To manipulate the stock price, she thought. She told me how he would come out of the closed door meetings with the CEO and CFO and immediately start asking for finished audit reports that he would go over and change then bring back to her to sign off on."

"Did she sign them?" Sid prompts her.

"She'd recheck them and they were wrong, inflated, but he would insist they were right and he was a partner and he ordered her to sign off. She was afraid she'd done something really wrong, like felony wrong, and she didn't want to go to jail."

"That's where Alison came in," Charlie can't keep himself from bragging about her. "That girl sure picked the right lawyer to open up to."

"What did you do?" Sid wants to hear the rest of the story.

"For six months the two of us collected paper, everything the executives made her sign. Then we took it to the SEC and they took it to a Grand Jury. The scary thing is that Amerigas is the President's favorite oil company, one of his biggest campaign contributors. Securities fraud in a corporation that big is one thing but going all the way to the Vice-President who used to be a lobbyist for Amerigas and maybe even the President is another thing altogether."

"I'd say so," now Sid knows why Charlie is so impressed. "Could it really go that far?"

"Only if there's evidence of some sort of a government cover-up or some sort of special treatment for the corporation or its officers. Probably not, but... who knows? Of course, I got out of there as soon as we gave the case to the SEC, so did Charlotte the accountant."

"How did you hook up with OceanSave?"

"They were the only ones that would take us both. No one in Washington wants to touch a whistle-blower. They're the worst kind of Judas in the old boy system. But OceanSave came to us. I was just about ready to go back to Chicago when OceanSave contacted me through a headhunter. They were great. I worked a deal for both of us."

"And that's where we met, at OceanSave," Charlie beams. "I asked her out before I even knew she was a superstar."

"The CEO of Amerigas called me a 'traitorous bitch' outside the SEC hearing room. He sure didn't think I was a superstar."

"Hey, consider the source," Charlie laughs. "From the likes of that crook it was a compliment. Here's the band."

Chapter Six

Headhunting

"*L*adies and Gentlemen, Senators and Congressmen, Lobbyists and Hookers, Staffers and Staffettes, Lawyers and all other assorted D.C. night-people, let's hear it for the hottest political rockers in Washington, M.D. Farrow and the Headhunters."

The band takes the stage in a rush, playing their instruments on the move with a rockabilly almost bluegrass sort of sound. The guitarist is a pretty boy of the curly-haired, open-shirted, achy-breaky sort. He immediately commandeers one of the two vocalist's mikes. The bass player is such a skinny, desiccated specimen of human waste that he would make Keith Richards look healthy. The drummer is just flat, balls-out strange looking, sort of like Animal from the Muppets with Buddy Rich's overbite. Those are the Headhunters and they are all hair and unshaven chins and jeans and boots and vests (but no cowboy hats, thank god) and they play hard for about three minutes before M.D. Farrow saunters up onto the stage, removes the microphone from its stand as if caressing an erect phallus, and starts to sing:

> Shorebreaks are my bass line,
> Seabirds sing my song,
> The ocean writes my lyrics,
> Seducing me to sing along.

Her voice is deep and throaty, caressing the words as if they were glistening grains of sand running through her fingers. Her voice speeds up into a plaintive wail, almost hymn-like as she prowls the front of the stage:

> The waves' white foam
> Breaks across the sea-beach of my mind.

The Ocean is my Holy Place
Never, ever, left behind.

The guitar player keys a rolling bridge that the bass and the drums
pick up, throbbing her into the chorus:

Water, wind, air and sky,
Sunrise and sunset,
Eyes and heart and the gentle sounds
I never can forget.
The ocean is my Holy Place,
So cool and free and pure,
No matter when, no matter how,
The ocean must endure.

The singer and the band drive and pulse their way through three
more verses, speeding up then slowing to a desperate hopeful plea in
the choruses almost as if Elvis had met Wordsworth for a gospel sing
in heaven.

M.D. Farrow is a different kind of rock star alright. Sid senses that
from the moment she takes the stage. Diminutive, almost childlike,
thin as a wraith, yet with intense flashing eyes that are older and angry.
Her hair is jet black and she never smiles at all. Her eyes are darkly
rimmed but her lips are bright red. She looks like a Goth hillbilly. As
Sid watches her in the throes of song-birth, he realizes that she is older,
tougher, more guttural than her small size at first signals. She delivers
the lyrics as if they are a plaintive prayer, a desperate ultimatum. When
the song ends she seems to collapse inward as if the deliverance of her
message has sapped all of her strength and left her hollow.

She takes a long moment to collect herself.

"M.D. is something else, isn't she?" Charlie leans into Sid's ear.
"She claims she's invented a whole new style of music. She calls it eco-
rock."

Sid nods, but can't take his eyes off the dark presence on the stage.
Even as she fights to catch her breath, she glares out into the darkness,
challenging the invisible audience.

"That was *Holy Place*. You've all heard it before. But this isn't a
damn funeral even if that monster in the White House up the street
wants it to be. C'mon, let's dance, like the Druids did under the great

trees, and our Native-American sisters and brothers did on the beaches of our great lakes and oceans. This one's a Washington song. It oughta git you movin'. One, two, three and..."

And the Headhunters launch into a swing dance thumper that gets the people out of their chairs and onto the floor. As far as Sid can tell it is a song about *"marchin' up the river to hand the man his head/marchin' 'til we change things here or all of us are dead."*

Not very happy lyrics those, Sid thinks to himself, but the band plays the song like they are at a rockabilly barndance.

"Eco-rock, eh? It's different alright. I'll give her that," Sid answers Charlie as the dance floor fills up and the two-steppers and the flailers start competing for exhibitionist space.

"I like to mess with her. I call it John Denver on speed," Charlie laughs.

"Yeah, with a touch of 'Kill my landlord' thrown in I'd say."

"I like M.D.'s music," Alison is much more serious than the brothers Castle. "Her lyrics are worth listening to, not like most of the repetitive rock crap or the ugly, misogynist rap stuff that you hear. Her words actually say something."

"Does she write it all herself?" Sid asks.

"Every word," Charlie brags, "with musical help from that skinny little piece of crap Wrig Jones, believe it or not."

Sid decides that Charlie is referring to the gray-skinned, hollow-eyed bass player who looks like he is about to keel over from either malnutrition or emphysema.

As the set wails on, the dance floor becomes an eclectic combination of a gyrating barndance and a sing-along choir.

"What's your connection to this M.D. Farrow?" Sid's curiosity finally kicks in.

"You don't know! You've really never heard of her?" Charlie's tone makes Sid feel as if he is so ignorant or so far out of it (or so old) that he is beneath contempt.

"Uh, no. Sorry, but I don't spend a lot of time searching the radio dial in the limo for the latest eco-rock," Sid answers with dyspeptic sarcasm.

"She's on the Board of OceanSave," Alison steps in between the brothers like a referee. "She's the head of the OceanSave political action committee and I work for her."

"In fact, M.D. introduced me to Alison," Charlie adds brightly.

"In that case, Charlie boy, you should be eternally grateful to her and Alison should probably damn her to the lowest circle of match-maker's hell."

Alison cracks up while Charlie tries to figure out what his brother has just said.

"M.D. is a good boss," Alison tells Sid between songs. "She is an incredibly intense person. She never goes anywhere without her lap-top. It seems like she's always typing things into it—ideas, song lyrics, names, addresses, notes."

"Yeah, mostly people she wants me to go talk to, I'd say," Charlie mock-complains.

"Actually, right now about all we talk about is L.A. The plans are already underway for next year's Earth Day march and rally. M.D. is in charge of the planning," Alison picks the thread back up.

"It's going to be in L.A., not Washington?" Sid is surprised.

"That's right. 'From the Tar Pits to the Sea' that's the logo she wants to use to spotlight the pollution of the ocean by the big oil companies."

"Why L.A.?"

"M.D. says we'll get twice as many people there. Maybe a million protest marchers. It'll be the biggest eco-march ever. They'll march to the Santa Monica pier."

"You sound like you like working for her and for OceanSave."

"I believe in what they're doing. It's not really law, mostly research actually. Sometimes I feel more like a private detective than a lawyer. But in her position M.D. needs a lot of information to fuel her lobby-ing efforts and political action strategies."

"Wouldn't you rather be practicing law in a regular firm?" Sid doesn't know why he is pressing her so hard. Probably because Charlie actually seems serious about this one.

"Oh, headhunters sometimes come after me now, prestigious lib-eral D.C. law firms, since we tipped the SEC to Amerigas. But this is what I do. I learned that at Amerigas. I learned to hate those corporate gangsters who think they own the world. With OceanSave I can actu-ally do something to make their life miserable, like they did for my accountant friend Charlotte."

It has gotten real quiet in the club. The band has left the stage and M.D. Farrow has taken the microphone all by herself. She has pulled up a stool to the front of the stage, adjusted the mike down to her small stature, and quieted the crowd with a silent, penetrating stare.

"This is the last song of the set and I'm gonna go acoustic for it. I wrote it when that warmonger in the White House invaded his last country. It's called 'Oil Whores, Bad Wars.'"

She starts to sing in that deep throaty voice and a hush moves through the packed-in mob in the club. Sid wouldn't have called it a rock or a country song. It is more of a folk protest song of the sort that hadn't really shown its face in America since Dylan and Baez back in the sixties of the last century. The redneck right wing has their super-patriotic, jingoistic, hillbilly paeans to America in splendid and smug isolation from the rest of the planet, so M.D. must have decided to counterpunch with some songs of her own about the realities of America.

Oil rich sands in foreign lands
His lust for oil prevails
While brave men die
And Mothers cry
And the night is pierced with lovers' wails.
(refrain) Oil whores, bad wars,
Can't separate the two.
The thieves and thugs that
Run our world
Never, ever, think of me and you.

Her song is any angry indictment, a plaintive howl. Sid can see how Charlie's whistleblower girlfriend could be attracted to M.D.'s militant anti-corporate mindset. Corporate whoredom could be the rallying cry of a whole new protest generation and M.D. Farrow aspired to be that generation's Dylan. Maybe eco-rock was not quite as silly a concept as Sidney Castle had first thought.

"Wow!" Charlie is the first to start clapping.

"That's a great song," Alison is clapping too.

"She certainly does have a presence," Sid says, but nobody hears him because the whole audience in the club is on their feet and clapping wildly.

M.D. Farrow just sits there on her stool with her head bowed as if the song has utterly sapped all of her strength. When they finish clapping, she stands up and looks out over the crowd with those probing black eyes as if trying to find her enemies. Then, she leaves the stage.

"C'mon," Charlie orders, ushering them both up from their seats at the stage-side table, "I want you to meet her Sid. She's a trip."

Sid isn't all that certain that he needs much more of a trip this night, but he follows along obediently as Charlie leads them backstage.

Others have beaten them to the throne of adulation. M.D. is sitting in a director's chair against a blank black wall with her lap-top computer already on her lap. A distinguished-looking 60-ish, silver-haired man in a thousand dollar Italian silk suit flanked by two 30-ish junior executives similarly but less expensively suited is handing her his business card and protesting way too much about how passionately he enjoyed her music.

He doesn't look like the eco-rock type, Sid can't help thinking as they wait for the suits to finish their audience with the dark queen. M.D. seems amused by the whole thing as she takes the distinguished gentleman's card and shakes his fawning hand.

"What's with the lap-top?" Sid whispers in Alison's ear.

"She never goes anywhere without it," Alison whispers back. "Major computer jock. She does everything with it. She's already programmed a CAD model of the Santa Monica Pier."

"She writes all her songs on it," Charlie gets in his two cents.

Sid notices that as soon as the three suits drift away, M.D. immediately enters the name and information on the business card into her computer.

Chapter Seven

In the Middle

"I meant it about driving to L.A.," Charlie had said as they left the rock club the night before. They had parted at the curb, Charlie and his girl taking one cab off to be by themselves, and Sid taking another back to the Belle Terre. He had slept well and hadn't given another thought to how he was returning to L.A.

Now Sid is sitting in the hanging garden under a gas heater eating breakfast when Charlie comes in all radiant lover's smiles and sunny morning enthusiasm. He doesn't even give Sid a chance to swallow his melon slices before he launches into his sales pitch.

"Hey, big brother, c'mon, let's pack up and head for L.A. We can rent a car right down on Dupont Circle. Go pack. I'll get the car and come back and pick you up."

"Whoa. Slow down firedog. I can't drive to L.A. It'll take four days."

"Maybe longer. That's the beauty of it." Charlie is gobbling the berries and banana slices off of Sid's plate.

"Charlie, I've got clients. I need to be back."

"No you don't. Two of the days are weekend. You know as well as I do that nothing happens in court on Mondays."

"You're out on bail. You leave and that makes you a fugitive."

"C'mon Sid. You're my lawyer. You know they're gonna drop those charges. Hell, the Natural Resources Committee of the House of Representatives bailed me out. Man, they've got great coffee here.

"OK, OK, you're probably right. But I can't do it. I've got clients."

"They're not clients. They're movie star dopers and child molesters and celebrity murderers. Man, I'd say a week off from your freak show is long overdue."

"I can't just go off the map like that."

"That's exactly what it's all about, Sid. Don't you see? It's the map. You won't be going off the map. For a change you'll be getting on the map."

Sid just stared at him. He had no idea what Charlie was saying.

"That's the problem. You're the problem with America, Sid. All you professional types. The people who make the decisions in the country. You're all in Washington or L.A. You don't know America. All you ever do is fly over it."

"So this is about America? I don't have anything to do with America?" Sid cringes when he hears himself saying that, not only because it is true and marks him as a cynical, uninvolved, materialist freeloader, but because he can see his comment igniting Charlie's face with evangelical ardor.

"Brother, you're my lawyer; you've got everything to do with America. I'm gonna show you America, OK? By car, OK? Hell, I won't even make you drive the whole time. No limo with your goon..."

"He's not a goon."

"Whatever. Just me and you in a... hey, in a Chevy. Remember those commercials when we were kids: 'See the USA in your Chevrolet.'" Charlie's enthusiasm is like a flash flood carrying Sid helplessly away.

"Just you and me in a Chevy in baseball caps. You can even leave your cell phone on if you have to, and I'm taking a videocam. I'm gonna film our trip across America. I'll use the footage the next time I talk to Congress."

Chapter Eight

Nightmare

*B*ack in L.A., Jerry Creogan is just finishing dinner. He's in *Duke's* in Malibu and has just polished off a sea bass in a Mexican vegetable sauce. His boss's black towncar is parked outside in the limo section of the lot and his cell phone sits glowing on the table next to the remains of the sea bass. Under his black jacket, his short-barreled .38 rests in its shoulder holster. When he left for Washington, Sidney Castle gave Jerry C. (as the other drivers and gunmen call him) a list of four things (besides manning the cell phone 24-7) to do. Jerry had spent the last three days working on them and three were done.

Jerry has a talent for digging people up who either have buried themselves alive or have been driven underground by people who don't want them around. It is just one of Jerry's many talents, all involved with violence of one strain or another. But unearthing people who are hiding out or trying to stay uninvolved is perhaps the most useful of Jerry's talents to Sid's particular needs as one of the two or three A-list criminal defense lawyers in Los Angeles. Often the people involved in Sidney Castle's cases were so rich, so famous, so powerful, or so connected that they really could make people disappear or at least want to disappear. That's where Jerry Creogan so often came in.

He had found the gift for digging up these *desaparicidos* in the five years he spent as a bounty hunter when he was a young man. That is how Sid had first met him and grown to admire the violent economy of Jerry's methods of finding people and convincing them that it was in their best interest to accommodate him. Early on, Sid became acquainted with Jerry on a freelance basis, but when Sid started to get famous, his cases more high profile, he had hired Jerry full-time as his driver, bodyguard, finder of missing (or hiding) persons, but most importantly, over time, his sounding board and only real friend.

Sid had been divorced for almost four years. In his business there had never been much time for dating. He'd had a couple of what the women involved had relentlessly (or hopefully or desperately) called 'relationships,' but for him they had never gotten far beyond the 'I have fun with you and we're pretty good in bed together' stage. He often wondered if what had happened between him and Beth had made it impossible for him to ever have a relationship again. That's why it was so good to have Jerry around because he knew at the end of the day when he got in the car or in the middle of the day when he had to go somewhere to see someone that Jerry would be there to talk to him as if he were a real person not the best and most expensive attorney in L.A. Then, of course, there was the time that Jerry had saved his life. Sid paid Jerry well, but the two of them had a relationship a lot closer than employer/employee. Jerry was like Sid's other brother and Jerry was Sid's only friend.

Jerry is still sitting at *Duke's,* nursing his coffee, stalling, trying to find a way to avoid doing the fourth thing that Sid had asked him to do. In the last two days since Sid had been gone Jerry had crossed the first three off the list, but the fourth one was still there and he looked at it with dread. In the last three days Jerry had driven down to Newport Beach to get a retired NBA player's signature on an affidavit stating that he had seen the female movie star in question leave his party at a certain time. Next he had driven out into the valley to find the car salesman ex-husband of a female wrestler who allegedly strangled her agent with her bare hands. This was a simple attestation that his ex had worked as a prostitute, stripper and mud wrestler in Las Vegas before relocating to L.A., bulking up and entering the grunt and hug business. Those two had been as easy as pie for Jerry, but his third customer lived in a rusted-out trailer behind a bean field up in Ventura County. He was a skinny little man who couldn't have weighed more than 115 pounds soaking wet, but when Jerry asked him to sign a paper attesting to a simple fact about a family member, the man went postal.

The basketball player was bigger than Jerry though not in better shape and had been very personable and cooperative. The car salesman was about as average a human being as Jerry had ever encountered and signed the brief statement of fact with a sullen despair that befit his buried life in an auto mall under the freeway. But the greasy little weasel was the meanest thing in southern California next to the rattlesnakes in the ditch lines. Jerry asked him politely and the little rat tried to stab him with a snap-open about eight inches long. Jerry broke his arm taking the knife away from him and then broke three of the fingers on his non-signing hand before he got his signature attesting to his brother's heroine addiction.

This fourth chore on the list, though, was different than the others, touchier. Jerry dreaded doing it because he had done it before and it had never gone well. Sidney had asked him to deliver some money to Sidney's ex-wife Beth. Jerry would rather have gone up against the skinny weasel with the knife any day.

Beth hated Jerry because Beth hated Sid, and Jerry was the only contact Beth had with Sid. Jerry didn't hate Beth. He actually understood pretty well why she acted the way she did, why she drank so much, and why she would tear off into a caustic firestorm whenever he showed up at her door. He had a cousin who was bi-polar and had actually talked to him about it, about the medicine for it, about how it made people think. After the first time that she had attacked Jerry, Sid had told him about Beth's case and what the depression did to her. Sid told him right away not to take it personally, that it was him that she was really striking out against, not Jerry. Nevertheless, Jerry still dreaded these monthly incursions up Topanga Canyon to the rundown shack around a curve across a muddy ditch where Beth Castle was methodically drinking herself to death.

According to Sid, she had been a legal secretary when they met— smart, ambitious, eager to learn, quite beautiful—working for another lawyer in the office where he had started off. Sid, totally sober, had told Jerry all of this the day he had reported back from delivering the first alimony payment. Sid sent the cash by personal courier via Jerry because Beth never opened her mail. She just threw it away as if it was an invasion from the outside world or was laced with anthrax. He sent Jerry with cash because Beth had become a virtual hermit and if he gave her a check she never cashed it. Sid had been married to Beth for three years. She had never told him about the depression before they got married and he had never checked her medicine cabinet to see what she was on. Jerry was a Sherlock Holmes fan and that would have been the first thing he would have done.

Jerry Creogan finishes his coffee, leaves a good tip and heads the car out of *Duke's*. Driving up the canyon, he steels himself for the names she's going to call him, the low slurs on his manhood and his intelligence she's going to scream at him, the scary things she threatens to do to Sid if she ever sees him again, the desperate and pathetic tears she's going to shed as she takes the money. As he pulls across the metal bridge over the slimy ditch in front of her shack, he wishes one last time for a man spoiling for a fight to answer the door, a big strong guy that he could easily subdue instead of the pitiful drunken harridan with whom he knew he was going to have to deal.

There are no lights on in the house when he pulls up, but that isn't a good indicator of anything. He knows that she often sits in the dark, drinking, hating the world (or terribly fearful of it). Sid has told him how within months of their honeymoon, she had started to change, how he had gradually learned that the woman he had married was really someone else. '*American Gothic* meets *Dr. Jekyll and Mr. Hyde*,' Jerry remembered Sid describing it in that strange Movie-Speak that he and his brother used a lot. "You remember in *Alien* how that monster explodes right out of the guy's chest," Sid has described his ex-wife's rages against him. Strangely though, and this was what Jerry had the hardest time understanding, Sid never blamed Beth or Beth's illness or Beth's rages for their breakup. Sid always blamed himself each time, once a month, when he got his report from Jerry on Beth's condition up in her canyon cabin. That was really why Sid sent the money up with Jerry. He wanted someone he could trust to look at her, speak to her, make sure she was OK (or as close to OK as she could ever be)..

Why me? Jerry thinks as he climbs up on her porch in the dark and knocks on the cheap, hollow door.

No answer right away.

Maybe she's passed out, he thinks, but he knows he can't just shove the envelope full of bills under her door. She'd claim she never got it, call the sheriff to harass Sid for her alimony money that she'd thrown away or hidden.

Jerry knocks again, still no answer.

Jerry knows she's in there, probably drunk, sitting in the dark. But it's not like her to not come to the door because she so enjoys calling Jerry names—"Oh, it's Sid's errand boy" or "Oh, Jerry, you still Sid's pimp"—and telling him what she thinks of her ex-husband. But to-night, for some reason, she's not leaping at the opportunity to scream obscenities at Jerry.

Jerry tries another volley of knocks and when she still doesn't show up at the door he knows something is wrong and he knows he can't leave without finding out and reporting it back to Sid. He tries the door. Locked. He circles the house. The back door is locked too, but a slider on a little side porch is open.

The smell of death hits him as soon as he is inside the pitch black-ness of the house. He feels his way through the living room to a lamp, but Beth is not in her usual drinking chair. He finds her in the bathtub, naked, dead, her head stuck in a large dark halo of congealed blood.

How am I gonna tell Sid this? Jerry's first thought signals where his loyalties lie. Sid had been predicting something like this happening to Beth for months. The booze kept the medicine from working (when she remembered to take it) and Beth had been sinking deeper and deeper into her alcoholic underworld of hate. "Give her the money. It's all she's got. She won't talk to me. All she does is scream obscenities at me. But check her out. Tell me if we need to take her out of that Ten-nessee Williams world she's built for herself up there in the canyon." *He saw this coming and now she's dead,* Jerry thinks. *Damn, how am I gonna tell him this?*

Jerry doesn't touch a thing. He calls 911 on the cell phone. 10:30 on a Tuesday night and it takes the county sheriffs and the morgue truck almost half an hour to come up the canyon. He waits outside on the rickety porch. He's been driving Sid to crime scenes for years. He knows the drill, knows exactly what questions they will ask. It is obvi-ous what happened. She was trying to take a shower, fell, hit her head, bled out. An accident.

Jerry knew that the facts of it didn't really make any difference. Sid would still blame himself, would still think inside his most pri-vate thoughts that there was something he should have done. But Jerry knew different. He was the one who visited her every month. She had been dead for years.

Chapter Nine

Shooting America

*W*ithin two hours the brothers Castle are on the road. Charlie has gotten his way right down to the baseball cap he bought for Sid in the gas station where they stopped for maps. The rental is, indeed, a Chevy, a nondescript 4-door Lumina that Sid wouldn't be seen dead in if he were in L.A., the land of the Four Horsemen of Mercedes, Porsche, BMW and Lexus.

"See the USA... in your Chevrolet," Charlie sings as he wheels the car off the beltway and onto the Interstate in Virginia." Who was that old chick that sang that on TV when we were little?"

"Dinah Shore," Sid answers from the passenger's seat, still in denial that he is really going along with this stupid road trip.

He has just talked to Jerry Creogan in L.A. whose reaction had been ultimately predictable. "Why the hell you wanna do that?" Jerry had asked in disbelief.

"Hold the fort and keep the phone on," Sid gave Jerry his instructions. "Tell Rosario to cancel my Monday schedule, rebook it for later in the week." And that had been that. Sid had just bought himself four days of freedom from his lawyer's life in L.A. Now all he had to do was sit back and live through four days with Charlie.

Sid had never unpacked in the first place, so it hadn't taken much to be ready to go when Charlie got back with the car. Charlie's luggage consisted of a medium-sized backpack and a large black hard shell case that could have housed anything from a guitar to a chainsaw to a submachine gun. In fact, it protected a Matsushita Future Cam, the state-of-the-art mobile videocam. It was the shoulder-slung videocam of choice of all the news jocks and hand-held indies.

"Where did you get that?" Sid asks when Charlie opens up the case in the trunk of the rental car to show it to him.

"OceanSave bought it for me," Charlie answers proudly as if he is showing off his first born.

"They just buy you toys like this whenever you ask for them? This thing had to cost big bucks."

"It's not a toy," Charlie takes instant umbrage. "And yes, it cost bigger than big bucks."

"Can you even work it? Since when have you become a, what, a video guy?"

"Videographer. And yes I can work it. The last six months I've been taking a crash class, hands on, from the best in the business, Matt Morris."

Suddenly, Sid is impressed. Everybody in Hollywood knows that name. Morris had put the whole documentary genre back on the map with his social consciousness films.

"You know Morris?"

"He taught me to operate the machine."

"No shit!"

"Yeah, no shit."

Pulling out of Washington, it was the videocam that really got them talking.

"What are you going to do with it?" Sid asks.

"I'm going to shoot America," Charlie answers dead seriously.

"Lee Harvey Oswald did that half a century ago," Sid makes a feeble historical joke.

"No, I'm gonna shoot all the good stuff about America. All the stuff that nobody ever sees, that you bigshots in New York and Washington and L.A. don't even know exists."

"Why? What good's it going to do?"

"Hell, everyone wants to make a movie," Charlie laughs. "This'll be ours."

"Ours?"

"Hell yes brother. We're in this together now. Butch and Sundance ride again, only this time we're gonna film it and it's gonna have a hell of a lot happier ending."

"Let's hope," Sid is still his skeptical self.

"I want to call it *Between the Devil and the Deep Blue Sea*. Get it?" Charlie announces.

Again, Sid doesn't have a clue.

"See, the Devil," Charlie explains, "is Washington and the way the politicians are betraying America and the Deep Blue Sea is L.A., the

Pacific, the west coast. My, *our* movie will be about all that's caught in between the two."

"Sounds like a boring travelogue for senior citizens in the public library," Sid scoffs.

"Maybe," Charlie laughs, "but it'll be a travelogue like no other. Morris is gonna help me edit it."

"Aha, a new genre. The travelogue as political rant."

Suddenly Charlie turns serious: "Dammit Sid, these people who are supposedly leading our country are stealing America right out from under our noses. They're taking the prairies, the mountain..."

"The oceans white with foam," Sid sings in a sarcastic mocking voice.

"That's right," Charlie isn't laughing. "They're polluting everything."

"Charlie, c'mon, you sound like a cross between 'God Bless America' and one of those Doomsday crazies carrying a sign that says '**THE WORLD ENDS TODAY.**'"

"The way things are going," Charlie finally loosens up and smiles at Sid's characterization, "that's about how I feel."

They drove in silence for a while through the rolling hills of Virginia toward the blue mountains to the west.

Sid busies himself with the maps, always the organization man. *If Charlie had his way*, he thinks, *we'd just set a compass on west and take any road that looks interesting.*

Charlie drives and fiddles with the radio button until he finds a song he likes, an old country-and-western song that the rockers had stolen back in the last century: "Freedom's just another word for nothin' left to lose. Nothin' just aint't nothin' but it's free," he sings along as he drives.

"How are we gonna do this?" Sid finally asks. "Which way do you want to go?" The maps are all spread out on his lap.

"How about the most beautiful way?"

"I gotta be there in no more than four days," Sid's voice is tight, barely able to disguise the 'what have I gotten myself into' panic that he is feeling. "We can't just be wandering around the country looking for beauty."

That cracks Charlie up. "Don't worry, we won't have to wander far. It's all around, just nobody wants to see it, much less protect it."

"Four days, got it. And if we're not pulling into L.A. in four days

I'll be hopping the nearest plane."

"Sid, relax. I'll get you back to your uptight celebrity lawyer life in plenty of time. Meanwhile, relax. You're worrying about ending your vacation before it even begins. You're thinking about getting back to work before your time-off even starts. You're being so damn Corporate American."

"OK, OK, but we have to at least pick a route, figure out what roads to take."

"Hey, big brother, I trust you. Just make it beautiful."

Sid suddenly realizes that Charlie is just being himself, is just staying in character. Charlie had always been the one who pursued beauty: in waves, in books, in women, and now in cross-country trips. Sid realizes that maybe he is missing a lot of things that Charlie is always looking for and talking about.

"We're on I-66 and another Interstate is coming up in seven miles, I-81,' Charlie is trying to help.

"OK," Sid has calmed down, "81 is good. Take it south. We can take it all the way through Tennessee to Knoxville than pick up I-40 West to Nashville and Memphis almost all the way to L.A."

"Memphis, home of Elvis Presley, and Nashville, home of M.D. Farrow, this is like a Country-and-Western odyssey," Sid doesn't know if Charlie is being serious or not.

"I doubt if Homer would be that excited about it," Sid tests the waters.

"Oh, but Jethro would," Charlie splashes back.

If nothing else, Sid has to admit, riding cross-country with Charlie will not lack for entertainment.

"81 through Virginia and Tennessee should be beautiful," Sid assures Captain Romantic. "First the Blue Ridge then the Smokey Mountains.

"Sounds good," Charlie is settling in with driving, changing channels at will. Fast food, gas station crackers and diet cokes, are their cuisine of choice, and stops are frequent.

Charlie unpacks the videocam for the first time at a pull-over right up against Mount Rogers near the Virginia-Tennessee-North Carolina line. A family in a Winnebago are also pulled over to take in the view and Charlie yells, "hey folks, can I put you in my movie?" The kids squeal with delight. The husband smiles and says "sure buddy." But the wife looks skeptical.

"Sid, go ask them where they're from, what they're doing," Charlie directs as he shoots. Sid obeys grudgingly.

"We're from Delphi, Indiana," the man answers proudly, "and we're taking the kids to see Washington, D.C."

"How old are the girls?" Sid asks for want of further direction from Charlie.

"Dawn is eight and Sunny is six," the man, all proud smiles, follows every movement of the camera as Charlie crosses in front of them shooting. Sid wonders if they are planning on naming their next daughter Dusk or maybe Twilight or perhaps Moonbeam.

"We wanna see the White House," the little girls shout as if they are on TV, "and the President."

"Do you like the President?" Charlie takes over the interview, shouting from behind the camera.

"Oh yes," the little girls bubble.

"How about you, Dad?" Charlie has got them right where he wants them now.

"Oh, I like him alright," the man says. "I'd like him a hell of a lot better if he and that Congress of his would do somethin'"

"That's a start," Charlie is ecstatic when they are back in the car and on the road. "That was great. A family of hicks from Indiana going to see the President. Morris ought to be able to do something with that."

Just outside of Knoxville, in Oak Ridge, Tennessee, a sign with a historic text catches Charlie's attention: "**HOME OF THE MANHATTAN PROJECT AND THE FIRST NUCLEAR REACTOR. NOW HOME OF THE OAK RIDGE ENVIRONMENTAL MANAGEMENT PROGRAM.**"

"Gotta love it," Charlie mocks as he shoots the sign. "You know what the Manhattan Project was, dontcha"

"What am I, an idiot?" Sid's contempt for the question leaves him wide open.

"Well, actually..."

"The A-bomb. Nuclear power. It all started right here. A lot of people say this is where we won World War II."

"A lot of other people say this is where we took our first big step toward destroying our planet. I gotta shoot this. Environmental Management Program. What do they think they can do? Pull back in all that radiation they let loose."

"It was the biggest war ever fought," Sid is only baiting Charlie now because Charlie is already one step up on his soapbox. "Built the A-bomb."

"Fucking A!"

Sid didn't know if Charlie was being sarcastic or just quoting their favorite line from *The Deer Hunter*.

Chapter Ten

Documentary

They shoot the defunct nuclear reactor in Oak Ridge, then Charlie sets up his camera in the parking lot of a Food Lion and asks people what they think of the nuclear reactor, what they think of the town's history, what they think of the President. He has a whole clipboard full of waivers that he gets anyone who will talk to him to sign. Matt Morris has told him he has to do that. He asks one old codger if he had been around when the historic reactor was still going, but the man says "no, I didn't live here then." When Charlie goes on and asks him if he knew anyone who was still around who had worked at the reactor, the man answers noncommittally: "Naw, they're all dead."

"But Charlie doesn't need waivers for the bumper stickers they start collecting from almost the very beginning of their trek. The first one that catches their eye reads: **"Your ridiculous little opinion has been noted."**

"Now that's the way that the President and Congress are treating America right now," Charlie says as he shoots it.

In Virginia they see lots of **"Virginia is for lovers"** bumper stickers but only one **"I've got the pussy so I make the rules"** bumper sticker accompanied by a cartoon of a very large, muscular, tattooed woman holding a frazzled cat by the tale.

In Tennessee, they collect **"Everyone has a photographic memory... Some just don't have any film"** and **"The Proctologist called... they found your head"** and the one Sid liked **"If you can read this, I can slam on my brakes and sue you."** Charlie's favorite was on a large SUV named Valerie that they saw walking across a parking lot in Knoxville. It was on a tee shirt not a bumper sticker, but on a woman that size it could have been one. On the front of her shirt was a picture of Elmer Fudd toting his trusty shotgun accompanied by the slogan as only he could say it: **"If you take away my guns, you take away my wife!"** On the back of her shirt was that wascally wabbit Bugs Bunny saying: **"I never knew he had a wife."**

When Sid is driving, Charlie sometimes just shoots out the window at a lake down in a valley or at high tension lines cutting a thick swath up the side of a dense pine mountain or a river running free between two green spring banks or the same river being penetrated by the pipes and fences of huge power plants, oil refineries, and factories. "Don't tell me that America doesn't mess around with Mother Nature," Charlie points his camera and laughs.

Tennessee is horse country just like its neighbor Kentucky to the north, and Charlie shoots rolling farms with white fences stretching out for miles and colts frisking in the cool spring sunshine. "You know, Seabiscuit was a California horse," Charlie picks up Sid's history lesson. "Beat the snot out of all these eastern horses."

In Nashville they shoot the huge baronial estates of the reigning Country and Western stars. One singer's high electronic gate at the mouth of the mile long driveway down through the rolling lawns to his mansion is decorated with a twenty-foot high guitar and banjo.

It is in Nashville that M.D. Farrow comes up. "Who is she?" Sid asks. "I haven't heard of her. Is she big outside of Washington and Nashville? Where'd you get to know her? Does she live in a big house like these?" It isn't really an interrogation. Sid is just healthily curious.

"I met her about a year ago. She's on the board of OceanSave. She's one of the most involved of all the people in the movement. One of the leaders. I like her ideas. She doesn't speak loud, but when she speaks the OceanSave people all listen. She's become the architect of almost all of our public policy."

"Charlie, she's a Country and Western singer, c'mon."

"I know, I know, but she's a really smart Country and Western singer. If you talked to her, you'd know it right away. She's a planner; she's a visionary; she's a revolutionary."

"C'mon, Charlie, she's an entertainer. Are you telling me that the policy-making of your organization is in the hands of this, this, hillbilly singer?"

"That's exactly what I'm telling you. Don't be deceived. She's not just a singer. She's all kinds of things. She's the one who planned that whole march in Washington last weekend, the one that got me testifying before Congress, the one that knocked the DC cops off their nut.

She planned it and it got us more publicity than we ever imagined."

"So what makes her so strong in OceanSave, what's her policy?"

Charlie thinks on that a minute: "I guess it's because she's fearless. She's not afraid of anything. That's why Alison idolizes her. M.D. says that our job is to agitate. That's the word she always uses. To get in America's face."

"So, a militant?"

"Oh yeah. Before M.D. we were like Gandhi wimps, but she put a whole new spin on protest. She doesn't care how much violence happens at our rallies. It only makes us look good, only helps our cause. If last weekend was any indication, we gotta say she's right."

"That's great," Sid's voice signals the skeptical caution that is coming," but you're the one who's out front, on the microphone, inciting her little riots. She could get you killed. Hell, you're the one getting the death threats, not her."

Charlie didn't say anything to that right away.

Sid thinks it might have sobered him, but it has only made him more thoughtful, almost guarded, as if he isn't quite telling everything. Criminal lawyers like Sid tend to have this sixth sense that warns them when witnesses aren't telling the whole truth and nothing but the truth.

"We all have our roles in the organization," Charlie finally decides what he wants to say. "I'm the media guy, the face man, the spokesman."

"OK, so you're the movie star and she's the director, but who's the producer. Who's bankrolling all these Earth Day and protest extravaganzas that you're putting on?"

"America does. All the people who think that the Congress and the oil companies are raping our country and screwing all of us in the process."

"Yeah right. And how much of it are you donating to the cause?"

"A lot of it."

"How much?"

"Ninety percent of the royalties from the book."

"Well, nobody'll ever say you're not committed to the cause."

"There you go."

"And how about your visionary, revolutionary M.D."

"All her money is in it too. She's not living in any big houses. Hey, this isn't just a game, Sid. We're all willing to do anything to save America from these profiteers. For them there is no future. All there is for them is profit now and the future be damned."

Once again Sid feels a regretful jealousy that he can't engage with the passionate energy that clearly rules Charlie's world while nothing but greed, excess, and decadence rule his.

In the early morning with the sun coming up outside Memphis, they shoot a freight train rolling out of a dirty railyard and it sets Charlie to singing *a cappella*: "Good morning America, how are you? Don't you know me? I'm your native son." Driving through the South, the names of the cities and towns call up all the ghosts of history and the Civil War battles they fought: Chattanooga, Chickamauga, Atlanta, Memphis, Corinth, Tullahoma. The names are like music but the history was a death dirge.

They shoot people too: a couple in Memphis who had lost a son in the war and hated the President for it so much that they had no fear of advocating assassination right on the camera—"I hope somebody shoots the sumbitch and they string the prick's body up on a lightpole like they did in the French Revolution"; a gay electrician in Little Rock who couldn't see why he couldn't marry the closeted cop he'd been living with for years—"I figure since he's a cop it oughta be alright, don't you?"; to the two brothers in the 7-11 parking lot in Fort Smith who lived across from a hog farm and were mad because America smells bad—"The whole country stinks," Tom the oldest complained.

"Smells like shit," his younger brother Bobby Red chimed in.

"Between the air pollution from cars and the water pollution from all kinds of human and agricultural waste..." ("and hog shit and cow shit and horse shit," Bobby Red interrupted him,) "...between all the different kinds of industrial pollution, the whole country just flat out smells so bad everybody oughta be walkin' around with a clothespin on their nose," older brother Tom clinched the argument.

When they hit Oklahoma and then the panhandle of Texas and then New Mexico, the country flattened out into a high desert brownness of dirt and scrub and long stretches where only telephone poles next to the road broke the horizon line between earth and sky.

They shot dry washes and boarded up gas stations and forlorn Indians selling beads and phony tourist crap out of rotting pick-up trucks next to the highway where the cars were going by so fast that the drivers could only pick them up in their rear-view mirrors. But now, mostly, Charlie shot oil wells pecking away at the southwestern earth. His camera couldn't get enough of their huge beaks bobbing up and down in a steady, relentless tempo of profit and gain at the expense of the helpless earth.

"If I lived out here and had to look at those things all around me all the time, I'd shoot myself," Charlie expresses his loathing of the oil rigs.

"We've got them all over L.A.," Sid protests. "They're everywhere. Right along the beach."

Charlie thinks a minute, knows his older brother is right: "I guess I just never paid much attention to them before. Too busy chasing waves and women."

"So what's the deal with this Alison?" Sid asks somewhere in west Texas or eastern New Mexico while Charlie is driving and the video-cam is taking a well-earned nap. "I like this one. She seems different from most of the girls I read about you with in the tabloids."

"You read those rags?" Charlie is appalled.

"No, I don't read them," Sid defends himself, "only their headlines in the line at the supermarket: **CHARLES CASTLE CAUGHT IN LOVENEST WITH SUPERMODEL** or **CHARLES CASTLE, THE OTHER MAN?**"

"Cute!"

"So?"

"You're right. Alison is different. I could marry her."

"Whoa there, cowboy. I've never heard you say anything like that before."

"I said I could. I didn't say we had plans or anything. We've never even talked about it. But you're right. She's different. Smart and good. We're both smart, you and I, but I'm not sure how good we are."

Sid didn't know exactly what Charlie meant by that but he didn't push for an explanation *(probably because he'd been thinking a lot lately about how not really good he was. Smart yes, successful yes, fairly powerful yes, but good?).*

"You know what I like about both Alison and M.D. They're totally committed to it, totally engaged."

"To what?"

"To making things better, to protecting what's good about America. They're the key to making all this work. Alison works with M.D. on OceanSave's policy. They're the brains behind all we do. They put the words in my mouth."

"Oh, great, so now you're a ventriloquist's dummy."

"Man, you're a real joy to talk to. Nooo, I'm not a dummy. But right now I'm a team player. We all have to be, or nothing's ever gonna happen."

"What do you mean?"

"M.D., Alison, OceanSave. They've got it figured out. The environment movement, the tree huggers, the green peacers, the Sierra clubbers, the eco-terrorists, none of it has ever worked. Too fragmented, too much competition, too much jealousy and disagreement and power-grabbing. But we're going to change all that."

"What are you talking about?"

"M.D. and Alison are trying to put together a summit."

"A what?"

"Did you ever hear of Tecumseh? The Indian Chief?"

"Yeah, sorta. Back east somewhere, wasn't he?"

"Yes. Indiana, Ohio, then in Canada."

"So what?"

"Tecumseh's our model."

"Model for what?"

"For bringing all the tribes together."

"What are you talking about?"

"Look, eco-politics is a huge cluster-fuck right now. Everybody disagrees, has carved out their own little piece of the eco-pie. It's just like Tecumseh. He was the last native-American chief to bring all the tribes together. He knew that they had to unite to keep the white man from taking their land. Tecumseh thought he was starting a revolution. Too bad he was only fighting a rear-guard action. His battle was already lost, but ours isn't. M.D. is planning a summit of all the eco-groups. After that she's gonna push for the biggest march, the biggest protest demonstration America has ever seen. So big they'll have to listen. So big it'll change the whole course of human events. And she wants to do it in L.A."

"L.A. Why?"

"Because it's America's last frontier, and the Evil Empire has got it dead in their sights."

"What do you mean by that?" Sid is starting to worry about his little brother. Charlie is starting to sound like one of those mad conspiracy theorists.

"L.A. is the next big stage for the oil barons. All of the oil companies are moving on L.A. You know why?"

"No, why?" Sid plays along.

"Because the administration is going to let them start drilling off-shore again. Right in the Santa Barbara Channel. They're all lined up and ready to go."

"You think it'll really happen?"

"Not if we have anything to say about it. California, the Pacific, it's the plum that Washington wants to pick. It's where the oil is. It's all there, just off shore, right within reach, and oil companies want it so bad they can taste it. Look at all the Washington types around the President in his government. They're all corporate. It's all about oil, I'm telling you."

Sid knew better than to argue with Charlie when he was convinced that he was right and had the evidence to back it up. And besides that, Sid didn't really care. Charlie was the involved one, the futurist, the passionate one. Sid could barely get through his life from day to day.

And so they drove on across the southwest, and as they drove they talked, and as they talked they started being brothers again instead of a lawyer and his client or a media star and the careless rich that he is attacking.

"I used to love it when we'd just hang out and talk," Charlie gets nostalgic somewhere in New Mexico. "At the beach, driving around L.A. when you were home from college. In those days you seemed to know so much."

"Seemed. You got that right. Not sure I know much of anything these days."

"Hey, lawyers always know the answers to the questions before we ask them, right?"

"Yeah, right." Both Sid and Charlie laugh out loud at that.

"Those beach summers really were fun," Sid catches Charlie's nostalgia bug. "Man, we went everywhere looking for waves."

"Remember that big day we had down in Newport?"

"Best ever." Sid indeed remembers. "Longest rides we ever had. Faces like pure silk. Curl like a railroad tunnel. Damn, I haven't gone surfin' in five years.

"Hell, it's all we used to do," Charlie sounds sad. "I still go out once in a while when I'm in L.A., but it's not the same."

"I know. It's hard to go back. About a month ago I was eating dinner with some people in a restaurant down in Newport, at the Balboa Pier. After they left, I was on my way to the car but for some reason I suddenly switched direction and walked out on the pier. I was out on the end by that greasy little diner and I looked south toward the Wedge and you know what?" Sid waits, but Charlie doesn't venture a guess. "There's a green light on the end of the Wedge now. Just like in *Gatsby*. Man, it seemed like some kind of an omen or something."

"Actually, that's pretty cool," Charlie is clearly caught up in Sid's grappling with the Pandora's Box of nostalgia that Charlie has opened.

"Yeah, it was. It was like the past blinking at me."

"We were out of some California version of *The Great Gatsby*," Charlie tries to lighten the sad sense of loss that he detects in Sid's voice.

"Yeah right, the Castle brothers, surfing princes."

"Hey, you gotta admit we weren't bad."

"Yeah, not bad at all," and Sid actually smiles at the thought of it.

"You still read so much," Charlie asks out of pure curiosity.

"Yeah, I do. Usually at night before I fall asleep. TV sucks so much."

"This is good. Remember we used to talk about books all the time when we'd be driving in the car. You never gave me a bad steer, especially Joyce. Joyce could have been a surfer."

That cracks Sid up. The idea of nearsighted James Joyce in coke-bottle glasses, a wool suit and tie, and a little black square hat standing on a surfboard is an image right out of Salvador Dali. "After I saw that green light down in Newport, I started reading Fitzgerald again. You know me and Fitzgerald. I've been reading him since high school."

"What are you reading?" It seems so strange to Charlie to be having a conversation like this with Sid. They could have been back fifteen, twenty years ago, two surfers, driving from beach to beach, talking about everything, even books they were reading.

"His California novel. *The Last Tycoon*. The one about the movies."

"I've never read it," Charlie admits.

"Man, it's great, actually a lot like you are talking about."

"How?"

"OK," Sid loves to talk about books. Charlie had often thought that if his older brother hadn't grown up to be such a smart lawyer that he would have made a great English professor. "It's set in the thirties, and in the beginning of the novel they're talking about how the country is going to hell and out of work people are marching on Washington and there's actually fear of a revolution. All the characters are trying to decide what they're going to do if the revolution comes. That's sort of how I feel these days."

"What do you mean?"

"All of the characters feel out of touch. The Bonus Army is march-ing on Washington and they're way out here in L.A. making movies. They finally decide that if the revolution ever makes it to L.A. that they'll have to go out and hide somewhere in the canyons until it all blows over."

"So how does it end? Do they all take off for the mountains?"

"That's just it. It doesn't."

"Doesn't end."

"Fitzgerald drank himself to death while he was writing *The Last Tycoon*. He never finished it."

"So the revolution never got to California?"

"Nope."

"And you're reading novels that are only half written?"

"Uhn-huh."

"Terrific. Well don't count on it this time. If M.D. has her way, the revolution will be in L.A. by next April and everybody out here will either have to decide to join in or head for the hills," Charlie laughed his carefree laugh, but Sid wasn't sure it was really such a joke.

Chapter Eleven

Purple Mountains

*J*ust before they get to Flagstaff, Arizona, Charlie and Sid take a detour north, up to the Grand Canyon and on into Utah.

"Why are we going this way?" Sid asks. "L.A.'s that way."

"Trust me," Charlie is dead serious. "You're going to see the most beautiful part of America you've ever seen. I've gotta shoot it. It's really what we're fighting for."

"I'm not fighting for anything."

"You will be. We all will be."

They drive to the North Rim of the Grand Canyon. Their parents had taken them to the South Rim a couple of times but they had never looked at it from this side. Standing on a natural bridge out over the canyon, they spot a thunderhead with rain already slanting down out of it coming straight at them off the South Rim which seems much closer than it really is.

"It's gonna rain," Sid, always the conservative one, warns.

"It's perfect. Look how dark and threatening it is coming straight at us. Matt'll love this. He'll make it symbolic. Wow, look at that lightning. It's like an old John Ford western. Remember that storm in *She Wore a Yellow Ribbon* or was it *Fort Apache*?"

"I don't know, but we're going to get soaked."

"Just let me shoot 'til it starts raining, then we'll make a run for the car."

"Terrific," Sid grouses as he moves to the railing that rings the top of the rock to get a closer look at the storm that is coming in. On his left hand's instant contact with the metal railing, Sid is knocked back four feet from the electrical shock. He ends up right next to Charlie, knocked flat on his butt.

"What the hell?"

"That railing, it shocked me."

"The railing knocked you down?"

"Yeah, c'mon, let's get outa here."

"I'm right with you."

Back in the car, they laugh about it.

"Hey, that was just a warning about your life," Charlie kids Sid. "The next time you get the full lightning bolt treatment."

"Very funny. Damn shock knocked me down. That railing must have collected all the electricity in the air."

"No, I like God sending you a message better. That's the version I'm tellin'."

They laugh about it all the way down the mountain. That day they shoot the sublime beauty of America, her wildest and most exquisite landscapes in Bryce Canyon and Zion National Park. It is beauty on such a grand scale that even Sid has to admit to Charlie that he is glad they took the detour.

"Gives you a kinda shock of recognition, doesn't it?" Charlie grins mischievously as he says it. "So pretty it kinda knocks you on your ass, doesn't it?"

"Very funny!" Sid can't help but laugh.

On the road south toward Las Vegas, Sid is driving and Charlie is playing back the day's footage on the videocam.

"Man, this is great stuff," Charlie is excited. "It's so strong and awe-inspiring. This is perfect for the film. It's what America really is."

"I'm glad we did this," Sid admits. "I needed a break."

"Hey, it's worth doing. We haven't taken a road trip like this for years. We used to do it all the time. It would refocus us, clean out our heads."

"Is that what we were doing? I thought we were just drinking beer and chasing waves?"

"Hey, brother, it's not like we're a couple of illiterate dumb asses. We've been doing what people in America hardly ever do, what more of 'em need to do, look at their country and look at themselves and realize how lucky they are."

"You think some documentary movie you're making could do that? C'mon."

"If it's done right, it could."

"No way. No movie could do that."

"That's what I want this film to do. That's why we're making it. I want people to look at it and realize how we've gotten off the track, how we've lost touch with our country. How Washington is letting the country be run by people with guns and right-wing Christian radio-stations and bigshots at Amerigas and USA Plastics and Teltech and PC-USA. Can you believe it? The big corporations and the Jesus-freaks are a political coalition."

Boy could Charlie talk. After a while Sid realized that the whole trip was just Charlie's rehearsal for what he was going to say on the talk shows and in the interviews when his documentary about America hit the theaters.

Sid was impressed. It hadn't been a tirade or a passionate overflow of heated words. Charlie had delivered that speech in a slow, quiet, evenly reasoned voice of total conviction.

"You sound like you want to start a revolution," Sid too is serious.

"We already have," Charlie grins. "You should have been in Washington, on the mall, last weekend. Four hundred thousand people Sid, four hundred thousand! Here read this," taking a stiff white business card out of his wallet and handing it over. "M.D. gives them out by the thousands. They're the calling cards of our revolution."

It was just a plain white card with the OceanSave logo followed by a quote.

"Read it'" Charlie demands. "It's Camus. That's what we're all about."

Sid reads:

> To abolish conscious revolt is to elude the problem. The theme of permanent revolution is thus carried into individual experience. One of the only coherent philosophical positions is thus revolt. It is a constant confrontation between man and his obscurity. It challenges the world anew every second.

"Camus huh?"

"Yeah, keep it. It's from *The Myth of Sisyphus*. M.D. says that that is our goal. Permanent revolution. The kind of revolution that teaches people that we can't let these destructive powers take over our world, destroy our very environment. Camus wrote that when the Nazi's were in power in France."

"I'll keep it," Sid tucks it into his wallet. "If nothing else it will remind me of where you are coming from when I see you on TV."

"It would be better if that quote pointed you in a direction to go."

Charlie is dead serious.

The lights of Las Vegas are just rising up out of the desert dark like a neon holocaust on the plain when Sid's cell phone goes off.

"Ah, California State Bird," Charlie chortles.

Chapter Twelve

Lost and Found

*J*erry Creogan internally flinches when Sid answers the cell phone. He has been trying to get Sid all day but Sid's phone has either been turned off or left in the car or simply ignored. But this time, almost nine at night, Sid answers, and Jerry has to figure out a way to tell him.

"Sid, hey."

"Jerry, how you doin'? You wouldn't believe it. We have just had the most spectacular day ever. Bryce Canyon, unbelievably beautiful. Zion National Park, awesome. Man, Jerry, you wouldn't..."

"Sid, sorry, but I've got bad news." Jerry's voice is racing now that he is started. "It's Beth. She's, she's dead. I found her last night when I tried to deliver the money."

Silence, as if the line had suddenly gone as dead as Sid Castle's ex-wife.

"Sid, hello, you still there?"

Suddenly America didn't seem so important. Suddenly Sid's worst nightmare had materialized.

"Yeah, yeah I'm here. What happened?"

Jerry can almost feel the despair taking over his boss's voice, the high exhilaration plummeting into the dark brooding moods that he had been noticing come on his employer and friend more and more often as he drove him around the city.

"She fell, Sid, in the bathtub. She'd probably been dead more than a day when I found her. She fell and hit her head, then bled out. I kept calling her to tell her I was coming like you told me to, but she never answered so I decided to just go up there and take a chance. That's how I found her."

"She'd been drinking, hadn't she? That's how it happened, didn't it?" Sid's voice is sputtering and missing as if his clutch is slipping.

"Yeah, probably. The coroner took one look at her and said 'accidental death.'"

I've finally lost her. I saw it coming, something bad like this, and I didn't do anything She is, was, my first love, the only woman I've ever loved, and I've lost her. I screwed it up royally. Dead, my god! His self-reproach raced through Sid Castle's mind in a breath of time.

"Sid, you still there?" Jerry fidgets in the car in L.A. holding the dead phone.

"What is it? What happened? Sid, what's wrong?" Charlie's voice in the car seems far away as if he is speaking from the bottom of a well.

Jerry and Charlie don't really know what is running through Sid's mind at this moment. But they both know Sid well enough to guess. *He's blaming himself,* both Charlie and Jerry are thinking simultaneously. *He's blaming himself. He thinks he's personally responsible for everything. He's the one who makes things work, who can negotiate anything. But he can't negotiate this.*

Charlie doesn't have to be told what happened. He knows it can only be Beth and he knows it's bad.

"Beth's dead," Sid finally tells Charlie. "Jerry found her last night."

"I'll be there as soon as I can," Sid gets back to Jerry on the cell phone. "I'll get a flight out of Vegas. I'll call you to pick me up at the airport."

"Screw that!" Charlie interrupts. "We'll drive straight through. It's only five hours. I'll make it in less."

Sid, into the phone: "Never mind. Charlie says we're driving. Meet me at the beach house in the morning, early, six."

Jerry Creogan, dead serious, knowing that he is stepping out of line but doing it anyway: "Sid, I've been thinking a lot about this all day. I think you shouldn't come home. I'll tell the papers you're out of town and can't be reached. I can bury her. I'll get the pallbearers. Just let me do it and don't put yourself through it. It's going to be a freak show."

Sid, weary now: "Can't Jerry. I have to bury her. She's mine. Get a good night's sleep. Be at the beach at six. I'm gonna need you big time tomorrow."

They didn't say much as they drove through the black, empty desert night. Charlie buried the Chevy's speedometer somewhere over ninety miles an hour and tried to stay awake. Sid sat straight up against the window. The desert nightscape sped by outside the window, but not as fast as the lost and self-hateful thoughts pulsing relentlessly in the dark landscape of Sidney Castle's mind.

I failed her is all he can keep thinking. *I failed her* is the demon that bares its teeth at him through the window as the car races through the dark Nevada night. *I failed her.*

The sun like a lurid bloodstain is spreading up out of the desert behind them as they come into L.A. in the morning. Ground fog sits on the highway between the stony hills. Beth's corpse waits in the morgue for her only ex-relative to claim her. Sid is driving now because Charlie started dozing off at ninety miles an hour somewhere around Barstow.

Charlie wakes with a start on the passenger side.

Sid greets him almost cheerily, having seemingly made peace with Beth's death while Charlie slept.

They get coffee at a gas station.

"Did you sleep at all?" Charlie asks.

"No. I will eventually. What I need now is to shower, then there's stuff I've gotta do."

"Can I help?"

"No. Get some sleep today. You can help me bury her tomorrow."

"OK."

Long silence as they come down into L.A. through the Malibu hills headed toward the beach. The sun coming up over the mountains sends a straight line of glistening silver light across the ocean to the horizon. As they get closer to the water, they can see the waves braking on the beach and the first surfers paddling out to catch them.

"That used to be us," Charlie points to the surfers going out, trying to cheer his brother up.

"Long time ago it seems," Sid's voice is sad.

"I'm gonna have a surfer's wedding, I think," Charlie doesn't give up.

"What are you talking about?" Sid is tired, slow.

"I'm gonna marry her, Sid. Alison. I'm gonna marry her."

"Yeah. Right. Surfer's wedding. Geez!"

"Yeah. Right. At the beach. In the morning sun. Just like this. I'm gonna teach her to surf."

"You're really serious about this one?" Sid's skepticism coats his voice like the morning after.

"Yeah, I am."

"Well, good," Sid softens. "I like this one. She's as smart as she is beautiful. Probably too smart to marry you."

"Actually that's what I'm worried about. She doesn't like my visibility."

"Hell, who would? I mean, you're getting death threats on a daily basis."

"She says she wants to have a marriage and a life that's normal."

"Good luck! Tell her the Castle brothers will never have that. We're too well educated."

That's what Beth had wanted to have too, Sid thinks, *but by the time I figured it out it was just too late.*

Chapter Thirteen

The CEO Backstage

The CEO, the titular head of Amerigas and one of the biggest contributors to the campaign war chests, is intimately involved with a rather impressive parade of that other species of tits in the Versailles Suite of the Louis XIV Hotel on Paris Place in downtown Washington. It is fat cat day and night for the oil industry in the nation's capital and though it is only early afternoon the revels have begun. The CEO's lobbyist handlers have provided him with no less than four of Washington's most prodigiously endowed professional women to serve his coffee, butter his buns and generally entertain him with their high spirits this sunny May Day afternoon. The CEO's head lobbyist and smiling Pandarus, the Director of this week's revels, has whisked them up via the freight elevator to the Versailles Suite and delivered them to his majesty the CEO like large bon-bons being served on a golden platter in the French court back in the good old days. But these particular bon-bons are the kinds of dessert that good old boys always like to sample after a tasty beer and barbecue luncheon. Some might feel that four of these overflowing bon-bons might signal a certain excess on the part of the CEO, the steward of the corporation's funds, dividends, and stock prices, but if those kill-joys could see the titillation that these four inventive bon-bons provide for the highly stressed CEO they would certainly excuse his indulgence.

But such dalliance can only last so long before it spends itself and grows dull. And other revels await as does the elegant silver gray limo parked in front of the hotel. A dinner with two of the company's most generously compensated and high ranking members of Congress at La Jardiniere in Georgetown, an amusing visit to a country rock night club to catch the act of the company's most vocal entertainment industry critic (a "diverting foray behind enemy lines" the honorable Congressman from Pennsylvania characterizes it), followed with whatever other nighttime diversions the Congressmen deem necessary to insure their continuing support and arm-twisting influence for the CEO's Amerigas interests.

Their dinner of bourguignons, truffles and soufflés handily dispatched, the CEO and his honorable guests proceed in their silver gray coach to the lively venue for the evening's musical entertainments. The streets are crowded around *Elmo's* in Georgetown. M.D. Farrow and the Headhunters are still packing them in nightly with their message-laced menu of eco-rock. The silver gray limo threads its way through the crosswalks and jaywalkers, the drunk-dialers and hand-holders, all the diverse revelers of a typical Saturday night in the big city tenderloin.

"She is the most vocal critic of the administration's environmental policy, the mother of all tree huggers," Pandarus the lobbyist regales his clients as the silver gray limo creeps along in traffic toward the club. "You're gonna hate her, hate her message, but she's the hottest act in Washington right now, her music is great, and she has a really sweet ass."

All that vital information dispensed in their briefing, the honorableCongressman from Louisiana leers: "I guess that makes us strange bedfellows tonight, eh?"

And the honorable Congressman from Pennsylvania cannot help but rejoin: "I hope not the strangest before the evening's over."

And the CEO just sits fat, full and happy in his slow rolling silver gray limo smugly confident in his control over his fellow travelers and their votes.

At their reserved table just off the stage in *Elmo's*, the drinks flow like the blood of empire and the dancers swirl around them like tribal dionysians in the heart of darkness. The number that most entertains the CEO and his political minions twangs out in the middle of the set. It is an upbeat, satiric reworking of two classic Country and Western tunes, and M.D. and her Headhunters give it a rowdy and fast-paced cowboy rendition:

Mama's got a laptop
And she checks on all the market news.
Daddy's got an Ipod
So he dials up all the rhythm and blues.
And there's a tapedeck on his tractor

That gives him and Rush and O'Reilly
A chance to schmooz.

Sitting at his table listening to the music in his gray silk suit and his elegant snakeskin cowboy boots, the CEO is quite contented, even pleased with himself and the way he has spent the day. It is an elegant life he leads and as M.D. Farrow's first set ends he decides in a magnanimous gesture of *noblesse oblige* to share it with the less fortunate masses.

"Let's go backstage and say hello to the band," the CEO suggests to his political puppets. "They're quite good, and I'd like to meet this Farrow person up close and personal." The CEO has always been prone to the jingle jargon of TV commercials and his vocabulary is often laced with their inanity. "Where's the beef?" had been his favorite rhetorical question concerning almost anything and everything for years.

So, with his mildly amused political sycophants in tow, he rises majestically from his table and leads them to the backstage area where he extravagantly tips a remarkably oversized black man with a shaved head and a black, skin-tight tee shirt that blares SECURITY across his chest to plead his case for a private dressing room audience with the Country and Western diva. What he gets for his fifty dollar bill is admission behind the curtains to a green room area where the Headhunters lounge around drinking beer and smoking cigarettes and picking at piles of fried chicken bits.

M.D. Farrow is not partaking in the between sets hilarity. In a corner, under a floorlamp with a super-bright three-way bulb, at a small computer desk the size of an end table, she sits working at her laptop computer. The CEO's entourage interrupts her labor. The lobbyist introduces the CEO and the CEO introduces his two political pawns and M.D. Farrow takes it all in silently like some tribal queen being greeted by a delegation of colonial subalterns. She knows that they are the enemy, the ravagers of all that she holds dear, the ultimate targets of her repressed wrath, yet she welcomes them with a nod of acknowledgement and an utterly neutral "hello" as if she is simply answering the door for some unexpected guests.

The CEO, utterly confident and secure in his power, unleashes the cowboy charm that always proves so successful with the women that travel in his elegant oil industry universe: "Loved your music tonight, Miss Farrow. You have a powerful presence onstage."

Though she says little, M.D. recognizes this greasily smiling CEO of Amerigas right away. His whole business and personal bio is already in her laptop and has been for more than two years. He is one of OceanSave's prime targets for exposure and she has been meticulously preparing his case all of that time. She knows all about the whores, the ridiculously expensive champagne, the corporate jets and private islands and million-dollar birthday parties masquerading as Board of Director meetings. It is the first time that the two have met and both are naturally curious. She has even gone so far as to place one of her people in the job of driver of his sleek gray limo so that she can keep close track of her prey. But tonight she tries to be polite, to tread lightly, to not tip him off to her plans for him and his company's downfall.

"I'm glad that you enjoyed our show," M.D. gives him the canned treatment for admiring fans, before cutting to the chase," even though we rarely see eye-to-eye on the oil industry's emerging public policy."

"Which one? Yesterday's or today's?" the lobbyist thinks he has made a joke that will cut through the confrontational tension that is beginning to build between the two principals.

M.D. and the CEO ignore him. They are intent upon measuring each other, gauging each other's strength.

"You are a strikingly original voice on the contemporary music scene," the honorable Congressman from Pennsylvania pipes up. "I remember when Dylan was writing music like yours way back when."

"So I remind you of Dylan. That's quite a compliment," M.D. surprises him with her graciousness, "but you are right, he was a long time ago and, indeed, the times they are a changin'," M.D. makes her own little joke but does it without smiling.

"Do you like my songs?" M.D. addresses her question directly to the CEO without the slightest hesitation.

"I really like your sound. You've got a great band," he replies evasively.

"That's not what I asked," M.D. won't let him escape, won't indulge or pamper him.

"Your songs are too politically charged for my taste," the CEO takes up the gauntlet still supremely confident in his material power.

"Good. They're meant to be," M.D. never raises her voice, keeps her tone level and her meaning precise.

"Ah, but we look at the world from very different perspectives, now don't we?" the CEO oozes charm as he smiling patronizes. "I find your view of the oil industry surprisingly naïve, yet you express it eloquently in your music."

"How is that?" M.D. is cold and frightening in the control she is maintaining in this subdued conversation.

"Well, you seem to make the oil companies your sworn enemy, the villains, when they really are not. They are the lifeblood of America. Without oil America ceases to exist as we know it today."

The manager of the club interrupts their pleasant exchange because it is time for M.D. and the Headhunters to go back onstage. But M.D. is not disappointed. She has no real interest in getting into a debate with a drunken CEO about matters that cannot be changed. Her curiosity has been satisfied. She has met him in person.

"Who was 'at?" her bass player asks through the blue haze of cigarette smoke.

"That is a patronizing prick and three of his many sycophants," she replies without the slightest tinge of humor.

Before she returns to the stage, she types for long moments into her laptop as if recording some vital information.

Chapter Fourteen

Hard Driving

The CEO's silver gray limo is parked in front of the club waiting for him. It is not a rental. It is just another vehicle in the Amerigas fleet. Once a newspaper geek did a count for a story on corporate waste and found out that Amerigas had more vehicles in its motor pool than the Maryland State Police had on the streets. The driver holds the limo door open for the CEO and his pawns. They disappear into its plush gray elegance. When the driver clicks on his turn signal, the ebbing traffic on Wisconsin Avenue seems miraculously to part like a sea of bobbing red taillights and the long gray limo floats out into it like an ocean liner navigating a regatta of pleasure boats.

"To Annie Monday's house in Chevy Chase," the CEO coughs to his driver through the cigar smoke. It is the most discrete and exclusive of whorehouses in the D.C. area and it is the CEO's standard operating procedure to treat his more influential minions to an evening of its exotic delights before sending them out once again to espouse and vote for the various humanitarian agendas of big oil in the discourse of the body politic.

The CEO's limo proceeds through the congealed traffic of Northwest D.C. and on out into the suburbs. Chevy Chase, Maryland is a sleepy bedroom community with wide lawns, ornate street lamps, and big sprawling Colonial and Georgian houses set back under ancient shade trees that cast shadows so black and deep that they can even swallow up a long silver gray limousine. The CEO gets out of his limo in the circular drive in front of Madam Monday's imposing front door to bid his guests good night and good professional coupling. Outside of the President's, the Vice-President's and the Cabinet wives, Annie Monday's houses the most prestigious collection of high-class courtesans inside the beltway. The CEO assures all three of his cronies that all of their evening's erotic expenses will be picked up by Amerigas and he hectors them to order nothing but the best in the way of both wine and women for their evening's diversion. The CEO watches his congressmen go with a benevolent grin on his face and an encouraging wave, all the time thinking: *Those hypocrites. United States Congressmen and they're following their dicks into a cathouse.* The CEO waits long minutes for his honorable guests to clear the door and the front parlor of the establishment then he follows them in himself for a short *tete-a-tete* with the Madam herself, Annie Monday. Again, only minutes later he emerges once again but with two statuesque courtesans in tow, one garish blond, the other vixenish brunette. This hastily arranged *ménage-a-trois* descends into the rear of the limo.

The CEO is happy now. He is totally in command, set free from the silly restraints that govern the lives of ordinary citizens. He orders his driver to proceed slowly back to his elegant French hotel—"Take your time. Cruise the monuments, the Capital, the White House, that sort of stuff. We're in no hurry. And yes, raise the screen."—before settling into the deep plush seats with his two ladies in waiting.

The CEO's driver marvels at the strange illusions of rich people. But the CEO is perfectly happy, secure in his regal power, his wealth, his ability to literally buy people for both the furthering of his business interests and the fulfilling of his personal perverse desires.

As the tinted screen whirrs up between the limo driver and the car's deep and sumptuous rear compartment, the CEO orders his two willing guests to immediately disrobe. As the sleek limo glides silkily through the spotlit city of monuments, the CEO proceeds to instruct his courtesans in some intricate sexual acrobatics performed upon each other for his entertainment followed by alternating oral exercises performed upon his now gleefully exposed self.

What the CEO didn't know was that this particular Amerigas limo had been provided with a hidden videocam by its undercover OceanSave driver and his whole little *ménage-a-trois* orgy was being recorded. Ignorant of his starring role and undaunted by his courtesan's mobile ministrations, he directs his two escorts to accompany him up to his room in his chandeliered hotel for the playing out of the second act of his little porno movie.

But little did he know nor could he ever have guessed from his vantage point on his throne of wealth and power and obscene perversion that the third act of his evening of political bribery and sexual debauchery was already underway.

Chapter Fifteen

Message in Blood

"**M**an, this guy can't get enough. Amerigas'll have to raise the price two cents at the pump just to pay for this guy's hookers."

"Manny, Manny, slow down. What happened? Tell me."

"Your guy dropped the two Congressmen off at that high class whorehouse in Chevy, but also came away with two hookers himself. They blew him in the back of the limo, then he took them up to his room for more fun and games."

Manny Kravitz, PI, key hole peeper extraordinaire, dirt-gatherer to whoever comes up with a week's retainer plus expenses, sometime paparazzi when he got lucky and took a conveniently embarrassing shot of someone with a recognizable name, is calling in from the sleek silver gray limo that he has been driving for the CEO of Amerigas for the last two days.

"Did you get him on tape?"

"Oh yeah, right down to the money shot with his eyes bugging out. This guy's a real piece of work. He's the boss of one of the biggest oil companies in the world and he's put by my count seven hookers on his expense account just today. I've got pictures of all of it. The Congressmen and the lobbyist going into the whore house, this guy coming out with the two girls, them doing him in the limo. The whole deal."

"Manny, Manny, slow down. That's great. Where is he now?"

"I just told you. He took the two girls up to his room in the hotel. I think he's settled in for the night. This guy's gotta be the horniest man in D.C. since Bill Clinton."

The CEO didn't sleep that night. He was too busy with his playmates in his penthouse room. His version of a *pied-a-terre* was a great faux chateau rising up above Pennsylvania Avenue only blocks from the White House itself. The Versailles Hotel with its high columns and marble staircases, its fluted windows and grotesque gargoyles perched at the tops of its columns and on the corners of its leaded mansard roof, provided the penthouse love nest where the CEO spent all of his Washington visits with his harem of hookers. He exercised his power through his sex, used his expensive girls and then threw them away like so many soiled seabirds after one of his oil spills.

Finally, morning broke over Washington and the CEO fell into a satiated sleep. Plastic gargoyles of the faux chateau watched over his slumber like ugly security guards. In the morning the plastic monsters watched room service come and go, watched the CEO dial the phone to summon his evening's entertainment, watched the two public courtesans disembark the private elevator and enter the penthouse to play this night. By eleven they were gone, and by midnight the CEO had retired to his canopied bed in the master bedroom. It was a clear night and the moon that had risen over the Potomac shone down with a pure white light on the wide-eyed, blindly staring plastic gargoyles who guarded the CEO's smug slumbers.

For three moon-drenched hours the plastic gargoyles guarded the sleeping CEO. For three cloudless hours the moon cast its spectral light over the dark sloping roof that protected the corporate penthouse. For three hours the human security below guarded the lobby and made their methodical rounds of the hotel's corridors, but even they were starting to doze off leaving only the plastic monsters on the roof on duty. But then a dark figure, slender, lithe, all in black, moved like a moon-cast shadow down the steep pitch of the eighteenth-century roof trailing a taut rope behind like a life-line. This silent ghost lowered itself over the edge of the roof and dropped down right in front of a gaping gargoyle to the sill of one of the CEO's penthouse windows and slipped in through the diaphanous curtains. The plastic gargoyle, half grotesque squatting man, half screeching bat, stared blindly at this descending figure but was incapable of raising an alarm, powerless to summon slumbering security.

The black apparition moves soundlessly through the penthouse rooms. A tiny pinlight sparks in its hand and lights its silent progress through the furniture. The CEO's bedroom is easy to find and the CEO himself even easier. His snores are echoing off the canopy of his bed like the burping of elephants. The black-clad figure hesitates not one whit. Drawing a folded piece of stark white paper written on in large red letters out of its black waistband and laying said message on the snoring CEO's chest, the ghostly figure snaps something sharply in its dark gloved hand, waits but a moment as the CEO awakes to the sound, then plunges the long thin blade of that switchblade knife down hard through the paper into the CEO's black heart. Wide-eyed in shock, the CEO tries to speak, to cry out, but all he can do is sink back into his pillows and die. The dark sheathed figure retires to its waiting rope. The plastic gargoyle screeches silently at the moon. The human monster in the bed stares straight up, eyes wide open, seeing nothing.

All of Washington awoke the next day to *The Washington Post's* headlining of the CEO's murder. On the front page above the fold, high profile murder took precedence over everything else. Two lines of high block letters all across the face of the page shouted: "**INDICTED OIL CEO AND PRESIDENT'S MAJOR CONTRIBUTOR MURDERED IN HIS SLEEP.**"

Only the police (who didn't release it to the media) and the plastic gargoyle knew what the note soaked in blood on the CEO's chest read: "**WE, NOT THE COURTS, SENTENCE YOU TO DEATH. MORE HEAD'S WILL ROLL.**"

PART TWO

Thunder and Lightning

Chapter One

Best and Worst

time passed. The seasons didn't change much in California, but in Washington the grim drizzle of April and May gave way to the high heat of summer. June gloom enshrouded L.A. and Ventura and Orange Counties. August and September burned molten on the beltway. Time and tide passed like the waves rising and falling on the beach and the tourists ebbing and flowing from the Capitol down the Mall to meet with Mr. Lincoln.

In September, Charlie married Alison, his golden girl. Sidney was his best man and M.D. Farrow was her maid of honor. Charlotte, Alison's whistleblower pal, gave the bride away with a bit of gender bending panache that was so very twenty-first century. Charlie got his surfer wedding on the beach just below the Santa Monica Pier complete with the bride's entrance to the Beach Boy's *Good Vibrations* down an aisle of standing surfboards. The bride wore a stunning white wedding gown with a full veil, a bare midriff and a blue ruffle where it ended at her knees symbolizing her commitment to the ocean. The groom wore an elegant, classic-cut tuxedo in the same ocean blue as the bride's ruffle with the pants starting with the conventional cummerbund but ending as a pair of baggies just below his knees. Both discarded their flip-flops to be married barefoot.

Sid stood next to his brother and looked longingly at the bride. All he could think of was his own wedding years before in the church in Santa Monica where he and Beth had lived, all very staid and conventional and promising in its normality. But all that promise had turned to pain and despair and betrayal and finally to Beth's funeral back in the first week of May.

Sid had buried Beth. Jerry and Charlie had helped him carry the coffin. The sun had been shining that day too but it hadn't shed any light on what had happened to Sid and Beth. Their marriage had been consumed by Sid's career and Beth's alcohol and pills, by Sid's drive to win every case, to build L.A.'s highest legal profile, to defend his way to the very top of the A-list, and Beth's insecurity in the company of all those rich and famous and decadent and almost always guilty people (no matter how many favorable verdicts Sid brought in). Oh yes, Sid blamed himself alright, for the death of his marriage, and for Beth's death alone in that house in the canyon, but most of all for his not seeing it coming, for his not understanding how his work, his ego, his fierce competitive drive, had driven Beth away, had consumed all the promise they had hoped for on that long ago wedding day.

That's what Sid couldn't help thinking about as he stood next to Charlie and gazed on Alison's beauty as they repeated their vows. Charlie was getting his surfer wedding at the beach just as he had day-dreamed it in the car driving cross-country back in the Spring, and Sid had gotten to know Alison a whole lot better over the summer. Of course, she had moved to L.A. to be with Charlie. But she was on a mission. M.D. had handpicked her to coordinate the Earth Day pro-test plans for OceanSave.

Sid hadn't taken Beth's death well, hadn't been able to get over the sort of human June gloom that descended over him after her funeral. Jerry had tried to cheer him up, but Jerry was a guy, and all of his "get-on-with-life" pleas to his boss and friend fell like the cliches they were on Sid's deaf ears.

Alison was different. She decided she would be Sid's nurse, Sid's shrink, Sid's lady with the lamp, Charlie's brother's keeper.

She always addressed him as Sidney and he always listened in-tently to every word she said. Over the summer they grew as close as two people who weren't lovers could be. She and Charlie and their wounded Sidney became an L.A. threesome that society was getting heartily sick of dealing with. By the time the wedding came around in September, Sid was back in the courtroom from which he had taken a two month hiatus and Charlie was out of the editing room which had pretty much held him captive most of the summer. Alison had been the one who kept life all together for both of them even while doing her organizing among the innumerable California eco-groups. She had finally convinced Sidney that he had to go back to work (because it was who he was and he was very good at it) and Charlie's documentary, co-produced with the notorious Matt Morris, was almost ready for release.

As Sid stands next to his brother and Alison on the beach listening to them exchange their vows, he realizes that he is in love with her. It comes to him as clear as the sunlight on the waves. She had moved to L.A. in June to open an OceanSave office in Santa Monica. Her job involved making contact with all of the California eco-groups, most already mobilized against the threat of offshore drilling. But she had gone out of her way to include Sidney in her and Charlie's reintegration into the world of L.A. They would invite him to join them for dinner. They even introduced him to the club scene where he was utterly uncomfortable. But he was happiest when all three of them went surfing. He hadn't done it for years, but he still had his board and it was like getting back on a bike. They had fun surfing and Alison was learning, but then Charlie had to go into the editing room on the documentary and the threesome outings stopped.

"Sidney? It's Alison. I'm on the freeway. Just got back from Ventura," she called him on her cell phone one afternoon when he was moping around the beach house. "How 'bout a Margarita at the Baja Cantina. Charlie's locked in the editing room with Morris. Yeah, just us. I had a great day. I need to celebrate." She had spent the morning with the biggest environmental group in Ventura County, the Channel Islands Protectorate, and they had come wholeheartedly on board in support of the Earth Day protest march "From the Tar Pits to the Sea."

He had gone and they had spent a nice afternoon and early evening, making a dinner on tortilla chips and salsa interspersed with salty margaritas on the rocks. Sid hadn't missed Charlie and all indications were that Alison had enjoyed the company.

After that there were other afternoons and evenings that Sid and Alison spent on their own. "Call Sid. He'll take you someplace nice. I can't get out of here 'til ten or eleven. He knows all the good places. Hell, he might even introduce you to some local gangsters or movie stars. Call Sid. I'll see you later at your apartment," Charlie encourages her more than once to use Sid for his stand-in to fill her early evenings. In a sense, as he stands next to Charlie at the wedding, Sid feels sad. Now those lazy late afternoons in beach bars or those runs along the beach walk from Santa Monica to Venice and back, just the two of them, were probably over. The documentary is done. Charlie and Alison are married. That changes everything Sid is sure.

"'Til death do us part," both Charlie and Alison pronounce the fatal words that seal the deal. Sid looks on as M.D. Farrow purses her deep red lips at that conventional wedding phrase. *M.D. is a strange one*, Sid thinks, *scary, sort of hillybilly gothic.* The beach wedding is only the second time that Sid has been in her presence. That first time, backstage at the rock club in Washington, he had been impressed by her talent, her way with words and song-writing ability certainly, but as he thinks back on it, the one thing that struck him was her intensity. He remembers her sitting in the dim glow of her laptop computer's screen against the back wall of that backstage area, everyone milling around her, and she seemed to be perfectly still, powerfully focused, suspended in a weird halo of light that gave her a kind of unearthly look. It had only been a momentary impression and a moment later M.D. had looked up and greeted Sid graciously at Charlie's introduction. But Sid still remembers and thinks it strange that through that whole encounter M.D. had never smiled. Her lips had remained as tight and intently set as a closed vice.

Alison's smile, as she tosses her bouquet in the air and throws her arms around Charlie's neck for their first married kiss, is as bright and sparkling as the glistening silver carpet of light unrolled out over the water to the brilliant sun presiding like an approving angel over the festivities. Sid breaks out the champagne and everyone toasts the bride and groom there on the beach with the high ferris wheel slowly spinning above them.

After the wedding they all head for Sid's beach house in Malibu. Sangria in pitchers, chicken breasts on the built-in deck grill, lounge chairs on the beach, and bathing suits and shorts for the reception. It is a strange mix of Hollywood and the hippies of a past protest generation, sort of twenty-first century Gatsby. As Sid tends the chicken on the grill, he marvels at how he and Charlie have found each other again. It had been that cross-country trip in April, that crazy eco-politics odyssey that had brought them back together. So much had happened in such a short time: the Congressional hearings, meeting Alison, the car trip and the shooting of the documentary, then the bad stuff dumped on them at the end of that trip as if the dark powers suddenly decided that too much positive progress was being made. Jerry had called to break the news of Beth's death and that same night, in the car, M.D. had told Charlie about the murder of the eco-movement's anti-Christ, the CEO of Amerigas.

That was a strange conversation, Sid thinks as he remembers it now. Through the clear panes of his glass patio doors, he can see M.D. Farrow and that skinny weasel of a bass player from her band sitting inside, out of the sun like vampires, both talking intently as they sit hunched over M.D.'s lap top. Sid remembers how that night five months before, driving across the desert from Las Vegas to L.A., Charlie had tried to call Alison on Sid's cell phone and M.D. had answered. At the time, Sid had thought it strange that M.D. would be answering Alison's phone in the middle of the night. Alison wasn't there, or at least wasn't in the possession of her cell phone, and that was when M.D. had told Charlie about the murder of the CEO. "That's funny, she's usually home by this time of night," Sid remembers Charlie saying after he had hung up. But again, it didn't seem to bother Charlie so Sid hadn't said anything.

After everyone has eaten, and the party has chilled out, and people are starting to drift away, and Alison is off changing clothes for their departure on their secret honeymoon, and the sun is starting to set out over the ocean, Sid and Charlie have their first chance of the day for a moment together. They step down off the deck and walk toward the water's edge looking right into the sunset.

"Great day, Sid, thanks."

"Hey, no problem, I'm the best man."

"Yeah."

Charlie gets quiet as they walk on toward the water. It isn't like him.

"Hey, you guys are really married," Sid breaks the awkward silence. "What was she thinking?"

"No lie. Believe me, I told her, 'buckle your seat belt.'"

"She's a great girl, Charlie," Sid suddenly turns serious.

"Yeah, I know. She likes you too. I keep tellin' her, 'you just don't say nice things about lawyers.'"

"Hey, thanks, and bite me."

"Look, seriously," now it is Charlie's turn to get serious. "You've saved my life with her this summer. Matt's had me chained in the editing room."

"Not a problem. It's not as if I had any kind of a life. Seriously, she cheered me up. She's a great girl."

"Yeah, I know. Man, I'm actually married. Ever thought I'd say that."

"Where are you two going?" Sid, brilliantly counterfeiting both joy and interest, changes the subject.

"A fancy new all-inclusive in PV. Just for a couple of days. I think she'll like it down there. No documentary. No politics. Just us, starting out together."

Sid just doesn't have anything to say to that. For just a moment he finds it hard to breathe, his throat tightening as if there is a noose around it.

The silence between them goes on a couple of beats too long as they stand looking at the sun starting to sink into the sea.

"I got another one of those notes, Sid."

"Death threat?"

"Yeah, reads like the same guy."

"Look, don't you think you should start thinking about security, now that you're married and all."

"Maybe. Hell, I don't know. It's just this one crazy. They're so intermittent."

"Yeah, but they keep coming."

"I know."

"Look, Jerry's bored as hell baby sitting me. I don't even have anything high profile coming to trial in the near future. Let me give him to you for awhile. He's the best. He'll jump at the chance. He'll take care of the two of you. Nobody'll get near you."

"What? Now?"

"Why not? He's in the house. He always keeps a packed bag in the trunk of the limo. You won't even know he's there."

"C'mon Sid. You want me to take Jerry along on my honeymoon?"

They looked at each other, the sun setting over Sid's shoulder, and neither one can keep from laughing.

"OK. OK. I got carried away," Sid has to admit.

"No, that's OK, I hear you," Charlie still has that impish grin on his face. "Maybe when I get back. Maybe Jerry is a good idea after all. But not on my honeymoon."

They start walking back toward the house. The sun is sinking faster and faster, being eaten by the sea.

"Hey, there she is. Gotta go," Charlie makes his break for the house. Jerry is taking them to the airport in the limo.

Sid stands anchored on the dark shore as Charlie bounces off toward his bride. Looking out across the water, Sid sees the lights of the ferris wheel on the Santa Monica Pier suddenly come on.

Chapter Two

The Premiere

The first of December and Charlie and Matt Morris's documentary is 'in the can' and they have rented the Georgetown Theater in the heart of Washington for the premiere.

"You gotta go with us to Washington for the premiere," Charlie had dropped this demand on Sid only a week before. "You were in on this film from the very beginning, our road trip, all that stuff we shot, it's in there."

Alison had called a day later. Sid had first thought that Charlie had put her up to it, but as she talked he decided not. "Sidney, I wish you would come with us to Washington. Charlie really wants you to see his movie. And I want you to come too. He'll be doing his Hollywood thing with that Morris guy. All the press, the cameras, I need somebody to keep me out of it. I don't want that kind of visibility. What I'm doing now, well…" her voice trailed off without finishing. When he didn't answer right away she sort of stuttered back to her original request: "I wish you'd go with us. It would make it so much easier for me."

"Hey, no problem, I'll go," hers was an offer he just couldn't refuse. "It'll be fun. Hell, I'm probably be the only one of you who has ever been to a Hollywood premiere before. I'll get you down the red carpet with no problem at all."

"Thanks Sidney. I'm so glad you're coming."

Sid was glad too, at least for a few minutes after he got off the phone. He was glad that in some small way he could be of use to her, them. Glad that he would just be in her presence for a couple of days. Glad that he could look at her and dream. He hadn't seen that much of them since the wedding. He had missed her terribly. But his exhilaration turned quickly back to the hopeless reality. She was his brother's wife. There just wasn't any negotiation room there. It was a situation that as a lawyer he knew well. All he could hope for was a compromising plea bargain. So he poured himself a scotch, and then another.

They take the red-eye out of LAX to Washington on a Thursday and Sidney has by far the reddest eyes. They sit together three across in coach, Alison by the window, Charlie in the middle, and Sid on the aisle. Charlie simply hates the concept of "First Class" while Sidney is used to nothing less. But he knows he is just along for the ride. He has been working hard and drinking harder since the wedding. His loneliness has been his only drinking companion.

"Hey, the three musketeers," Charlie jokes as they fasten their seat belts, "off to slay the dragons or tilt at windmills just like Butch and Sundance and Etta heading for Peru."

"Something like that," Sid corrects him like an older brother. "You just crammed three novels and our favorite movie into one mixed metaphor."

"Alrighty then," Alison laughs at both of them unleashing that radiant smile of hers that takes the edge off of even the most numbing hangover.

In the air, Alison quickly falls asleep against the window as the darkness closes around them, but Charlie wants to talk and Sid can't sleep anyway.

"Washington loves this Hollywood stuff," Charlie tells Sid something he already knows. "They'll all be there, Senators, Congressmen, lobbyists and hookers. Not very often the movies come to town."

"I'm looking forward to seeing what you and Morris have put together. I hope it's not just another one of his rants." Sid's head hurts and his mouth is dry and he wishes he hadn't said it as soon as the words were gone. This film means so much to Charlie. But worst of all Sid realizes that he has just given Charlie a soap box and now he is going to have to listen dutifully all the way to D.C.

"It's not," Charlie takes off, "even Matt said that. He said just the other day on the phone that this one is really different from all the others. Then he said a funny thing, at least I thought it was funny. He said it is a lot more poetic that his others. Imagine that, Matt Morris and 'poetic' in the same sentence."

"That's like someone saying that Arnold Schwarzenegger is a sissy boy."

"OK. OK. Very funny. But when you see it I hope you change your mind. We tried to make a movie about beauty and evil, about evil trying to rape beauty, about America and the people who are trying to destroy everything that's good about her."

Charlie is really off and running now. Sid's head is throbbing, his seat belt is buckled, and I really am *in for a bumpy ride* he thinks.

"I know it's just a movie, but it's a small part of something bigger. It's pressure. It's keeping the heat on these bastards. Here's the real deal, Sid. We're in a revolution. It's for the soul of America, for the life of the twenty-first century. They don't care about America. All they care about is money. Did you know that all the big oil hot shots are moving to L.A? You know why?"

"No why?" Sid is utterly uninterested yet feels he has to keep up his side of the conversation. "Is this another one of your conspiracy theories?" His ingrown negativity, his outgrown criticism, rise up against all of his better judgment to bait Charlie.

"Hardly. These guys are right out in the open, cocky as hell because they are sure the government's gonna let them start drilling offshore again. It's been fifty years. Right there in the Santa Barbara channel. They're all lined up and ready to go."

"You think that will really happen?" Slight interest pushes past the dull throb of Sid's hangover.

"Not if we have anything to say about it."

"Who's 'we'?"

"Forget I said that."

"Who's 'we'? Your ecological groups? C'mon."

"Just forget it, Sid. Hey, it's Chinatown."

And with that, Charlie just shrugs his shoulders and grins, albeit, at least it seems to Sid, uncomfortably.

Sid's head still hurts and an awkward silence settles down between him and Charlie. As if heaven sent, Alison picks that moment to wake up, rub her eyes like a kitten, take a healthy slug from her water bottle, and turn to her other two musketeers.

"Hi honey," her hand comes up and darts a quick caress across Charlie's cheek, but then she looks full into Sid's face and cringes. "Sidney, are you OK?"

"Yeah, yeah, I'm fine. Charlie's just been depressing me about the end of the world plus I've got the mother of all headaches."

"Poor baby. Here, take some of these, take three," and she passes him her water bottle along with the pills, "they'll help."

And they do. By the time they land in Washington Sid feels almost good enough to face food. Sitting at a counter in the airport over postmodernist breakfast inventions, Charlie gives them their schedule for the day. The premiere in Georgetown isn't until seven but he is tied up most of the day doing TV interviews with Matt Morris. He consigns Alison to Sid for the afternoon. "We'll all go in a rental limo," Charlie scripts their evening. "Matt and I will get out first. There'll be a red carpet, cameras, the whole deal. They'll stop the two of us. You and Alison can get by down the red carpet while they've got us in their sights."

"Thank god," Alison's relief is genuine.

"No problem," Sidney is the only one who has been to premieres before and is fully confident that no one will notice him slinking by while the bright lights and the cameras are focused on his brother.

"Sidney and I will be just fine while you movie stars are doing your thing," Alison assures her husband, her smile like sunshine and her voice lapping like a gentle wave.

Charlie drops them at the hotel and keeps the cab to go meet Matt Morris for their interviews. It is only ten o'clock.

"I'm meeting some girlfriends for lunch," Alison announces as the bellman leads them to their rooms. "You ought to get some sleep."

"Yeah, I will, I should," when he is alone with her he often has trouble expressing himself.

Alone in his room he tries to sleep but he just lies there in the dark staring at the ceiling like some impotent Hemingway character impossibly in love. He wishes his brother didn't exist and that Alison and he were the lovers in a world of beaches and bungalows and eternal sunshine. He knows he can't live like this for long, a third wheel in their love affair. *It's all so Casablanca*, he thinks with a wry inward smile. He longs for her to look at him the way she looks at Charlie. Across the darkness, through the locked door to the adjoining room he hears her come in from her luncheon. She's probably napping now he thinks and the ache of his loneliness is as palpable as his headache was earlier. In the darkness and the silence he feels miles, oceans, eons apart from her, the vast distance between her liking and his love. Finally he falls hopelessly asleep.

The premiere is a brightly lit affair. In fact, Georgetown blazes with the hot fire of celebrity. Charlie, Alison, Sid and Matt Morris make a foursome in the long black limo that Morris collects them in. Morris has done this before. He instructs the limo driver to park on a side street in Georgetown two blocks from the theatre to insure that their arrival timing is precise.

"We'll let those fat-ass windbags get in first," he explains.

"He means the politicians," Charlie translates.

"Then, we invited some of the rubes that got in."

"He means they brought in some of the people, ordinary people, that we interviewed on camera," Charlie continues his translation.

"Then an actor friend of mine is going to do this great cut-out bit with our fearless leader and that faux-virgin wife of his."

"That is a nice touch," Charlie can't hide his amusement. "This comedian friend of Matt's who does stand-up in comedy clubs is going to escort two life-size cardboard cut-outs of our President and his Virgin Queen down the red carpet. We all wrote a whole stand-up routine for him to do at the microphones."

"Alrighty then," Alison says it with that ironic little lilt that implicates in a nice inoffensive kind of way how stupid it all is.

"What's this 'alrighty then'?" Morris has this acute case of rabbit ears, prides himself on missing very little of what goes on around him, which is probably one of the reasons his documentaries are so entertaining. He seems to have a talent for capturing peoples' voices at their funniest, their most intelligent for their capacity, their most plangent.

"It's just something my grandmother used to say."

"It can mean anything from 'that's nice' to 'screw you'" now Charlie is translating for Alison.

"Omigod, Charlie, you're married to Annie Hall!"

"Who's Annie Hall?" Alison probably knows and is just baiting Morris, successfully.

"Good lord!" he mutters and hits the redial button on his cell phone to check if the rubes and the cut-outs have started down the red carpet yet.

When they finally pull up to the red carpet in front of the theatre at 7:15, Morris suddenly goes all chivalric, turning to Alison and magnanimously gesturing "Ladies first." He knows full well that her stepping out of the limo in her strapless, almost backless, flowing, ankle-length, bright red dress is going to immediately catch the attention of every camera and reporter in the crowd. And he knows that after all of them pose the question "Who is that gorgeous woman?" he can step out of the limo and collect all of the good will and admiration that her striking dress and her natural beauty have generated. As she steps out of the car, she is temporarily blinded by the camera flashes and the wolfish teeth of the ravenous massed press. Morris climbs right over Sidney to follow Alison out of the limo, but he does it with charm, raising a forefinger to Charlie and Sid and saying: "In the movies, it's all about timing."

Outside the limo, Alison is quickly forgotten as Morris and Charlie take center stage. The radical filmmaker and the surfer revolutionary are both dressed in counter-culture evening wear, Morris tie-less in basketball shoes, Charlie also tie-less in cowboy boots. Waving and toothy they walk the red carpet to the microphones like hippie royalty going to court. Sid and Alison, follow them down the red carpet and pass by as if they were invisible.

"The best thing we can do is just go to our seats once we get inside," Sid whispers to Alison as they pass through the crowd like ghosts. "It'll be fifteen minutes before they stop feasting on those two and no one will bother us in the theater."

Sid is right. He has been to these things before in L.A. The lights are dimming for the film before Charlie and Matt Morris make it to the roped-off section in the middle of the theater reserved for Morris's crew. Sid can read the excitement in Charlie's face. It is the flush of celebrity. This is Charlie's world, Charlie's bully pulpit.

The lights go down and the film begins with an orchestral overture in direct imitation of *Star Wars*. Huge white block letters rise out of the bottom of the screen and solemnly march into the background across a star-massed, black, night sky

Movish strikes again, Sid chuckles to himself as everyone in the theatre recognizes the allusion as the start text ceremonially marches up the high screen:

"Beware of the leader who bangs the drums of war in order to whip the citizenry into a patriotic fervor, for patriotism is indeed a double-edged sword. It both emboldens the blood, just as it narrows the mind. And when the drums of war have reached a fever pitch and the blood boils with hate and the mind is closed, the leader will have no difficulty seizing the rights of the citizenry. Rather, the citizenry, infused with fear and blinded by patriotism, will offer up all of their rights to the leader and do it gladly so. How do I know, I know this for this is what I have done. And I am Caesar." (101-44 BC)

Matt Morris's head is going around as if it's on a swivel. He is not looking at the screen at all, only at the audience.

"Look at 'em, Charlie," he leans in and whispers. "They're reading every word. We've got 'em."

The next scene is a helicopter shot of Washington with the Capitol in the background, the camera slowly circling high above the mall, the monuments, the White House, the seat of government. As the camera circles down over the White House it levels off and at low level slowly buzzes the length of the mall from the Capitol shimmering over the reflecting pool and pulling sharply up over the Lincoln Memorial.

But then the same scene is repeated, only this time in black and white. It is a similar helicopter shot, historical footage of a bygone anti-war demonstration when the organizers turned the mall into a huge graveyard with coffins and headstones lining the reflecting pool and the steps of the Lincoln Memorial to symbolize the soldiers killed.

From the coffins on the mall the cut goes straight to brilliant, sun-drenched shots of huge, coffin-like rock formations rising up into a cloud-brushed Wedgewood sky.

"That's Bryce Canyon. We shot that," Sidney leans across to Charlie and Alison and whispers excitedly, then recoils, embarrassed, at his outburst of emotion.

"It sure is," Charlie grins at his famously cynical brother's loss of composure. "Pretty cool, huh? You're a moviemaker, Sid. There's a lot of the stuff we shot and a lot of other California stuff in here."

Charlie Castle's and Matt Morris's *The Devil and the Deep Blue Sea* lives up to its title. All through the film Charlie's scenic shots of America, his surfing and skiing and hiking footage are juxtaposed to hilarious speeches by government figures (in one the Secretary of the Interior argues that offshore drilling platforms make great artificial reefs for fishing) and startling hidden camera footage of oil company executives partying with hookers. It isn't a long film, but it seems to rocket by, the striking images bombarding the viewer at a breakneck pace and the damning words of the talking heads embedding in the audience's mind like pieces of shrapnel.

The film ends with scenes of horror, the ocean coated in oil, black waves breaking on the filthy beaches, sea birds blackened and unable to spread their wings and fly, toxic fogs hanging over Los Angeles darker than any space ship's shadow over an American city in *Independence Day*.

This time it is Charlie leaning across to Sid: "No way the message is gonna be lost on any audience," he whispers as the huge, apocalyptic words "***THE END***" march up across the screen from bottom to top as had the words of the opening. "That's what could happen to America if Big Oil gets away with this scam."

Afterwards, when the lights come up and the raucous applause subsides, Charlie and Matt Morris, the surfer radical and the notorious film-exposer, take the stage and thank everyone for coming. Surprisingly, considering the size of Morris's ego, Charlie gets the last word, probably because Morris knows that Charlie will thank him profusely for being a wonderful mentor (which Charlie does in spades). But, Charlie has always been a genius with a microphone and Sid knows (and certainly Alison is learning) that Charlie's last words to this captive, utterly enthusiastic audience won't be some lame thank-you to an already established media icon. That's just not Charlie's kind of "seize the day" style! Instead, when he finishes thanking Morris, Charlie just stands there at the mike, looking out over the crowd, letting the packed theater go awkwardly silent.

Finally, he breaks the silence in a quiet, firm, almost conversational, neighborly, confiding, plea for consensus and solidarity: "You know, everyone," he begins, taking them all in, "it's *our* country, *our* world, not theirs', not these oil company thugs."

That was it—short and sweet. *This time Charlie took his cue from Hemingway's minimalism*, Sid thought. The standing ovation lasted for long minutes.

Chapter Three

The Inner Circle

After the premiere, the press dispersed to meet their deadlines and Charlie and Matt Morris commandeered the limo to take them to their late-night talk show interviews (Morris's manager has booked two, one on local TV, one on radio), leaving Alison and Sidney in front of the theater to fend for themselves.

"I'll get us a cab to go back to the hotel," Sid suggests.

"No way. It's only ten-thirty," Alison protests. "I told M.D. and Charlotte I'd meet them at the Bastille Wine Bar."

Unexpected change of plan. Sid wonders why there has been no mention of this earlier.

"Funny name for a wine bar?"

"It's a cool place. Very intimate. It's broken up into little rooms, you know, like cells in a prison.

"Aha! Hence the Bastille."

"Hey, way to go Einstein."

Sid hesitates, wondering where he fits into the rest of her evening. Alison picks up on his uncertainty right away.

"You wanna come with me? It'll just be a lot of catching up. I need to report on how the arrangements are going for the Earth Day March in L.A."

Sid hesitates again.

"Really. Sidney. Come along," she reassures him. "We both need a drink."

"OK. Why not? I told your husband I'd get you back to the hotel safe and sound."

"But not necessarily sober," she laughs.

They decide to walk through the chilly December evening to the wine bar. M.D. actually has a "cell" (as the maitre'd, or perhaps jailer would be the better title, calls it) reserved. She must be an influential regular because when Alison mentions "the Farrow party" the pompous martinet behind the reservation desk immediately gets all fussy and escorts them to their private little cell in the back. They are the first to arrive and are well into their first glass of Pinot Noir when the others materialize out of the shadows.

It is somewhat of a crowd. Not what Sidney had expected at all. As they had walked across Georgetown, he had envisioned himself as a fourth wheel on a sort of business girls' night out. But M.D has brought her whole entourage: Charlotte as expected, but also two of the three headhunters, the weasely chain-smoking bass player and the drummer with the exploding hair.

Joining them at the table, M.D. Farrow seems initially startled to see Sidney with Alison, but immediately recovers her dark charm and greets him with her cold vampire hand outstretched across the table.

"Mr. Castle, good to see you again."

"Sidney, please."

"Yes," and Sidney is immediately ignored as both M.D. and Charlotte reach over the table to give Alison greeting hugs.

Those formalities accomplished, Alison takes over and introduces Sid to the others.

"Sidney Castle, Wrig Jones ..." (the skinny bass player who is from the north side of Chicago and whose mother named him after the ballpark down the street) "and Fleming Bangler ..." (originally from Indiana but much more comfortable pretending to be from Texas).

"Hey, I'm Flem Bang, how ya doin'?" the drummer, all Texas down home friendly, holds out his hand to Sid.

"What?" Sid feels like he has missed something in the exchange as he takes the extended hand.

"Huh?"

"Flem Bang. That's his stage name," M.D. responds to Sid's puzzled look. "He thinks it makes him sound like Slash from *Guns and Roses* or The Edge from *U2*.

"We just think it's stupid," Wrig Jones mutters sourly.

"Flem Bang?" Sid repeats it, but it is all that he can do to keep from laughing.

Sid mutters something inane about really enjoying their work and sits. The introductions don't go any further because the waiter interrupts to take the newcomer's orders: cabernet sauvignon for M.D., pinot grigio for Wrig Jones, and just ice water for Flem Bang.

"Hates wine" Wrig Jones makes a condescending excuse for him, "hoosier hillybilly," he adds lighting a new cigarette off the stub-end of his last.

Settled in, the businesswomen begin to catch up. They start with Alison's married life, move to Charlotte's orientation and growing experience as Alison's replacement in the OceanSave Washington hierarchy, touch on M.D. and the Bands' successful gigs here and there, recording sessions, newly written songs, all just harmless wine bar conversations. The men say little. Wrig Jones smokes incessantly. Flem Bang can't take his eyes off of Charlotte. Bored, Sid gets up and goes to the men's room, winding the long way through the narrow corridors of the snug little rooms, trying to peek into them as he passes but only getting quick unsatisfying glimpses of romantic couples stroking each other. When he returns, M.D. and Alison have disappeared, Charlotte leans on Flem Bang's shoulder stroking his scraggly hair, and Wrig Jones smokes sullenly into his pinot. Sid briefly wonders where the two went and what they are talking about.

"How are the arrangements going?"

"I've contacted all of the groups."

"Good. Are the numbers there?"

"Yes. They will be. These California groups are publicity pros. They're ready to start selling it right after the first of the year."

"Good. Any candidates for the special assignments?"

"Yes. Two. These groups seem especially suited for the security and the kind of diversions we want."

"Who are they?"

"One's an anti-lumbering crew in northern California. They're like a right wing militia almost. Scary people. About half and half men and women, some Indians. They are hippies, when they're not up north in logging country they all live on a farm in the canyons above Malibu probably dealing drugs to support their dissent. They just hate the government."

"Who doesn't?"

"Yeah."

"You think they'll be good for what we want?"

"Yeah, they're frustrated."

"How frustrated?"

"Very. They see how it is, how nobody, not the press, not the government, takes us seriously. They want to make a real statement, turn some heads,"

"What do you mean? A real statement?"

"I don't know. Nothing specific. Something the cameras will really like."

"The other group is even scarier. Led by a heavy-duty Gulf War vet, rides a Harley and flies a helicopter. His issue is very simple and clear. He hates dumb wars fought for bad reasons."

"Can we control them?"

"I think so. I talked with the leader. He calls himself Black Jack Daniels. He wants to be a part of anything that will embarrass this President and this Administration in Washington."

"Good. I'll come out in January and I want to meet with those two. Set it up."

"Okay, but there's one other group. You asked for the most radical ones, right?"

"Right. Who are they?"

"All women. A sort of motorcycle gang but not into drugs or crime or anything illegal. Environmentalists."

"An eco-motorcyle-gang?"

"Yes, they call themselves *Dykes on Bikes*."

"Oh, I've *gotta* meet them," M.D. smiled with relish.

"No problem. How are things here?"

"They're getting interesting. The grand jury meets next week."

"So?"

"Both cases are on their list."

"So they have anything?"

"No. We don't think so. We better get back."

Though they have been in the alley outside, they pretend to have been to the ladies room. Nobody has much to say when they sit back down.

Sidney watches them after they return. M.D. seems to have this strange hold on Alison as if they have some secret that they don't want to share with anyone.

"We booked a concert in L.A.," M.D. volunteers. "In January."

"Good. You'll get a break from the winter," Alison answers with small talk, the weather.

It just seems strange to Sid. *These people don't seem to have much to talk about,* he thinks. If only he knew.

A grand jury? There weren't any witnesses. No way. I got off that roof and was long gone before anyone even knew he was dead.

In the dim candlelight Sid's gaze moves from one to the next to the next all around the table, wondering.

That bastard's chauffeur, our detective, he's on ice. They can't touch us. Nobody deserved killing more than that bastard.

He wondered what each of them was thinking, what their secrets were. They were such a strange gang of conspirators. M.D. so dark and mysterious; Charlotte so seemingly innocent yet all over that walking shag rug; Wrig Jones with smoke coming off of him like he was ready to spontaneously combust; Flem Bang looking like a Hell's Angel who has lost his way and wandered into a fern bar.

I've gotten it done, the dirty work. We're about ready to go all the way. What we've got on Amerigas will go all the way to the White House.

Sid couldn't help thinking what a group of misfits they were, yet they made music together, organized political actions together, some were most likely sleeping together.

I'm the only one who could have done that job. Murdering that SOB was the most satisfying thing I've ever done. Nothing is ever what it seems. There were no witnesses.

Who knows what they all were thinking? Sid doesn't. As his eyes trail around the table he can only imagine.

"How is it going for the permits for the march?" M.D. breaks the contemplative quiet with a procedural question.

"I've started the process," Alison reports. "They don't like it, but they'll have to give them. I'm not telling them how big it will be."

"I could help with that," Sid volunteers (he knows not why, probably to impress Alison) "Your organization could probably use a good lawyer in L.A."

"You have no idea," Alison makes a joke out of his offer. Everyone around the table laughs, some less nervously than others, except for M.D. Farrow.

"Are you committed to this cause?" he could feel her eyes burning right through him even in the dim candlelight.

"No," he answered her honestly, "not like you, but I can help. *Pro bono*, of course. My little contribution to your cause.

"But you are a criminal lawyer. We're not criminals."

"I know, but I know all kinds of people in the system in L.A. I'm sure I could be helpful."

"That is a very generous offer, Mr. Castle."

"Sidney."

"Yes, Sidney, thank you." M.D. Farrow's utter inability to smile (even when being gracious) continued to amaze Sid. She was scary like some zombie out of *Dawn of the Dead* or some other cheap horror movie. "I'm sure Alison will take you up on your offer."

"What were they all so on edge about?" Sid asked Alison in the cab.

"Do you remember the murder of the CEO of Amerigas last spring?"

"Yeah, sure."

"A grand jury starts meeting this week and that is one of the cases that they are reviewing. They were all called for questioning after the murder. The DC police spent a lot of time on M.D. and Charlotte before they gave up. Not so much on Wrig and F.B."

"Probably just trying to corroborate the others."

"Yeah, I suppose. Anyway, they're all wondering if they're going to be called again. Stupid, huh?"

"Not really. A grand jury is a pretty intimidating thing. Who do they think killed the CEO anyway?"

"Nobody knows."

Chapter Four

Groundswell

*C*harlie Castle's and Matt Morris's documentary on America and oil first goes viral in short clips on U-Tube planted by Matt's minions, then goes national in almost a thousand theaters a week later. People love it, not only on the coasts in Washington and L.A. but in the middle too. People from Arkansas and Iowa and Ohio see themselves in the funny, goofy, confused and pissed-off people that Charlie and Sid interviewed as they drove across the country. It is as if the whole country was just waiting for someone to take on these belt-way politicians, challenge the self-indulgent excess and expose just how much America was getting screwed.

Sid and Alison and Charlie, the three musketeers, hop back crosscountry (with Matt Morris in tow) for the L.A. premiere of the documentary. This premiere, with its spotlight sweeping the sky over Hollywood, its limos and red carpet, its clamoring paparazzi and fawn-ing media whores (one TV channel sends L.A.'s All-Alliterating news team—Rick Rodriguez, Deborah Dicenzo, Pedro Peres—to cover the festivities) has the same basic ingredients of the Washington premiere, but is much more relaxed, much more California copasetic, because it is just a much more familiar occurrence. Charlie and Matt Morris are the news show and talk show guests *du jour*. Like a political tag team, Ecology and Art, the Abbot and Costello of the environment, they are led out as the daily dog and pony on every news show, afternoon TV coffee clatch, and late night talk show in L.A. They know it will all subside in a week or two, but for the time being Alison and Sidney are pretty much left to their own devices.

Jerry Creogan, however, is much busier. Sid has insisted that he take over as Charlie and Matt Morris's limo driver. So for two weeks Jerry has been carting Butch and Sundance around L.A. and Burbank and wherever else there seems to be a camera and a microphone.

Jerry doesn't mind the work. He would do anything Sid asked him to do and they had talked months before about Jerry going temporarily to Charlie as a bodyguard as long as the death threats kept up, but the limo driving and the bodyguarding has cut in on Jerry's nightwork, on a job that even Sid doesn't know that Jerry has taken on. It is a part-time job, granted, but one that Jerry has pretty wholeheartedly thrown himself into. As he himself said to his first client, "you can take the man out of bounty hunting, but you can never take the bountyhunter out of the man."

A year before, a priest from Jerry's neighborhood in San Pedro had come to him. Jerry wasn't a churchgoing man by any stretch of anyone's imagination, but somehow this padre had heard about his bountyhunting past. In the best tradition of St. Paul and the Blues Brothers, Jerry felt like he was being summoned on a mission from God. The priest asked him to find the seventeen-year-old daughter of a Mexican couple who were his parishioners. Jerry took on the job *pro bono* as Sid would have described it. It had only taken him two weeks to find the girl. She had started out doing crack with some hip-hop freaks in Venice and ended up making porno flicks in a suburban tri-level with a swimming pool in Chatsworth. Jerry had broken as many cameras as he could find while he was taking her out of their little improvised studio.

Her parents shook his hands and thanked him with a fervor usually only reserved for saints and angels. They said that he had brought her back from the dead, saved her from the grave, and it all made him feel so good about himself that when the priest showed up a few months later with another "resurrection" job Jerry took that one too. And another after that. And he never took any money for these jobs. He saw them as his ticket to humanity, maybe even into heaven. He was working on just such a job when the whole documentary entourage returned from Washington and Sid installed him as Charlie's limo driver.

Unfortunately, Matt Morris came along with the package. So while Charlie usually went home to Alison after the talk show tapings or the live news show appearances, most nights this Morris character wanted Charlie to show him the L.A. sights. Morris was a drinker and Jerry quickly got used to pouring him into the limo barely coherent or ambulatory at about thee AM in the morning sometimes in the company of some bimbo so excited to spend time under a so-called filmmaker that she didn't care how drunk, slurring and slobbery he was.

But this Saturday night is different. Jerry has gotten a real break in his latest bounty-hunting case, that of a soccer player who has run away three weeks before. The boy was an A student, an athlete, supposedly a good kid, and his parents didn't have a clue why their kid had split. Jerry had gone to the school and had made the kid's friends so uncomfortable that they had finally given him the probable reason. The kid was gay and couldn't tell his parents. But worse, his friends thought that the kid had been exploring his newly realized sexuality with some much older gay men. It is a phone call from one of these high school friends that has given Jerry his lead as to the young soccer player's whereabouts. He'd been seen on the 3rd Street Promenade in Santa Monica "with two guys that looked like bikers or leather freaks or something like that" Jerry's teenage tipster had described the sighting. As soon as he drops Morris at the airport and asks Charlie for the rest of Saturday off, Jerry goes straight to Santa Monica. He has been poring over pictures of the kid for three weeks so he's certain he can recognize him on the street, but he's not sure that this one will be a win-win situation, not at all sure that the boy will really want to be liberated from his leather Svengalis. Jerry waits four hours, but they finally show up at Starbucks on the Promenade just like he thought they might. A good thing too as the sweet coffee was starting to gurgle menacingly inside him. Jerry lets them get their mochas and frappicinos. Jerry lets them settle in at a table under the ferns near the sidewalk. Jerry lets them sip for long peaceful minutes before he sits down uninvited at their table.

"What are you doing?" the thin balding business-type in the black leather sport jacket and blacked pressed jeans seems violated by Jerry's joining them.

"What the hell is your problem?" the thick biker-type in the leather vest, the earring and the tattoos seems angry at Jerry's intrusion.

"I want the kid. His parents asked me to bring him home. His soccer coach misses him."

"You what? No way," growls leather biker.

"What if he doesn't want to go?" whines leather accountant.

Jerry smiles amicably and shakes his head benevolently: "Sorry guys. Not an option. He's going with me. Now how do you want to do it."

"Do what?" biker barks.

Jerry decides that his side of the conversation is over.

The kid still hasn't said a word. He just sits there sipping from his paper cup.

"Sammy, c'mon, lets go. Your parents are worried sick about you."

"I don't want to. They'll never understand." The kid isn't a mute.

"See. He doesn't want to go," razor-head biker doesn't say it nicely and starts to stand up over Jerry. Really big mistake.

Jerry's fist drives into his groin like a mongoose striking. Leather biker collapses to his knees with his breath exhaling like a huge mouth fart.

Leather lawyer, still sitting down, backs his plastic chair away from this tiny burst of violence. "Omigod," he gasps out in a whisper, both hands going to his mouth in fear.

"Sorry about that." Jerry is being very polite as he steps around the pile of bald head and leather doubled over on the ground and pulls the young man to his feet with one hand around the kid's bicep. "Didn't really want to hurt him, but I'm double parked."

"Omigod," the leather banker bends toward his broken butch boy-friend in horror.

Jerry, with a grip on his runaway soccer player's arm, is already out on the sidewalk, headed across the pedestrian promenade, before any-one in the coffee shop has even registered what happened.

The kid seems more confused than frightened. He is impressed by Jerry's limo, surprised that his parents sent a limo to get him. Jerry goes along with the kid's scenario. By the time they hit the 110 into Pedro the kid is getting over the luxury of the limo and getting back in touch with reality.

"Do they know where I've been? About, about me?"

"No, not yet. I haven't told them."

Dead silence. The kid trying to process that.

Jerry actually feels sorry for him.

"This is bad. What do I tell them?"

"You've got to tell them the truth because if you don't I will. I have to give them a full report. I'm a private detective and they paid for me to find you," Jerry lies.

"Tell them everything?"

"'Fraid so," Jerry's voice is filled with the resignation of the inevi-table. "They're so worried about you. They'll be so happy to have you back. It won't be so bad. OK, it'll be bad but it won't be totally bad. They'll be so relieved that you're safe. Just tell them. They'll handle it.

Look man, it's the twenty-first century. They'll handle it."

"Wow. They sent a private detective to get me in a limo. Cool."

"Yeah, cool." Jerry is starting to get disgusted. This kid may be a good soccer player but he sure isn't the sharpest crayon in the box. "You run away again and I'll come and get you in your mother's minivan with her driving."

Chapter Five

Computing

M. D. Farrow's laptop sits open before her all the way across America in the 747. In Jerry Creogan's limo, after he picks her up at LAX, she consults her laptop all the way to her white filigree hotel on the beach in Santa Monica near Alison's OceanSave office. Her weasel of a bass player is, as ever, in attendance upon her, but she never lets him near the laptop. It is like an electronic extension of herself, a receptacle for all of her ambient thought, a register of all her friends and enemies, a blueprint for all of her (and OceanSave's, one would presume) future plans. It is the brain of the braintrust, the hub of the inner circle, the engine that drives the movement, and it goes wherever M.D. Farrow goes.

The holidays in L.A. have been more of the same for Charlie and Matt Morris. Another opening, another show. The L.A. premiere of *The Devil and the Deep Blue Sea* mirrors the Washington extravaganza. But finally the holidays end, the documentary is all legal for Oscar consideration. Matt Morris leaves town but M.D. Farrow flies in.

M.D. Farrow has come to L.A. to meet the players, record in her laptop the progress in the planning of this new year's Earth Day March, the eco-political Big Event that M.D. Farrow hopes will shake up the world. Her plan is for this march and its attendant message to trigger a tectonic shift, an eco-quake in the political landscape. She wants this march to send a message that they will understand in Washington.

For Alison, M.D.'s visit goes beyond stressful. Not only is M.D. her boss coming to evaluate for the first time the infrastructure that she has set up for the mother of all marches, but M.D. has singled out a handful of highly volatile leaders of some of the less reputable, most radical, one could say least stable, groups that inhabit the seismic landscape of California eco-politics. Why these particular groups? Why not the bigger, more mainstream, more credible and Gandhi-like groups that will deliver the bulk of the marchers? Does she want to persuade them to get on board with the less radical groups? Is she trying to build consensus? Does she have special plans or designated duties for these particular groups? Who knows? Probably only M.D. and her laptop.

M.D. is scheduled to meet with Black Jack Daniels (not his real name as one might guess considering that everyone changes their name once they cross the Hollywood city limits), an ex-Marine Gulf War vet still bitter that he wasn't allowed to drive all the way to Baghdad in '91 and put Saddam Hussein's head on a pike personally. Black Jack is the leader of a protest group calling themselves the Eco-Vets. They verge on a para-military cell. All their literature, their posters, their banners, the bumper stickers on their trucks, even their tee shirts oppose and revile the administration's oil wars. Their logo is a dark Satanic vulture sitting on a gas pump ringed by the slogan **"Dead American Soldiers. Big Oil Profits."** Black Jack's group is made up of a volatile mixture of trigger hungry military veterans and wannabes plus bikers and rednecks and other assorted strains of criminality, but the largest percentage of Eco-Vet members are the parents and spouses and siblings of young Americans killed in the oil wars. Without exception, utterly unanimously, all of these hate the government that sent their children, brothers, sisters, husbands and wives off to their deaths in the name of oil profits.

M.D. is also scheduled to meet with Maud Gunn, the Amazonian leader of the Southern California Dolphin Society as well as the motorcycle gang *Dykes on Bikes*. Despite fronting an organization originally dedicated to the protection of one of the most intelligent and friendly animals known to man, Maud is universally feared as one of the angriest, most unbending, utterly hateful ecological advocates in the history of the western world. At six foot one and two hundred and ten powerfully body-built pounds, Maud looks more like a Raiders linebacker than a Free Willy spokesperson. Her public displays of pique aimed at politicians who disagree with her make Bob Knight's chair throwing and disagreements between hockey players look like child's play. True to her last name she always goes out heavily armed. Once, at the entrance to a Congressional Hearing in Washington, at the metal detector, the TV cameras captured the security guards removing three different guns and a switch blade knife from her imposing person. Needless to say, Maud is very security minded. She has also been, for at least three years, high on the international security watch list for potential assassin candidates. As Alison puts it to Charlie and M.D., she is "one really scary environmentalist." Charlie just laughs and nicknames her the Econator.

M.D. is also scheduled to meet with Edward J. Macalester, the micro-chip billionaire who heads up Channel Island Conservancy, by far the biggest and most substantially endowed of all the Southern California eco-lobbies. Macalester is sinfully young for a billionaire, only 36, and in his two thousand dollar Italian suits and his Lamborghini sports car he presents a rather marked contrast to Black Jack and Maud, yet he is no less avid, and no less capable of decisive action than they.

M.D.'s agenda for her visit is a full one and no wonder that Alison is nervous about her boss's review of the troops. Charlie and Alison are accompanying M.D. to all of her meetings and Jerry is their driver and bodyguard at Sid's strenuous insistence. The weasel, of course, goes everywhere with M.D. silently souring the proceedings like bad breath. Alison makes the introductions, reviews the previous talks that she has held with the principals, then, to Alison and Charlie's initial surprise followed by their confused wondering and suspicious curiosity resulting finally in their somewhat hurt resignation, M.D. asks them to step out and leave her and the weasel alone with these leaders that have been recruited to the cause. In the limo, after the first meeting when M.D. has asked them to step out, Alison asks why.

"I need to be alone with them," M.D. answers without the slightest hesitation or self-consciousness. "I need to gauge their seriousness, their commitment. You have done a wonderful job in setting all this up Alison, but I need to be alone with them face-to-face."

And that is it.

Jerry has a different take on the whole situation. That night, reporting in to Sid at the beach house over a stiff scotch, his only reward for a long day of driving all over L.A. with the eco-trust in tow, he gives his version to Sid who, as usual, is well ahead of him in the scotch column.

"This Farrow woman and that sleazy little ferret she drags around with her are weird, like zombies or vampires or something like that."

"Jerry, Jerry, you make it sound like your day was one long horror movie."

"No. No. It was OK. It's just that those two are so strange. They never say anything. She's always got her nose stuck in that notebook computer. As soon as she gets in the car she has Charlie raise the partition. They tell me where to go on the speaker phone. All so damn secretive. Charlie does whatever she says. What's the deal with that?

That woman's scary. She's like Elvira, Queen of the Damned, without the cleavage."

Sidney is drunkenly amused at Jerry's horror movie concern: "You make it sound like this is all a bad movie," he chuckles.

"Yeah, I know. But they're so different, so cold, so East coast. You think Charlie's in over his head?"

This is the first thing that Jerry has said that Sid takes seriously. He too has thought of Charlie's political involvement with OceanSave in exactly those terms. Even three sheets, this offhand comment by Jerry sobers Sid.

"Tell me more about what went on today," Sid presses Jerry. "Where did you take them? Who did they meet with? Did you hear anything?"

"Didn't hear much at all," Jerry answers. "She kept putting up the partition. But I don't think Charlie and Alison heard much either. The zombie lady kept sending them out of the meetings. They'd go in with her and that sleazy little hillbilly, but then pretty soon they'd come out again and hang out with me in the car."

"Who did she meet with?"

"First stop was at a place called Eco-Vets, a sort of warehouse/club-house, big place, in Carson, with a bunch of bad lookin' dudes hanging out, do-rags and bikers vests, that sort of bad ass costuming, 'hey look at me I'm a gangster.' Big dude in Army boots and camouflage pants and a khaki tee shirt that says **HOW DID THEIR SAND GET ON TOP OF OUR OIL?** meets them at the door with a scowl on his face."

"You're right, it sounds like a bad movie."

"At the end though, when they come out, the big Army guy is smiling and the Farrow zombie actually gives him a little Hollywood hug as they say goodbye. Like I said, strange."

Sid just shakes his head and shrugs that he has no clue what it means.

"The next place we stop, this unbelievable huge dyke meets them at the door. This is in Malibu right by the pier. Nicer digs. Window has a huge dolphin etched on it. This woman looks like a pro football player, really. Gotta be a body builder. Same deal, they all go in, then after a while Charlie and Alison come out. Then when they leave the huge dyke walks out to the car with them and the two women hug each other. It's like Elvira hugging Arnold Schwarzenegger."

All Sid can think is that M.D. Farrow is having great success in bringing allies over to the cause.

"Then they had me drive them all the way up to Santa Barbara," Jerry continues his picaresque narrative, "to this mansion up in the hills overlooking the ocean. Big gate with security, wrap-around driveway, huge Spanish hacienda, pools, verandahs, garages, all that stuff. Smells of big money. Fairly young guy meets them in the entranceway. Same deal for the meeting, only this time when they leave the zombie only shakes hands with the guy. But they seem friendly, even though I think it would take dynamite to make that Farrow woman smile."

Sid is bemused by Jerry's version of the M.D. Farrow tour of the southland radical landscape. He goes over it in his mind the next morning when his head has cleared, but still has no ideas. It is the last day of the Farrow woman's whirlwind tour and it is devoted to intra-office meetings of the OceanSave brain trust. Jerry drives M.D. and the weasel to the Santa Monica office where Charlie and Alison are waiting for a morning of strategy sessions. Sid is occupied all day in the courtroom defending the latest movie star druggie on his client list of celebrity screw-ups. By two in the afternoon Jerry has delivered M.D., her laptop, and her weaselly wingman to LAX for their flight back to Washington.

"That Farrow woman is scary," Jerry says for the umpteenth time. "Thank god she didn't stay too long."

"Oh she'll be back," Sid assures him cynically. "It sounds like she wants this big march to be her masterpiece, like wrapping Mount Whitney in orange plastic or turning the 10 freeway into a huge card section that spells out "**DEATH TO BIG OIL.**"

Ironically, Sid isn't that far off in his cynical exaggeration. Their lives getting back to normal, he invites Charlie and Alison to a Lakers game the next night. It is meant to be a carefree three musketeers evening hearkening back to the summer, but before halftime in the comfort of the law firm's private sky box Sid can no longer restrain himself and asks Alison: "So, how'd it go? She sure was in and out of town pretty fast." Good lawyer that he is, Sid wants to hear their first person version to compare it to Jerry's third person limited narrative of the two-day tour.

Alison is reticent, as if not really willing to bring Sid into the loop. Her hesitance could stem from either fear of or protectiveness for the motives and purposes of both M.D. Farrow and OceanSave. But Charlie has no such hesitancy.

"M.D. seems a little uptight these days. The march is four months away, Alison's already got eighty percent of it in place, and M.D.'s running around talking to all these marginal freaks about their minor roles in the deal. Seems like she's micromanaging to me."

Alison is mildly annoyed at his take on it: "Look, we're trying to stage the biggest protest march since the sixties, since the Vietnam War, since Martin Luther King on the Mall. She's just trying to get us on message, all on the same page."

Kobe drains another 25 footer below and whirls away pumping his fist.

"We spent all morning yesterday talking about the message and all we came up with is one word," now it is Charlie's turn to be mildly annoyed.

"Maybe that's all we need," Alison counters.

"Great. But I'm supposed to be the spokesperson for this whole operation. I'm the one who is going to be on camera. What do I do, just keep repeating it over and over?

"I think she's counting on your vaunted creativity," that last dripping with sarcasm, "to mold our message around that governing concept."

"You mean to spin it whatever way works best for the audience we're trying to convince that this is important."

"Hey, way to go, Einstein. And everyone says that Stanford is just a party school."

"Man, you two sound like that screwy political couple from back in the nineties. You know, Clinton's hillbilly strategist and Bush's P.R. girl."

"Carvill and Matalin?"

"Who?" Charlie truly has no clue.

Alison is smiling broadly: Carvill and Matalin? Us?" Sid thinks she has taken it as a political compliment rather than as the offhand joke he intended.

"So what is the one word?" Sidney tries to get them back on message.

"What word?" Charlie is trying to follow the game and the conversation and not doing very well with either.

"Have you ever seen pictures of the Belfast murals?" Alison suddenly is all seriousness, really is on message. "M.D. went to Belfast last year. That's where she got it. The word is 'Resistance'."

Chapter Six

Past Crimes

*M.*D. Farrow and her smoking weasel return unobtrusively to Washington. No limo awaits them at the airport, only Patriot Security—gray men in gray suits—which serves a subpoena on M.D. requesting her presence the following week at the Grand Jury hearings into the murder of the CEO of Amerigas. How do they know her whereabouts? How do they know that she is arriving on this particular flight? Questions she cannot answer but which raise alarms in her suspicious mind, for M.D. is also quite security conscious. She closely scrutinizes the official-looking ID cards of the process servers and records their names and numbers on her everpresent laptop. No one questions her right to do it... yet.

M.D. has been waiting eagerly for her grand jury summons. She knew she would be called because she was originally questioned when the CEO was murdered almost nine months before. Now she has less than a week to poison the Grand Jury investigation. She consults her laptop and immediately dials *The Washington Post*.

Two days later, M.D. with her entourage in tow—Wrig Jones the weasel, Manny Kravitz Private Investigator—marches into the editor's conference room of *The Washington Post*. Manny has been living in style, out of sight in plain sight on a tab footed by OceanSave. M.D. has kept Manny on ice all that time. She has set up this meeting with the two reporters she personally requested from the city editor with the teaser on the phone that went "I have an eyewitness to what happened the night before the CEO of Amerigas was murdered in the Versailles Hotel last April." That was enough to whet the newspaper's curiosity.

From the moment she enters the conference room, there is no doubt who is in control of the proceedings. The reporters know who she is, what her politics are, have done their morgue research, but they really have no idea how big of a story she is going to dump in their laps. They don't yet have any idea of the shockwaves this story will send through the grand jury's deliberations when it hits, through all of Washington and its oil-driven government, through the whole lobbying industry of Washington.

Introductions are offered by the reporters, but M.D. does not reciprocate. They know who she is and she will present Manny, her witness, when she is good and ready. Awkward silence. M.D. sits down. Others follow on opposite sides of the conference table. Reporters are poised, laptops open. M.D. prolongs the awkward silence by slowly opening her laptop and logging in, ignoring her eager interrogators. Finally she looks up from her booted-up screen and demurely invites them to begin: "Gentlemen?"

"Ms. Farrow," the shorter and younger, tie and sportcoated, of the two reporters pauses, waiting for her to correct him or tell him how she wants him to address her, but she says nothing, just waits.

"You said that you had information pertaining to the murder of the CEO of Amerigas," the older and taller, tie and shirtsleeved, of the two reporters cuts in and wards off the second awkward silence.

"Yes I do. This is Mr. Emmanuel Kravitz. He is a Private Investigator and he witnessed the complete profligate lifestyle of the Amerigas CEO leading up to that person's murder. Especially the events of the night before he was murdered."

The two reporters are typing so fast that their fingers are dancing. All of a sudden they have a salacious, sensational, paper-selling window into the degenerate life of one of the most powerful (and rich), most influential (and politically connected), Capitalists in America. They know all too well that when one of the marquee American names, an utterly recognizable, headline-compatible name, goes this far over to the dark side that the vast gullible American public will eat it up and, like Oliver Twist, beg for more. It is stories like this that can give the stodgy, old, journalistically cautious, ostensibly ethical *Washington Post* the same cachet with the reading public that *The National Enquirer*, *The Star* and *Us* magazine enjoy. Nothing sells papers like celebrity and political sex.

M.D. Farrow proves a surprisingly amenable source for the two reporters. She doesn't handcuff them. She doesn't negotiate any guidelines that don't allow them to name names. She basically gives them total access and pretty much the whole story. The reporters actually think they are getting the truth, the whole truth, blah, blah, and nothing but the blah. Now who are the gullible ones? Because there is never such a thing as the whole truth. Einstein proved that. All truth, all reality, is relative and the two reporters are only being fed as much of the truth as M.D. Farrow chooses to feed them. Manny has had almost nine months to rehearse this story and he has it down pat, especially his own protestations against all that the CEO did. Manny Kravitz portrays himself much more as Phillip Marlowe than as the keyhole-peeping pond scum that he really is. M.D. just lets him talk away. She has rehearsed his story with him countless times. In fact, Manny has gone over his story so many times that he has reached the point where he fully believes every word of it. Metareality is great. It can take the unreal and make it seem real with ease. Manny gives the reporters everything except the name of who might have killed the CEO.

After Manny completes his performance, the two reporters still have a few questions left and they turn to M.D. for the answers:

Why did OceanSave have a private detective surveilling the CEO of Amerigas?

Where has this witness been for the last nine months?

Why have you, the CEO of OceanSave, brought this witness forward at this time?

M.D. listens attentively (though she never smiles) and then declines to answer: "Gentlemen, first of all, I am not the CEO of OceanSave. We don't have a CEO. That's what oil corporations have. Secondly, I am under a Grand Jury subpoena in the investigation of this very case. I am scheduled to testify next Tuesday in closed hearings. Until then, I cannot answer your questions, but after I testify, unless of course a gag order is extended by the Grand Jury, I will be happy to answer all of your questions in full. Thank you." And with that, she gathers up her ubiquitous laptop and leads her minions out like a triumphal envoy of truth out of the clattering newsroom of the enemy.

Backstage at *Elmo's*, Wrig Jones smokes and listens as M.D. talks her way through their day. Both are drinking red wine, M.D. picking ravenously at small squares of hors d'oeurves-cut pizza as she talks. As ever her laptop sits glowing on the table like a time bomb. It is only eight o'clock. *The Headhunters* don't go on for another hour, but they both seem tired from their day of communing with the national media.

"*The Washington Post* are just a bunch of chickenshit journalists who still think that just because that bum is President of the United States they owe him some sort of fair and balanced story. They still think that just because his Big Oil buddies get to go to State Dinners at the White House that they can't be the worst kind of crooks who steal from their own employees pension funds and pick all of our pockets in the name of supposedly lower oil prices. Screw *The Washington Post*. Screw Big Oil. They don't give a shit about America. We're gonna bring them down, baby. Every one of them. I've got them all bookmarked in my favorites. They're all marked for a fall, every one of them. I wish I could kill them myself, cut off their heads like those terrorists in the Middle East do to our people sent over there to fight his wars. My father worked for their type thirty years. My daddy worked his brains out for people like them, like that Amerigas monster. Then one day they just fired him, him and four thousand other people whose salaries were too high. Then they went into bankruptcy and they didn't pay his pension. Just like that, like he'd never even been there. I came home from school one day and my daddy was dead. *The Washington Post* wants to know why? Let 'em dig that story up. I hope they do. I hope they're good enough. That's why I went to *The Washington Post*. What we did today is send out the first tremor. It doesn't take long for a tsunami to drown a whole country. We know that. But something has to start the shift in the earth that makes the tsunami start to build. That's what we're doing, setting things in motion. The other thing we did is turn their whole Grand Jury whitewash upsidedown. They took this whole deal to the Grand Jury because that keeps all the scandal, the bribery, the hookers, the crooked accounting, the price gouging, all of it behind closed doors. That's the Washington way. But now they can't do it. They've got to show that the CEO was not the victim they want him to be. These people all have to be brought down. All of them. From the oil companies to the lobbyists to the crooked politicians right to the White House. Amerigas is just the tip of it all. They're all guilty and we need to make them pay for a change."

No tears. No wavering voice. No loss of control. Just cold hate and sharp anger. A witness to one of her low decibel rants like this (like Wrig Jones) might wonder how she could possibly go on stage and sing with all that hate and anger boiling within her. But either Wrig Jones is too burnt out on cigarettes and wine to care or he knows full well that it is just her way of warming up to go onstage, her way of stoking the passion she needs to deliver her angry protest songs. The real value of Wrig Jones to M.D., the most attractive aspect of his smoky, weaselly persona, is possibly that he is simply such a good listener.

Chapter Seven

Security Issues

*C*harlie rarely thinks of Sid except when they are together. Charlie is too busy being a media star, tossing his surfer locks, commenting on clips from his documentary, and providing trenchant mocking anti-administration political commentary for TV interviews, magazine photo ops and newspaper reporters. He presents a People's Choice Award on a hokey TV awards show in January, for god's sake! Charlie is really putting OceanSave on the map, and in the process becoming a true thorn in the side of the Big Oil Administration.

Sid is directly the opposite. He thinks of Charlie all the time. In fact, Charlie has become a somewhat unhealthy obsession for Sid, splitting his consciousness, testing his capability for brotherly love. All over Alison. Only Sid knows when he wishes that Charlie was dead so that he could have Alison. Only Sid feels the terrible guilt of his fratricidal fantasies. Wishing Charlie dead in his secret soul, Sid obsesses over keeping Charlie alive. Charlie's security is all that Sid cares about after Alison. Again and again Sid insists that Jerry Creogan must bodyguard Charlie, at least until they find the sender of the threatening notes. Charlie, probably out of some natural instinctive conviction that he is some sort of immortal sun god like Apollo, laughs off Sid's concerns, steadfastly refuses Jerry's babysitting, though he rarely turns down a ride in Sid's limo. Undaunted, Sid nags both Charlie and Jerry like a shrewish wife until neither of them (or Alison either) can stand to listen to him anymore and Charlie gives in and Jerry moves over and Alison breathes a sigh of relief.

Now Jerry is Charlie's full-time bodyguard when Charlie is in L.A. (and Sid is pushing for Jerry to accompany Charlie on all trips as well). In fact, Sid is driving Jerry to distraction while Jerry is driving Charlie all over L.A. Sid and Jerry's cell phones are like a hot-wired circuit between the two brothers. When Charlie sneezes in Beverly Hills, Sid catches cold in Malibu, and Jerry is the infectious carrier. It is getting to the point that when Jerry's cell rings and Sid's number comes up, Jerry doesn't want to answer. But he always does, and Sid always asks the same question in one way or another:

"Jerry, hey, how are things going with Charlie? You keeping an eye on him?"

"For god's sake Sid, I'm almost living inside his pants!"

"Now that's a scary thought," Sid tries to turn his paranoia into a joke.

But all of a sudden it is no longer a laughing matter.

Charlie is flying into L.A. from Washington where he has been meeting with members of Congress for OceanSave.

Jerry, in the limo on the way to LAX to pick him up, is caught in traffic on the 405.

Sid, fantasizing about Charlie's plane crashing and Charlie's widow becoming all his alone, calls Jerry on the cell phone to make sure that everything is OK.

Charlie, flying coach as usual, is in the middle of the plane and it takes him a while to get off. He is in the usual trudging crowd as they descend the escalator and walk the long tiled hallway to the baggage carousels. Coming through the arrivals door, Charlie spots the sign immediately. It is held by a large, somewhat swarthy man in a grey suit with a chauffeur's hat on his head and it has Charlie's name on it in large black letters. Only Charlie's name is spelled wrong: "Charley" not "Charlie." Small thing, and Charlie in his usual heedless way just shrugs it off as he approaches the chauffeur holding the sign.

"Hey, I'm Charlie Castle. Where's Jerry? He was supposed to pick me up."

"Uh Jerry, oh yeah, Jerry got delayed and sent me in my limo," the driver seems confused, but Charlie doesn't pay much attention. It has been a long flight and he just wants to get home to Alison.

"Delayed? How come?"

The limo driver with the sign still seems confused, unsure, almost nervous. "The car's out front in the limo lot," he finally decides. "Can I get your luggage?"

"Don't have any. Just this," Charlie waves his backpack at him.

"OK then, shall we go," the driver with the sign coaxes him and Charlie starts to follow.

"Charlie. Hey Charlie, over here."

Charlie's head is turned by a deep voice bellowing from the sliding door. It is Jerry Creogan's voice across the crowded arrivals hall and the first suspicion enters his mind.

"What the? Hey, who are you?"

The limo driver drops his sign and runs for the door.

Charlie, his mouth open in surprise, then realization of what was happening, watches the man go as Jerry fights his way through the crowd to Charlie's side.

At the sliding door, another man in a similar grey suit seems to join the fleeing limo driver as they push their way past luggage-laden travelers and out into the night.

"Who was that? What did he want?" Jerry, always suspicious, is already asking as he comes up beside Charlie.

"I don't know. He said he was a limo driver and you sent him."

"I didn't send him. I got caught in traffic."

"What's going on?"

"I think somebody just tried to snatch you."

"Snatch?"

"Kidnap you. Somebody just tried to kidnap you, Charlie. Maybe Sid's not so crazy. Maybe you gotta start being more careful and I gotta start payin' more attention."

In the limo, the first thing Jerry does is report into Sid. He hates saying it, but he admits "you were right. Somebody just tried to snatch Charlie at LAX."

Dead silence on the line.

Jerry knows that Sid is just thinking, turning it over. He waits.

Charlie has less patience. "Put us on the speaker phone," he orders Jerry who plugs the cell phone in and flips the switch. "Sid, its Charlie. Jerry's right, somebody just tried to kidnap me. Have you talked to Alison today?"

"She's been up in Ventura all day. She should be on the way home now."

"Where are you?"

"At the beach."

"OK, we'll come there. Get Alison on the phone and tell her to come to your place too. I don't want her going home alone. Something's up and we need to talk about it. Jerry and I will be there in..." he looks at Jerry to finish his sentence.

"Less than a half hour," Jerry figures.

"Get Alison right away," Charlie urges.

Sid's heart doesn't stop racing until he hears Alison's voice on the cell phone. He wishes he hadn't had that third scotch but it is too late. He feels tactless, doesn't really know what to say to her, but this is not just a time-of-crisis phenomena. He is usually rather tongue-tied around Alison, so much he wants to say and so little that he can. This time, however, he really does have something to tell her and he does, bluntly, straightforwardly, and her reaction is "Omigod!"

An hour later they are all together in the Malibu house.

"Who would want to kidnap Charlie? And why? Who benefits? Who thinks Charlie is a good target? Why would they do it? Money? Political reasons? Why?" It is Alison who is deluging Sid and Jerry with questions as if they are some sort of counter-terrorism experts. Charlie is not saying much. He seems stunned, sort of like Luke Skywalker finding out that Darth Vader is really his father.

Sid's mind has been racing ever since Jerry's phone call from the car. He has turned all of these questions over dozens of times already: "Probably not money. There are a lot richer targets for kidnapping out there in L.A. than Charlie Castle. Has to be political in some way, but how?"

"These guys were amateurs," Jerry adds his two cents. "I don't think they were mob or gang guys. They gave it up as soon as I interrupted them and ran like a couple of scared chickens. Amateurs."

"OK, amateurs, but why?" Sidney is thinking out loud now. "To shut him up? Someone who doesn't like what he's saying? To blackmail us to stop OceanSave? To stop the march? To question him? Maybe that's it. Maybe they were Patriot Security and they wanted to question him."

"Or," Jerry cuts in again, "it could just be this guy who keeps sending the death threats."

"Some radical, fanatic," Sid still speculating.

"Or it could be some muscle hired by the oil companies or Amerigas to get Charlie and OceanSave off their backs."

"I like that one," Sid sounds like some studio executive greenlighting a high concept idea for a movie. Charlie's brush with kidnapping has become a kind of parlor game for the four of them, like a real life game of CLUE, Amerigas in the airport with the fake limo driver.

Charlie finally snaps himself back into the land of the living: "Well, whoever it was, they failed."

"This time," Sid growls at Charlie's naivete.

"They failed and it's not going to do us any good trying to figure out who did it because they're gone."

"All the more reason to make sure it doesn't happen again. I want Jerry with you full time, and I do mean full time, until all of this blows over or until we catch whoever it is who is after you."

Now Alison has become the silent one as Sid, seizing the unaccustomed role of leadership, starts plotting the future security of his brother's comings and goings. Perhaps the realization that she is the wife of a live target is just sinking in. Her quiet is that of a person suddenly readjusting her hold on reality.

"Jerry will lay out a whole system of procedures for moving around L.A., for entering and exiting buildings, for traveling, for attending public functions, even for when you are at home inside your own space. He's an expert at this, trained for this, we have to listen to him."

Jerry listens to Sid talk about him and he is gratified by the high level of trust and respect that Sid invests in him, but he is also slightly daunted by the heavy responsibility that goes along with Sid's confidence in him. Jerry knows that no bodyguard, no matter how well trained or how good, can guarantee the safety of anyone in this day and age in America. Sid seems to think that Jerry is some superstar among bodyguards and unfortunately Jerry knows better.

"Boy, I need a drink," it is Alison who shatters the tension of their family conclave.

Everyone subscribes to that idea. Another scotch for Sidney, beers for Charlie and Jerry, a white wine for Alison, and except for Sid who is at the sipping stage of the evening, everyone's first drink disappears as if they were crossing a desert. Their seconds make things smoother and turn them back to talking.

"Hey hon, you're gonna love this," Charlie remembers the news he has brought from Washington. "The Grand Jury findings are out. No indictments in the CEO's murder came down. After they listened to our witness tell what happened before that prick got murdered, they just decided to leave the whole thing alone."

"They don't want to push it any further because they know how many heads could roll," Alison speculates. "Typical Washington."

"M.D. says *The Washington Post* stories scared them off, or else somebody else testified and conned them into a cover-up, maybe pled national security, invoked the Patriot Security Act. Who knows?"

"What *Post* stories?" Sid doesn't know about any of this. All he remembers is him and Charlie getting the news of this Amerigas CEO's murder the same night they got the news of Beth's death, that night in the car driving back from Vegas to L.A. at the end of their crosscountry trip.

Alison takes up the burden of explanation, fills Sidney in on the private detective planted as the CEO's limo driver, OceanSave's orchestrations of the whole murderous mess, M.D.'s intentional leaking of the real story (or one of the real stories) of that night to The *Washington Post*. Even Sid, drunk as he is, can't help but think that this is pretty melodramatic cloak and dagger for a group like OceanSave to be right in the middle of.

"This can't be good for OceanSave," Sidney drunkenly blurts.

"All we were doing was collecting evidence to use in discrediting the CEO when he finally came to trial, and he would have come to trial if someone hadn't killed him first," Charlie glibly offers the party line, fully rehearsed and impeccably delivered.

He lets it go, but something still bothers Sidney about this whole CEO murder thing. He can't put his finger on it, but it just seems strange to him. Tonight though, he is just too drunk to pursue it.

Charlie changes the subject: "What about the march? How is that going?"

He is addressing Alison, but Sidney gathers that when Charlie and Alison are alone this is a regular topic of their conversation. He seems genuinely interested. She seems relieved to be off of the whole CEO murder topic.

"We walked the route."

"Who?"

"Me and some of the leaders of the major participating groups."

"That Black Jack guy? That big dyke?"

"Yes, they were there, part of the group. There were at least twenty people. It's a pretty long walk from the Tar Pits to the Santa Monica Pier. About nine miles. The route will pretty much follow Olympic Boulevard parallel most of the way to the 10 freeway. It took us about three hours to march it."

"You're gonna march a million people nine miles in three hours through the middle of downtown L.A.? No way!" It is Sidney not Charlie who is expressing this skepticism.

"No, we're not going to do it that way," Alison's eyes spark. She is proud of her planning powers, the responsibility that M.D. and OceanSave have bestowed upon her as their L.A. strategist. She is eager to show how she has solved this problem of the march's staggering numbers. "We're calling it 'Rolling Thunder,'" she explains. "Black Jack actually came up with that name. He said it was some famous operation during the Vietnam War. He's, like, some kind of military historian I think."

"He's like a big middle-aged biker thug if you ask me," Charlie mocked her.

"Bite me," Alison was not to be deterred from chronicling her triumph. "We're gonna start at the tar pits with a core group, maybe ten thousand people. That's doable downtown. They have twice that many runners in the L.A. Marathon every year. Then, along the route there will be staging areas where other groups will join us as we march. I want the marchers to build as we go along. By the time we hit Santa Monica there will be four hundred to five hundred thousand people marching. Then another five hundred thousand will gather on the beach in Santa Monica and be waiting to join us when we get there. They'll fill the beach all the way south toward Venice and all the way north toward Will Rogers. A million people. The biggest march ever, not just Earth Day, EVER.

"Do you really think you'll get those numbers?" Charlie's PR-oriented mind is already spinning those numbers into terms for media consumption.

"They'll come. They'll be there." Certainty is firm and confident in Alison's voice. "It's a question of pride. That's the message we're putting out to everyone. California is the most environmentally conscious state in America. We have to turn out in the biggest numbers ever. The people will come. They'll come from all over America, not just California. We've got the buses. We've contacted every single group, the smallest to the biggest. The word is out. Oh they'll come alright."

"Can the streets, the beach, handle those kinds of numbers?" This time it is Jerry's curiosity that forms the question.

"The beach, no problem. It's big enough to handle another million people. But we're still in negotiation with the cops about the route," Alison hesitates for the first time in this laying out of her blueprint.

"What's the problem with the route?" Charlie presses her.

"We start out on Olympic and that's fine," Alison answers. "They're cool about that. But I want to come right down the 10 freeway. They're not too cool with that."

"Yeah right," Charlie mocks, "they're going to shut down an L.A. freeway for a protest march."

"Maybe not," Alison looks daggers at him, "but it's going to be an awful lot of people and maybe we can just walk anywhere we want to."

That shut Charlie up and Sid and Jerry are both trying to figure out exactly what she just said.

"You thinkin' of just takin' over the Santa Monica freeway?" Jerry is actually grinning at the idea. "Like hijackin' a freeway. Cool."

"It's really gonna piss off the cops, sweetie," Charlie too seems pretty relaxed with the idea.

"Hey, five hundred thousand marchers, a couple of thousand cops, crowd control's gonna be a pretty hopeless security issue for them," Alison beams.

"Wait a minute. What if your crowd gets out of control?" Only Sid is shocked by Alison's scoff-law idea. "What if it gets violent?"

"It might, but not for long. The cops won't be able to do anything. We'll be like a tidal wave coming down that freeway."

"For god's sake, Alison, you're not planning a protest march, you're pushing for full-fledged revolution," they all look at Sid, see that he is drunk, excitable, and decide to ignore him.

"The confines of the freeway walls itself will provide us with security. All we have to do is lead the crowd into one left turn down the widest ramp. We'll be marching on Olympic, do a jog on 20th Street in Santa Monica and go right down the ramp. The only way the cops stop us is if they start shooting and there's no way they're gonna do that. There won't be much traffic because everyone will have been warned away from Santa Monica because of the march anyway."

"Cool," Charlie had to admire his wife's vision.

"Out there," Jerry signaled his approval too.

"You're all nuts," only Sid seemed to sense the danger in this public relations stunt. "It's five hundred thousand people, and another half a million waiting on the beach. If something happens, if it gets out of control, it could be a disaster."

"Really, we've looked at all that. Security issues have been right up front in all of our discussions."

Why did Sidney feel like he was hearing a meticulously rehearsed text, a party line, something that Alison had composed or had been told to say if any doubts were ever raised.

"Security issues, security issues," Sidney is drunk, his head is pounding, he knows he has to sit down, the room is starting to spin, the moon out over the ocean turning over, "everything is security issues anymore."

Chapter Eight

Chinatown in Malibu

*T*he deck of Sid Castle's Malibu beachhouse is an exceptional venue for ocean sounds, glorious sunsets, and hung-over meditation. Strong coffee fuels Sid's morning meditations as the waves break below and the heat of the sun burns off the ocean fog. What he has isn't really a headache. It is more a thick fog of guilt for his own weakness.

Surprisingly Sid remembers almost everything that happened the night before. He remembers the phone call from Jerry about the kidnap attempt on Charlie at the airport. He remembers his own frantic attempts to call Alison. He remembers their talking into the night about Charlie and Alison's security, about the Grand Jury findings in Washington (something still bothered Sid about that murder that he had heard about almost when it happened), about the plans for the huge Earth Day March that Alison was forming. But most of all he remembered with regret his own ineffectuality.

He had been too drunk to make his points, too drunk to be taken seriously. He had utterly failed in getting them to see how dangerous the world around their radical fantasies could become. He tried to warn them but they didn't listen to him because he was just a drunk. They all knew how smart he was, how well educated, how L.A. connected, how streetwise and executive suitewise, but they didn't really hear him. They didn't listen to what he said because in their here and now he was already drunk and showing signs of it before they even started the conversation.

Charlie is the idealist, Sid sips his strong coffee and looks out over the waves, *and Alison is the radical organizer willing to take risks to orchestrate her epic spectacle*, Sid worries most about her, *and Jerry will go through a fire-storm for all of us*, every day Sid feels thankful for Jerry's loyalty. *But I'm supposed to be the realist in the crew*, he is plagued by his own insubstantiality. *They need me to help them figure out what to do, and I'm too damn drunk to be trusted.*

Sid stands up from the chaise lounge and goes into the house, to the kitchen, where the half-empty bottle of Dewars sits on the counter from last night. Even as he walks toward it, Sid thinks about pouring himself a morning drink, hair of the dog, starting this day as he has started so many others in the recent wandering years of his useless life. Instead, he takes the large bottle still uncapped from last night, and in one decisive motion pours its remaining contents down the kitchen sink.

"Man, what did you do that for?" Charlie is in the kitchen doorway in his shorts and a tee shirt, just awakened, and has witnessed Sid's angry act of self-loathing. "That's a lot of expensive scotch going down the drain."

"Yeah, it is." Sid looks despairingly at his bright-eyed younger brother. "You want some coffee?" Sid runs away from trying to explain. He realizes that they all must have slept over last night.

On the deck, the hot coffee burning away the fog for both of them, Sid apologizes. "I'm not much help to you guys. I'd had a few drinks last night. Sorry. I didn't know things were going to blow up like they did."

"Hey, it's OK, no problem. All of us got caught by surprise by what happened at the airport. Everyone was upset."

Sid doesn't push the issue. He is reticent to draw more attention than need be to his own ineffectuality. He knows that he is drinking too much, knows that all the booze befogs his usually sharp analytic mind. For some strange reason he suddenly pictures himself as Paul Newman in that movie about the drunken lawyer, but he can't remember the film's title. He knows he needs to set aside the booze but he can't do it. He shades his eyes from the hot sun. It stabs at him, lays bare the guilt and regret he feels. He wishes he hadn't poured out all the scotch. He wants a drink now. He knows it would numb his regret, mask his guilt. He feels as if he's let everyone down and he knows that it all began with Beth.

"You know," Charlie breaks the long silence that ebbed in between them, "I was thinking about those guys at the airport last night. Jerry says they were total amateurs. They ran at the first glitch."

"So?" Sid is mildly curious.

"So, I think they were Patriot Security."

"Patriot Security? You mean government agents?"

"No, they weren't good enough to be real agents, not FBI or CIA. Patriot Security, like those Rent-A-Cops they hire for airports".

"What are you saying?" Now Sid was more than curious.

"I'm saying that maybe someone in Washington sent some of their private army of Patriot Security thugs to kidnap me, take my voice out of circulation."

"That's a little bit overblown, isn't it?" Sid is stone sober now. "The President sends some thugs to kidnap you?"

"Maybe. I don't think so." Sid can see that Charlie is deadly serious and honestly troubled by this possibility. "They just looked like and felt like government agents, Sid. They acted dumb enough to be, like, Army intelligence or something like that." And Charlie laughs a funny little laugh.

"Yeah, I always thought that using 'intelligence' to describe those people was an oxymoron," Sid picks right up on the joke, the irony of it.

Jerry joins them on the deck having already poured himself a cup of coffee.

Charlie runs his theory past Jerry.

Jerry gets a good laugh out of it.

"Hell, that's as good a read on it as anything we came up with last night."

"It's like Chinatown, guys," Charlie says.

"How so?" Sid knows what Charlie means but Jerry doesn't.

"*The Verdict,*" Sid suddenly remembers the name of the Paul Newman drunken lawyer movie.

"You don't always know what's goin' on," Charlie does a passable Jack Nicholson imitation. "Nothing is ever what it seems."

Now Alison joins them, also coffee'd up, and her presence sends Sid plummeting back into his abyss of regret. "Anyway, sorry I wasn't more help last night," he feels compelled to debase himself once again now that Alison is here. "I'd had too much to drink."

"Hell Sid, wasn't for you those bastards in Washington probably would have had me in jail two years ago," Charlie reassured him and Alison reached over and patted the back of his right hand.

Did Paul Newman get the girl in the movie? Sid couldn't remember. Alison's touch was magical. It made Sid forget all of his guilt and re-grets and self-loathing. It rededicated him as the in-resident version of their guardian angel. He vowed to himself that he'd watch Charlie and Alison's backs, try to ward off all of the bad vibes that the failed kidnapping and the upcoming march were giving off.

The deck of Sid's Malibu beach house is a good place for planning and plotting and trying to see things clearly. It is a wonderful place for escaping the empty sounds of the two cities and listening to the natural sounds of the sea and the sky. It is a place of withdrawal and meditation well out of earshot of the hectoring demands of the two cities. Nonetheless, the Earth Day March is only two and a half months away and from Sidney's Malibu deck on a clear night the Santa Monica Pier glitters in the distance, a sparkling necklace of light gleaming on the dark breast of the ocean, its ferris wheel a delicate bauble spinning slowly against the moonlit sky.

Chapter Nine

Echoes of Unease

*T*wo weeks pass and M.D. Farrow and *The Headhunters* complete their bi-coastal emigration. They set up shop in a Venice Beach dive bar, The Boardwalk Café, and it doesn't take long for their message to get out. They fit in well with the hippies and the homeless and the dreadlocked Rastafarians of Venice and their music is also right at home with the dope-smoking, ocean-loving, sun-worshipping denizens of L.A.'s most radical beach town.

Thursdays, Fridays and Saturdays are the *Headhunters'* nights onstage at the Boardwalk. M.D. has contracted for only three gigs a week for two months because that takes them through the Earth Day March as well as gives them some freetime to enjoy the California sunshine. At least that is M.D.'s argument.

"That's a laugh!" Sid mocks M.D.'s reasoning when he hears it from Alison and Charlie. "That woman and her rocker friends are like the Addams Family, for god's sake. Friggin' vampires. They're skin hasn't seen the light of day in years."

Sidney isn't reading Alison and Charlie very well these days. He can't tell whether they welcome M.D.'s and her everpresent weasel's help with the preparations for the big event, or whether they wish she had stayed in Washington. But from all that Alison says, M.D. isn't taking over Alison's pointwoman role in the organization of the march at all. If anything, M.D. is serving as a good buffer for Alison since M.D. seems more interested in the most radical groups of their massive coalition that Alison has put together. M.D. and the weasel come up with the idea of giving more militant groups responsibility for the security of the march, making them the cowboys who will ride the outer edges of the crowd on each side and herd them forward along the route.

Things actually seem to be proceeding pretty smoothly. Alison is running around with all the California groups like a wedding planner on speed. Charlie and Jerry are on the road from Tucson to Phoenix to Gallup to Las Vegas to Reno all the way to Salt Lake City flogging the Ocean Save message and drumming up support for the Earth Day March in L.A. hopefully in the form of bodies on buses. M.D. and *The Headhunters* are benignly playing their weekend gigs in Venice and then seemingly just hanging out with the Eco-Vets or with the Eco-Dykes. And Sid is just sitting in his Malibu beach house watching and worrying until Valentine's Day changes everything.

Sidney's deck hanging out over the ocean in Malibu is a wonderful place for monitoring the sounds of the sea and echoes of approaching events. History washes up on the beach in front of Sidney's deck like sea-borne warnings of things to come. Fragments of reality are flung up on the beach below Sidney's deck like the remnants of past storms and battles and revolutions and terrible natural disasters, earthquakes and volcanoes, tsunamis and hurricanes. As Sidney sits on his deck and listens to the ocean, what he hears is no longer as soothing as it used to be, as inviting as it once was. The waves crash upon the beach, dash madly at the deck, like ignorant armies or incited mobs, out to undermine the fragile ecology of the shoreline. Sidney sits and listens to the sounds of violence coming relentlessly nearer, crashing angrily just offshore. Then comes St. Valentine's Day, the day supposedly reserved for love.

It is a well-planned, well-executed, very military operation.

7:30 in the evening of February 14th. A large brown canvas-covered Army-looking truck pulls up to the Main Gate of the U.S. Marine Armory on the Navy Shipyard grounds in Long Beach.

7:31: the truckdriver in the Marine camo uniform climbs down out of the truck's cab to show the young marine sentry in the gatehouse his manifest papers. As the young guard examines them, the camouflaged driver pulls a scarf up over his nose and sprays a knockout gas in the soldier's face. Immediately, the driver takes the gassed soldier's place in the sentry box, waving the truck (which has magically acquired a new driver) on through.

7:33: the truck proceeds across the base along empty alleys between ancient quonset-type temporary buildings to the high warehouse that looms like some feudal keep over the peasants' hovels of the abandoned nighttime military base. Two sentries with rifles guard this main warehouse and they sit up on their benches by the office door as the truck rumbles up to them.

7:35: The driver and the armed soldier riding shotgun disembark the truck cab and engage the two warehouse sentries over manifests for a weapons transfer beneath the only light over the warehouse door. As they converse, weapons hanging casually at their sides, two dark shadows, all in black and ski-masked, glide silently out from under the canvas flap at the rear of the truck, and circle the sentries necks in instantly paralyzing choke holds.

7:38: The truck backs into the warehouse through its now-raised metal overhead door and, its canvas flap thrown back, spits out four more dark-clad shadows in ski-masks.

7:40: Specific crates, coffin-sized, designated by the driver working from a diagram, are packed tightly into the front of the truck's cargo space against the wall of the cab.

7:45: Smaller crates, again specifically designated by the driver's map, are packed tightly into the truck.

7:48: Two fifty-caliber machine guns complete with ammunition cases fill the remainder of the truck's cargo space leaving only enough room for the six shadows to re-enter and pull the canvas flap down over themselves.

7:51: The truck is once again underway, proceeding slowly, benignly, across the quiet base, picking up its replacement sentry at the outer gate, and trundling off into the Long Beach night.

A full four minutes pass before an officer returning to base pulls up at the gate, is not challenged by a sentry, and realizes that something is wrong.

Six more minutes pass before the two disabled sentries at the weapons warehouse are pinpointed. Alarms are sounded. Gates are closed. The whole base is shut down. Long Beach police and the California Patrol are alerted, but it is all too little, too late.

Ten more minutes pass before the surveillance video tapes have been played back and the brown Army truck has been identified as the vehicle of intrusion. But by that time said truck is already across the Vincent Thomas Bridge into San Pedro and dispersing its stolen cargo into six smaller vans which are departing in different directions as fast as their payloads are received. The authorities won't find the original brown truck abandoned behind a Sears store on Hawthorne Boulevard until late the next morning.

It is a flawless commando strike that even the victimized military have to admire for its smoothness and daring, all of which leads them to suspect that it was planned and executed by one of their own. But who? And why?

On his deck in Malibu Sidney listens to the ocean crash, records its disturbing sounds, but he knows nothing of this commando raid on the weapons depot. No one does. The military at the Long Beach Naval Base are directed to keep all details of the incursion under wraps.

"So as not to alarm the general populace" the directive reads. The Long Beach Police and the Highway Patrol are advised that it was simply a drunken misadventure by some base personnel and are thanked for the recovery of the abandoned truck. To all appearances, the military cover-up is as flawlessly executed as was the commando raid. Yet, unknowingly, Sidney is uneasy. The huge march is only six weeks away. Alison, Charlie, everyone involved is going about their appointed business, plans seem to be falling into place, yet still Sidney feels uneasy. The march is so big, so unwieldy. And his brother Charlie is still a primary target.

Chapter Ten

Many Voices

" *C*alifornia is not a cash cow for Washington to milk. California is not a sunny insubstantial playground for the politicians in Washington and their oil company cronies. California is not America's garden of Eden sitting innocently out here in the West waiting for Washington's original sinners to cause its unfortunate fall."

When Charlie gives a speech, he doesn't mess around. He takes a stage, seizes a microphone like a zealot preacher totally dedicated to saving the world and all his listeners from fire and brimstone.

"California and the whole American West is vulnerable. We are under attack. And it effects us all. Our mountains, our fertile agricultural valleys, our deserts, our coastlines, are all in Washington's sights. Why? Because the West is all tied together. The water from the snowpacks of the mountains irrigates our fertile valleys, quenches the thirsts of people as far away as Phoenix, San Diego and L.A."

When Charlie talks, with his sunny blonde surfer good looks, his wide bright welcoming smile, his sun-crinkled eyes and his lyrical stirring voice, women swoon, men compare and everyone listens. He creates a kind of rapture, a moment of suspension when his message subsumes all the other mundane realities of his listeners' lives.

"California is Washington's prime target. The Washington profiteers see California as their high dividend stock, their most attractive take-over target. Washington wants oil. They fight wars for it. They overthrow governments for it. They overlook torture and murder and women being executed for misdemeanors for it. It is all about oil. And Washington is willing to sacrifice our oceans, our beaches, our whole western way of life for the oil they covet in their greed." Charlie is on his message now, has cut quickly to the very center of the eco-threat.

Sid's voice is all inside but is no less intense in its worry for all that could go wrong with the headlong careening of all around him toward the Earth Day March now only five weeks away. In Sidney's mind, they are all playing with fire, tempting fate. Sid knows what Charlie can do to an audience. Sid has listened and marveled at Charlie's mesmerizing oratorical powers. Sid sometimes fantasizes about what Charlie might be like in a courtroom with that voice, that eloquence, that seductive power. *He'd never lose a case,* Sid decides as he moves slowly from painting to painting, sculpture to sculpture, collage to collage (the special exhibition) in the Norton Simon Museum in Pasadena. It is Sunday March 19th in L.A. and Sid has fled the emptiness of the Malibu house. Only a month left until the big Earth Day March. Charlie is off giving speeches. Alison is off lining up March support and volunteers. Jerry is off guarding Charlie. Even MD and the Headhunters are nowhere to be found. And Sid has vowed not to take a drink all day even though there is nobody around to see whether he does or not. This museum in particular has always been a place of refuge for Sid, a place where he can get away to some peace and quiet where he can think. Moving slowly through the museum, he can shake the cobwebs off of his mind and see reality a little clearer.

"California has always been vulnerable in all sorts of ways. Los Angeles is a huge city with a split personality, split between a sprawling automobile oil-dominated urban economy and a sun-drenched, wave-washed, beach paradise. Yet L.A. sits on a major faultline and lives under threat of most of the biblical plagues—drought, fire, crop devastation, mud slides, gang wars and movie stars. Now Washington wants to get in on the act of messing with the fragile ecology of the West." Charlie isn't even talking loud, not screaming, or ranting, or waving his arms. He's just talking straight to the crowd, engaging their rapt faces with his blazing blue eyes as if he is pleading to each of them individually to involve themselves in the fight against the evil of Washington trying to ruin California in the greed for oil.

As he prowls the museum Sid can almost hear Charlie giving his stump speech, the "Save the West" speech they have all fallen into calling it. He can almost see Jerry lurking off to Charlie's right on the steps to the stage, scanning the crowd. A Van Gogh peasant in a yellow hat reminds him of Charlie, a Botticelli Madonna of Alison, a dark Rembrandt man of business of a worried Jerry. Usually the museum can take his mind off of things, but not today. Sidney takes it as a sign of just how worried he is about all of them, as a warning of just how dangerous a game of anti-government protest they are all playing.

"We're all in this together," Charlie gives them all a stake in his message. "Every family—black, white, brown, yellow, Mexican, Asian, Indian, white middle-class Caucasian—every family that has ever packed their kids into the family car and gone to the beach on a sunny California afternoon, every surfer who has ever ridden a wave into a California beach, every fisherman who has ever cast a line into the vast Pacific, every Californian who has ever stepped out into the January sunshine and thanked their lucky stars that they weren't in Minneapolis or Chicago or Boston knee-deep in snow. Every one of us needs to join the fight against what Washington is trying to do to our world."

Charlie is rehearsing his Earth Day speech certainly, but he is also beating the bushes, recruiting the footsoldiers for the eco-resistance. Everything Charlie says is consciously designed to infuriate the Imperial President and the Do-Nothing Congress, to expose the Big Oil cronies, to influence the spineless, to cajole the clueless, to open the eyes of the blind, to bombard the ears of the deaf, to educate the dumb. And maybe along the way convince the American people that protecting the ecology of the West is their last chance, their place to make a stand.

It is this ever-present incendiary tone of Charlie's speeches that so worries Sid as he drifts into the museum's special collage exhibit. Some of the works strike Sid as really stupid: a group of Robert Rauschenberg brown segments of cardboard boxes and grocery bags or the Bottle Rack that Marcel Duchamp bought in a store, put his name on, and called art. But one box collage by Joseph Cornell pulls him in close with a kind of fatal attraction. It is a fairly large wooden box with a glass front furnished with a variety of French found objects that for some reason verge on the prophetic for Sid.

"I'm not running for President. I'm not running for anything," it is a riff that Charlie manages to insert in almost every speech he makes. Alison calls it his "trust me" line. "I'm working to make sure that the government, the politicians in Washington, the big oil interests, don't run over us."

One of the reasons that Charlie is such a powerful speaker, can get people to listen to him and take him seriously, is because he actually believes in what he is saying, actually is convinced that what he is saying is right and true and good and the government he is speaking out against is dead wrong.

The Cornell box that has wrested Sidney's attention is titled *Hotel du Nord* (*Little Durer*) and was created in 1950. It is overwhelmingly

French and makes Sidney, as his eyes inventory the objects that populate the box, think of the French Revolution. For Sid this box of found objects is eloquent and expressive, transports him into a world of historical-aesthetic memory that conjures images from sources as diverse as Wordsworth's *Prelude* and Broadway's *Les Miserables*. The young peasant boy in the box with his folded hands and sad, pensive look is the child of revolution. The tusked boar and the fanged dog, both rabid in their bared hate, are symbols of the repressed anger and barely controlled lust for violence of the people. The self-portrait of Durer marks the bemused distance of the uninvolved artist, his disengagement from the social milieu of revolution. The total effect upon Sidney of this strange collection of things in this glass box is powerful. It is probably just the particular day, his particular mood, the impending massive protest march, that causes Sid's fascination with this particular collage, this particular set of images. Or is it something else? Something threatening? Something bigger than Sid senses bearing down upon them all?

"Another Charlie, Charles Dickens, once wrote 'It was the best of times. It was the worst of times,' well if he were here today he'd say that this is the most screwed up of times. Our leaders in Washington are lying to us. The leaders of our economy who control the oil are ripping us off. The leaders of our military are fighting utterly unnecessary wars that are costing the valuable American lives of young men and women who have no idea what they are fighting for. The sad truth is that all they are fighting for is oil."

For Sid, standing in the museum staring at that box of revolutionary images, revelation comes slowly as if it has been stalking him for a long time. He realizes that all of the people around him, all of the people important to him, are involved in revolutionary action while his own life is one big muddle of inaction. While Charlie and Alison and MD Farrow are manning the barricades to save the ocean, to save the world, he is mired in a slough of despond, sinking in an alcoholic flood. Sidney can see his own startled dimly reflected face in the glass front of the box collage, his lost face superimposed upon the hopeful face of the small peasant boy of the eighteenth century. *Why is everybody involved but me?* Sidney thinks. *Why are they all so hopeful?*

"It's all about power. Our Imperial President and his oil barons are like Prince John and the Sheriff of Nottingham in the Robin Hood story that we all know so well. They are constantly raising our taxes in the form of oil prices and now they want to take over our land, our beaches, our ocean. That is what this year's Earth Day March in Los Angeles is all about. We must show significant resistance to their power. We must show them that hundreds of thousands of us are all together, united, in resistance to them. We must show them that they can't run us over."

I've got money, Sid thinks. *I've got status and even a kind of celebrity, or maybe notoriety, as a trial lawyer. But I don't have hope. All I've got is cynicism.*

Jerry Creogan moves quickly into position right in front of Charlie as Charlie moves out from behind the speaker's podium and descends the steps from the stage. Jerry has never really taken the time to analyze his role as bodyguard in great depth. For example, he has never really pondered the fact that when Charlie is on the move, he, Jerry, is little more than a bullet shield. His job is to catch the bullet meant for Charlie. Sidney had contemplated the reality of Jerry's job.

"You're sort of like the catcher in the rye," Sidney had said to Jerry the day he presented him with the two new Kevlar bulletproof vests and insisted that he and Charlie wear them whenever they are involved in a public function.

"Who's the catcher in the rye?" Jerry had asked innocently, not the least embarrassed that he didn't know.

"Oh nobody," Sidney resisted the temptation to be pedantic and condescending. He liked Jerry too much. "Just a character in an old novel. Just make sure you and Charlie wear the vests. I've just got a bad feeling about all this, the speeches, the March."

"Yeah, I know what you mean," Jerry had agreed in his typical laconic way. "There's always so many people around trying to get at him. It was a lot easier just being your bodyguard. At least we usually knew who didn't like you at any given time."

Even the art gallery couldn't jar Sidney's mind away from worrying about Charlie and Jerry. It is a rainy March Sunday and the sky off the ocean in Malibu is gray/black and gloomy when Sid gets home. The beachhouse is quiet and empty and dead. Sidney is already fighting the temptation to have a drink even as he passes through the entranceway switching on the lights. The flashing digital window on the telephone answering machine catches Sidney's eye as he moves through the dim house. Three messages. One from Alison from her car saying that she has a headache and is heading home for the evening. One from Jerry saying that Charlie's speech went well and they are on the freeway heading home to L.A. Routine stuff. Everyone checking in. But the third message stops Sidney in his tracks, makes the hair stand up on his neck as if some alien presence has infiltrated the silent, empty world of the beachhouse.

"Hello, Mr. Castle, this is Veronica Velasquez, Channel 6 news. We've done a couple of interviews after your trials." As soon as he hears her voice on the machine Sid goes on alert, attends closely to her every word.

"This afternoon we received a disturbing phone call concerning your brother. We record all incoming calls to the station and because this is a threatening one I would like to play it back to you in hopes that you would be willing to comment upon it."

The tape goes silent for a moment, and then a low raspy male voice, very much Darth Vader-like, comes up:

> Charlie Castle, surfer punk, we know that you and your Eco-Nazi's hit that armory. Who do you think you are? Your great March is a joke. We will attack you if you march. We will take you and kill you if you continue to rabble rouse. You and your tree hugging kind are traitors to America. We will seek you out and destroy you.

Even as the tape is winding down, Sid is formulating his reaction in his mind. He would like to just ignore the call, the newswoman, but he can't ignore the threat. This one is different from all the others. This one keeps saying "we" instead of "I." This one sounds like the voice of some right-wing militia calling from their training camp out in the woods eager for an assassination.

Sid calls the TV station, all the while fighting to remain calm. He gets the Velasquez woman who before he can say anything interrupts to inform him that his call is being recorded and that his voice could be used on the air.

"Fine. Fine. No problem," it is all Sid can do to keep from cursing her Big Brother efficiency. "My brother Charlie and I want to thank you and Channel 6 for apprising us of this threatening phone call. We receive calls like this on a regular basis and we treat them seriously, but rarely are their threats carried out." And with that Sid just let it go. He had learned from years of experience dealing with the L.A. news people that the less you say to them the less ammunition you give them for dissecting your every syllable. Sid carried it off succinctly, but he saved the message on the answering machine for Charlie and Jerry to listen when they got home.

Chapter 11

The Ferris Wheel

The view from the top of *The Arizona Hotel* on Ocean Boulevard in Santa Monica is a real stunner. From up there not only are you treated to the whole panoramic expanse of Santa Monica Bay from Point Dume to the Palos Verdes, but you are directly overlooking the Santa Monica Pier with its amusement park and restaurants and hordes of strolling tourists gaping at the surfers showing off on their very public ocean stage. At sunset as the burnished ball of fire sinks into the slate grey sea, a burst of colors—orange, pink, gold, red, burnt umber—erupts into the darkening sky in an almost volcanic array. Dusk settles into twilight then quickly into a deep darkness that magically triggers the lights on the Ferris Wheel that towers over the pier. It rises over the lower lights of the tilt-a-wheel rides like a revolving kingly presence in all its computer-lit glory.

Looking back from the pier toward downtown Santa Monica, *The Arizona Hotel* immediately catches your eye. It is a very retro, mustard and turquoise colored, eight storey hotel out of the fifties of the last century. It stands out because it represents the only real color in the whole Santa Monica skyline. Looking back from the pier toward the city, your eye darts immediately to *The Arizona* because it is different, colorful, old. It is flanked and towered over by bran' new, stark white, twenty storey, skyscrapers that look down like hulking bullies on this shorter, older, quainter beach hotel. If you were looking down from the 18th floor rooms of the *Sheraton* or the *Marriott* on *The Arizona*, you would see a nice, expansive flat roof decorated for a beach party and furnished with beach chairs and chaise lounges paired off for sunbathing, picnic tables spotted about, and potted palm trees all along the outer railings of the roof to shelter it from prying eyes and even provide a little shade.

Red Adams (Not his real name, but the one he went by onscreen) and Debbie Longo (one of Maud Gunn's *Dykes on Bikes*) checked into *The Arizona Hotel* right around the first of April. Red is one of Black Jack Daniels's boys, well no longer a boy, fifty four years old, grey in the hair and long in the tooth, an out-of-work (not retired) stunt man, a Gulf War vet, one of those guys who thinks he is still twenty two and looks all the time for ways to prove it. Debbie really is only about twenty two, or at least somewhere thereabouts. When Red Adams first saw her, the first thing that crossed his mind was "what a delicious piece of ass!" Then he found out that she was a lesbian. For about three days as they camped out in their room at *The Arizona* pretending to be a couple, Red was a very unhappy cowboy and kept begging Debbie to "say it isn't so," but she would just laugh at him and tell him to pay attention to what he was doing.

Debbie came and went on her motorcycle and Red drove a battered red Toyota pickup. By the tenth of April they had amassed ten surface-to-surface shoulder-fired rockets in their hotel room on the eighth floor of *The Arizona* right next to the stairway up to the roof. They stood them all up in the room's only closet and padlocked the door. They tipped the maid well and she didn't speak English anyway so nobody knew what they were keeping in their cupboard. Then all they had to do was sit back and wait. In lieu of what Red wished Debbie would let him do, they played gin rummy and drank coffee. In the evenings, they'd go up on the roof to smoke and watch the ferris wheel on the pier spinning out its computer-operated designs like a magic lantern.

Chapter 12

The Laptop and the Oil Rigs

With the March only three weeks away Washington beckoned. M.D. wanted a face-to-face to go over all the final details, so Alison flew to Washington the second week in April to put the finishing touches on the logistics of the March. Charlie stayed in L.A. to give more speeches, keep the fires fanned for the lead-up to the March. The media were starting to check in as Earth Day loomed and Charlie was appearing on TV, talking on talk radio, and doing print interviews on an almost daily basis.

Even as the wheels touched down at Reagan National, Alison was already thinking of getting back to L.A., to Charlie and her new life. Her legs were curled up under her in the narrow seat. The plane wasn't full and she had all three seats to herself. As the plane started the long taxi to the gate, she thought about them in bed that morning, kissing themselves awake, then making love one last time before he took her to the airport. *Charlie is such a child,* she thought. That was one of the things she so liked about him. He was still that fearless teenage surfer with the whole world before him.

The plane lurched to a stop at the gate and those three funny little bells rang, jangling Alison out of her warm reverie and back into the Washington world of M.D. Farrow. Moving through the airport she noticed the ubiquitous presence of Homeland Security. Men in blue uniforms seemed to be loitering at every turn. They looked like gas station attendants with guns. With the three-hour time change from the west coast to the east, it was seven o'clock, after dark, when Alison touched down. She knew that M.D. and the Headhunters would be getting ready to go onstage. She was scheduled to meet with M.D. the next morning at ten. She was eager to meet with M.D. She felt that everything was coming together for a great Earth Day March in L.A. and she couldn't wait to tell M.D. all about it.

"We've put almost everything together on the internet. Ads and videos of Charlie on YouTube, Instagram, Snapchat, Facebook, Linke-dIn, the works. Hundreds of blogs. I've tried to light up the blogo-sphere like a Christmas tree. Charlie is making appearances and doing media almost every single day. It's all coming together. We're going to have a million people for the March. I know we will," Alison gushed excitedly as she reported to M.D.

They were meeting in M.D.'s hotel room, the two of them, plus M.D.'s constant companion, the skinny, greasy, little weasel of a bass player who always seemed to be in silent attendance upon her, always lurking in the background smoking. M.D. sat on the loveseat dressed completely in her usual black, her jet black hair curling around her face like snakes. Her everpresent laptop sat next to her close at hand and her eyes constantly darted at its screen as she talked. Her hands fingered its keys in anticipation even when she wasn't looking at it.

"You've done a wonderful job of organizing all of this, Alison," M.D. responded to Alison's runaway enthusiasm in the even voice of either an accountant or a bored shipping clerk. "And the March will be so impressive. A million marchers, yes, excellent! You've got us over the first hump."

"I'm sure there will be a million," Alison repeated herself. "That ought to catch the world's attention."

"Well that's just it, isn't it?" M.D. jumped up and paced the room like a restless panther. "A million is all well and good; in fact, extremely impressive. But... ," she paused in mid-stride and raised a pointed fore-finger at Alison, "but how do you get the other three hundred and seven million to pay attention to them. That's the rub."

"All the world's media will be focused on this March," Alison thought she had the answer to M.D.'s question. "We'll get their atten-tion. Charlie will do that with his words. The whole world will hear his speech from the pier, at least parts of it."

"It will take more than words to move the masses, to catch the attention of all America, more than words," MD waved her hand as she paced, then plucked a cigarette from the weasel and took a long contemplative puff as if trying to decide what more to say. She gave the cigarette back, sat back down, and pulled the computer nervously to her lap as if it had been out of her hands too long.

"Oh Alison," she sounded quite sincere, "you've done a wonderful job. You've given me my million. Now get them to the pier and I'll do the rest."

After Alison left, M.D. Farrow, like the wicked queen in *Snow White*, turned to her skinny headhunter and laughed out loud. "That little yuppie bitch is so naïve, so romantic, so, so...childish."

Smoke was coming off the weasel like steam rising from a sewer. He just looked at M.D. and shrugged.

"She doesn't even imagine how different this March is going to be." There was a wolfish avidity in M.D.'s voice. She wasn't really talking to her weasel. She was talking more to herself, to the air, perhaps to her private gods. "The whole world is going to remember it. Other Earth Day Marches have taken place and gotten a sound bite on the Evening News, a long shot of a huge crowd on the Mall in front of the Lincoln Memorial. There may be hundreds of thousands of people at the March, but the impact lasts about one day. 'Oh yeah, it was Earth Day today. That's nice. We should plant a tree sometime.' One day if that. Then everyone goes back to their little bourgeois life and forgets all about it."

The weasel lights another cigarette.

M.D. prowls the room, unable to stay still.

"Well not this year. This March is gonna have some legs. This March is gonna stay in people's minds and consciences lots longer than that. This March is gonna make California more important to the American people than any Middle East oil country with an unwinnable war going on."

She curled herself on the loveseat like a sated cat and pulled her laptop to her.

In the plane cruising home to L.A. Alison had plenty of time to think. In the hotel room, M.D. had been so strange, scary, had a mad, driven look about her. *What had she meant when she said 'I'll do the rest,'* Alison thought. *I come bouncing in with my positive reports and my contact logs and my crowd estimates and it sets her pacing like a mad woman. Strange.*

Alison went back over their meeting. M.D. had been pleased with her work, had said so. Then M.D. had gone off on the big Gulf Coast oil spill of 2010. Alison remembered M.D.'s rant almost verbatim: "That drilling platform blowing up and leaking for two months was only a warning. Those damn derricks are everywhere! Or will be soon if we don't do something drastic. There are bills in Congress right now, all written, all ready to go, but stalled because the Gulf oil spill is still too fresh in peoples' memories. One is to end the off-shore drilling ban completely. But that's not all. The Federal Bureau of Land Management is proposing to sell oil and gas leases in previously protected wilderness areas like in Utah. And another one is set to restart building that pipeline from Canada to the Gulf. Oh, and here's a good one" and at that point M.D. had laughed maniacally. "The Ohio senate, without any public debate, amended a budget bill to open all state lands, parks mainly, but maybe even Lake Erie, to oil and gas drilling. And the President totally supports all of them. It's oil. It's just flat all about oil."

As Alison's plane glided over the California coastline headed for LAX, she looked down and dotted in the water as they flew were the oil platforms. She remembered a month or so before driving down the PCH from Santa Barbara with Charlie after he had given a speech and seeing the oil rigs sitting out in the water with the Channel Islands for a backdrop. Charlie had pointed them out to her.

"That's what this is all about," Charlie had said. "Those oil rigs out there in the water are like a whole horizon of guillotines just hanging over our heads."

Chapter 13

Preparing the Lightning

Black Jack Daniels and Maud Gunn were strange bedfellows. Especially considering Maud's pretty obvious sexual orientation. Political bedfellows maybe. Bedfellows in anarchy maybe. In fact Maud's compadres, who wore tee shirts that read "*Dykes on Bikes,*" had actually worked as extras on that hit TV show that had "Anarchy" in its title and motorcycles in its credits. Strange bedfellows perhaps, but on this sunny early April Day in the city of Carson just off the 405 freeway in Southwest L.A. Maud had just arrived on her Harley at the warehouse home of the Eco-Vets to find Black Jack Daniels lounging in the sun by the front door in a tattered folding beach chair. Black Jack liked the irony of the Eco-Vet operation being in Carson just a stone's throw from the B.P. Oil Refinery that was the industrial lifeblood of this wasteland community in L.A.'s rustbelt.

Dismounting, Maud didn't waste words on any greeting: "My bikers are ready. We know how we're going to snatch him. It'll be the biggest kidnapping since the Lindbergh kid. What about you?"

Black Jack just sat grinning up at her. He loved to mess with big, muscle-bound Maud. She was so serious. So damned easy. "Maudie. Maudie girl. Relax. You're too intense. Wound way too tight. Not even a friendly 'hello' or 'how ya doin?' for your friend Black Jack. Be sociable Maudie. I'm glad to see ya."

"Bite me, you red neck prick! I'm just reporting in. You're supposedly runnin' this show so I'm tellin' you that my biker girls are ready."

"Good. Good." Daniels decided he wasn't going to get anywhere joking with her so he might as well get serious. "It's almost here, isn't it? Our big day! I'll make the lightning and your bikes will provide the thunder."

"I'm gonna do it myself on my bike and I'll have two other bikes both backing me up and clearing my way." Maud Gunn was all business.

"Damn, you'd have been a good soldier. I'd have had a real place for you on my squad in Baghdad or later in Kabul. We'd kick some major towel-head ass. C'mon in, I want to show you what we've got," and he waved for her to follow him into the warehouse.

But it wasn't really a warehouse. It was more a maintenance hanger crossed with a military armory. The front room that you entered from the doorway was little more than an innocuous clubhouse. A bar with four barstools and a refrigerator, a couple of tables with cheap folding chairs, air hockey, a pool table, the kind of room you would expect a group of washed-up veterans would hang out in telling war stories. But in the back of this front a normal, innocent-looking door opened into the real Eco-Vets playground. The front club room had a low drop ceiling. The back of the warehouse had no ceiling at all and the curved roof was high enough to hanger two combat helicopters capable of transporting their pilot and two other men and enough weapons and other armaments to light up the sky over Carson like the fourth of July.

"Whoa," Maud Gunn actually took a step back in surprise. "This is not how they looked the last time I saw them."

"Yeah, pretty cool, huh. The black paint jobs really make them look bad ass, don't they?"

"They sure don't look like the two pieces of junk I saw a month ago."

"They were right out of the salvage yard then. You know how old these choppers are?" But he didn't wait for her to answer. "They were used in Vietnam, or a version of them was. Bell Iroquis. All the way back to Vietnam."

"A black paint job on an old chopper is great," Maud was still shaking her head, "but will they fly?"

"Already have, this one's mine. I had her up yesterday. For a month me and Karl over there, another one of the best helicopter mechanics and pilots in the world," Black Jack was certainly not lacking in self-esteem as he pranced like a peacock in front of his recreations, "have been retooling these two babies. They're fighting fit and ready to go. They're flying as well as anything I flew in Iraq and we don't have to worry about any blowing sand on this mission. You want a beer?"

Abruptly as that, Black Jack Daniels turned on his heel and headed back into the Eco-Vets clubhouse.

Maud Gunn impolitely turned down his sociable offer and headed out the front door back to her bike. She'd gotten what she had come for, evidence that this thing they had been planning was really going to happen. She climbed on her Harley and kicked it into ignition.

"Lightning and thunder, huh," the look on Maud's face was probably as close as she ever came to smiling at a man.

"Total firestorm," Black Jack grinned insanely back at her like one of those skeletal death's heads painted on the helicopters he flew in combat.

Chapter 14

The Star Chambers

*I*n the grand jury room at the Justice Department M.D. Farrow sat patiently, her laptop open on the table before her, and answered all their questions without hesitation.

"Please identify yourselves for the recorders" was the first thing the Federal Prosecutor ordered them to do.

"I'm M.D. Farrow, Chairman of the Board of OceanSave. We are an eco-conscious organization of more than one hundred thousand members dedicated to the reduction and ultimate elimination of fossil fuel energy use in order to combat the global warming and subsequent ecological breakdown that it causes. This is Mister Wrigley Jones, my personal and legal advisor. And you are?"

The prosecutor wasn't really expecting that question and hesitated a moment but then decided to humor her and reply: "Federal Prosecutor for the District of Columbia Michael Anderson."

Without any hesitation M.D. appeared to type his name into her laptop. At that prosecutor Anderson turned to the seated panel and rolled his eyes. Turning back to her, their eyes met and her utterly unwavering stare once again made him ever so briefly hesitate before embarking upon his questioning. M.D. Farrow answered each question directly and without the slightest hesitation. But between questions her fingers leapt to the keys of her laptop. Wrig Jones sat slumped next to her the whole time looking as if he was in gut-clenching pain (probably from nicotine withdrawal).

"Yes. We at OceanSave placed one of our people, a licensed private detective, as a chauffeur for the CEO of Amerigas Corporation in order to gather information on what we felt were his criminal activities."

"Yes, for months we observed him and gathered information on all of his questionable expenditures on prostitutes, alcohol, drugs, and especially on the buying of access and influence in Washington political circles."

"No, we did not choose to take this information to the FBI or to your Federal Prosecutor's office for two specific reasons. First, it would have ruined the undercover situation that we had created and second, we did not entertain a great deal of confidence that the Federal Bureau would put our material to any substantive use."

"Yes, our surveillance demonstrated that the subject was closely associated with Mister John A. Samuelson the lobbyist."

"Yes, our undercover chauffeur drove the CEO and his various passengers the whole evening in question, the evening of the CEO's murder."

"Yes, I would be happy to retrace his steps that evening. He entertained two Congressmen, members of the House Energy Committee, at a famous Washington restaurant. He then transported these two Congressmen to an equally famous house of prostitution in suburban Chevy Chase where he commissioned the proprietress to have those Congressmen entertained in whatever manner they chose for the rest of the night. He then departed that establishment in the company of three prostitutes whom he had commissioned for his own entertainment and returned to his hotel where he was found murdered the next morning. All of this material was given by me to the D.C. police in an interview the day of the discovery of the murder." To the amazement of all the listeners in the room, M.D. seemed to deliver this narrative without ever taking a breath.

The questioning went on for almost an hour. Frequently M.D. would make the prosecutor wait for her answer while she typed notations into her laptop. Finally he grew impatient of her almost robotic alternations of her answers with her typing.

"Ms. Farrow, can I ask you what you are typing so diligently into your computer?"

"Yes, I am just keeping a record of this interrogation."

"I wouldn't call it an interrogation," Prosecutor Anderson replied. "Neither you nor OceanSave is accused of any crime. We are just trying to collect information."

"Of course, as you say. But I must keep my records."

"I suppose. OK. Well then. Do you or your OceanSave organization have any evidence or research material or information concerning the CEO of Amerigas Corporation that would be useful to this Grand Jury or to any pending Congressional investigation into the business practices and subsequent murder of that individual?"

"I don't know. Perhaps. We have collected a great deal of information. As you have witnessed today, I am happy to answer any questions you may have pertaining to this man and what we view as his criminal business practices. However, we do not know who murdered him. Our surveillance was ended that night when he entered his hotel with those three prostitutes."

After that, the questioning became somewhat half-hearted. The members of the Grand Jury itself actually had very few questions for the two OceanSave representatives. One Juror, after consulting Prosecutor Anderson, did ask an interesting question that actually did give M.D. Farrow a moment's pause.

"What do you think the note on the knife in the man's chest meant?" the juror asked.

"It read: 'WE, NOT THE COURTS, SENTENCE YOU TO DEATH. MORE HEADS WILL ROLL.'" Prosecutor Anderson refreshed all of their memories.

"I have no idea," M.D. stared off into space as if trying to find meaning in the air.

Outside on the steps of the building Wrig Jones immediately lit a cigarette and M.D. breathed deep the fresh April air as if she had spent the whole morning imprisoned in a deep dark cave.

"There you go," Wrig muttered through a cloud of grey smoke, "our tax dollars at work. Ain't America great?"

"They don't have a clue," M.D. was staring steel-eyed into the distance, down the mall toward the dome of the Capital. "They can't see us coming. Hell, they don't even know we're here, but what is worse they don't care. They're so busy grabbing all that oil money for themselves they can't even sense what's happening in America, how many people are sick and tired of their way of doing business. They don't have a clue."

And then she suddenly smiled, even as Wrig Jones was lighting a second cigarette off of the first. It was as if she got a spontaneous breath of inspiration. "Wrig, c'mon. I'll show you how clueless they are, how out of touch." And she marched him straight across the mall and into the gallery of the House of Representatives.

"There, there's one of them." M.D. pointed down. He was with the CEO that night until he got dropped off at that whorehouse. Do you think the Grand Jury suppoened him?"

M.D.'s arm swept across the whole panorama of the House chamber. "There, there's our government in action. Two thirds of the seats are empty. It's all just an empty spectacle, a façade of government. Nobody's really governing." She sank back in her seat and just stared down at the turgid movement on the House floor.

"This has all gotta change," she whispered in a tight, controlled murmur. "They have to change their ways, and it all starts with oil. That's the key. Take a good look at them down there. A storm is coming down on them, on this country, a flood of violent awakening. Maybe it will wash them all away and we can start over."

"Aw screw 'em," Wrig said with his usual eloquence. "Let's git otta here."

Chapter 15

Gonna Make a Revolution

Four o'clock in the afternoon on the deck of Sid Castle's Malibu beach house. Sid is just sitting there looking out to sea. The burning sun is still high against the watercolor blue sky over Point Dume. Not a cloud. A day as clear as the eyes of a four-year-old child. Sid longed for that kind of clarity, that sense of innocence. All he ever dealt with was guilt, his own, his clients. He made his ridiculously excessive living on guilt. His own excesses fueled the personal guilts that plagued him whenever he was alone like this. He'd been to his office today. He still had on his suit pants and white shirt, but had discarded his coat, tie, shoes and socks. Then he had just sat down in the nearest deck chair and gazed at the vastness of the Pacific spread out before him.

He'd been sitting there staring out to sea for probably a half hour. He hadn't even made himself a drink yet. He may not have moved but his mind was racing. Alison, Charlie, his dead Beth, even Jerry, all the people in his world seemed to be rising up out of the ocean to feed his guilt, confuse him. He had these strong feelings for his own brother's wife. He loved his brother unconditionally, would do anything for him, yet all he could think about was Alison, how if Charlie wasn't there then maybe... . Then he blamed himself for Beth and he knew that Jerry was worried about him like a mother over her wayward child. And all of them swam helter-skelter in his mind like crimes he hadn't yet committed but already felt guilty for.

Then his cell phone vibrated in his pocket and he jumped straight up as if he'd been shocked. It was Charlie, stuck in traffic with Jerry out on the 405 driving back from Carlsbad down south.

"Sid, hi, hey, how about dinner? Alison is all the way up in Washington State. Let's batch it tonight. You, me and Jerry. Let's cook at the beach house. I'll do steaks and salad."

"Yeah, sounds good." Sid had felt a pang of disappointment that Alison wouldn't be there, but in the mood that he'd been buried in since he got home having Charlie and Jerry there could only be good for him. "Actually sounds real good. How far out are you?"

We're only around Newport Beach on the 405. We'll take the 10 into Santa Monica and pick up the coast highway at the pier. I'd say about an hour and a half."

"OK. Alison left us all kinds of salad stuff. I'll go to Von's in Malibu and get some steaks and beer. What kind do you guys want?"

There was a brief pause as Charlie and Jerry consulted on this momentous decision, but then the verdict came down: "Dos Equis Amber."

"Dos Equis it is then, "and all of a sudden Sid felt better. He had something to do, something constructive, something he didn't have to feel guilty about. He could buy beer.

But the real fact of this whole matter wasn't about bachelors or steaks or what kind of beer to get. The real fact was that Jerry and Charlie were both worried about Sid. Jerry had brought the subject up in the car when they hit the freeway out of San Diego.

"I'm worried about Sid again," was all that Jerry said, but Charlie knew exactly what he was talking about right away.

"I know, so am I. He's been hitting it pretty hard again lately, hasn't he?"

"Yeah, that's it. I mean, he always drinks, but these days he's drinking a lot more, and he seems depressed. He's just not himself these days since, well, since Beth."

"Yeah, I've noticed. It's complicated, I know. He seems really jumpy. The booze doesn't even seem to calm him down. I think Alison is the only one who does. He seems to relax when she's around."

So the two of them hatched their plot to have dinner at the beach house with Sid since Alison was still out of town, and that's when they called him from the car.

The three of them didn't eat until after eight. On the deck after dinner Sid and Charlie lit up illegal Cubans. But Jerry didn't do cigars. They didn't fit his lifestyle. Besides, in the car he had suggested that he should leave the two brothers alone so that Charlie could talk to Sid, try to fathom what was bothering him, try to cheer him up, try to get him to stop hitting the bottle so hard. In effect Jerry dumped all of his worries about Sid on Charlie's shoulders and, claiming fatigue and dislike for cigar smoke, fled off to his apartment over the garage. But he wouldn't leave until he extracted Charlie's promise to stay over at the beach house. Sid wasn't the only one that Jerry worried about. His worry about Sid's drinking was almost maternal, but his worry about Charlie's safety was one hundred percent professional. No way Charlie was going to get assassinated by some redneck militia crazy on Jerry's watch.

After Jerry had gone, Charlie used him to break the silence that had fallen over him and his older brother. It was an almost Conradian night scene, the two of them sitting silently in the darkness of the deck overlooking the sea only visible as shadows behind the glowing tips of their burning cigars. Down the bay in the distance the lights of the ferris wheel on the Santa Monica Pier blinked and pulsed like a magical firefly pirouetting over the water.

"Jerry sure is a worrier, isn't he?" Charlie broke the mounting silence.

"Yeah, and with good reason," Sid jumped on Charlie's nonchalant tone not even suspecting that Charlie was just trying to draw him out, out of his guilty isolation since Beth's death, out of whatever it was that had Sid in its clutches. "Hey, Charlie, remember John Lennon, Martin Luther King, it's the guys who raise their voices, who lead the protests, that the crazies out there, go after. Remember those damn threat notes."

"C'mon Sid, we haven't had one of those for over a month. Whoever it was packed it in."

"Who are those guys?" Sid chuckled in the darkness as he tossed Charlie one of their favorite Movish lines.

"Yeah, yeah," Charlie scoffed. "You think they're still out here looking for us like Joe LaForce and his posse, right? Well they're not."

"Yes they are. I know it. Jerry sure as hell believes it. When are you gonna get with the program?"

"Hey, I'm totally with Jerry's program. Look here. He made me tie these chips to all of my shoelaces. Like the chips they give you for a marathon. These are GPS Homing Devices so he can always know where I am. Good lord, I take my shoe off and he comes running with his gun drawn," Charlie and Sid both had a good laugh at that.

"Charlie... .do what Jerry tells you," Sid got back to serious fast. "Pay attention to Jerry. Stick close to him. He knows what he's doing. He's a pro and he does what he does really well."

"I know that. I know that," Charlie reassured Sid enough for their back and forth to lapse back into that dark Conradian silence. They sat and smoked for long moments.

"You know Sid, I'm not the only one Jerry is worried about."

"Oh yeah, who else? Not Alison?" and a real note of alarm crept into Sid's voice.

"No. Not Alison at all. You. You. I've noticed it too. You're hitting it pretty hard these days. The booze I mean. Since Beth died I mean."

"I'm OK. I'm OK. Yes, I've been drinking a lot, I have, but I'll calm down. I'll walk away. I always do. I just don't have a pressure case right now. One will come soon. They always do. Then I'll focus again. You know I will. You guys all have a lot more serious stuff to worry about than me."

"Sid, look, none of us could do any of this stuff without you."

"Hey, pay no attention to that man behind the curtain," Sid tried to laugh him off, but Charlie wasn't going.

"No, seriously, I think sometimes we look like we take you for granted. But we don't. Me especially. God knows how many times you've gotten me out of jail. I know you've always got my back."

"Are you kidding? You guys are the best entertainment I've got. Dinner and a show. You are all a very, I mean very, welcome relief from the L.A. lowlifes I have to deal with on a daily basis."

"Sid, you're deceptive you know. Some people think that you're a lowlife."

"They're probably not that far off."

"Yeah, imagine that," now Charlie was finally getting into the more comic mode of the conversation, the Movish mode. "You just can't handle the truth!"

"Look, what we've got here is a failure to communicate."

"Ah," Charlie took a deep puff on his cigar, its tip blazing bright for a second, and exhaled, "I love the smell of Cubans in the evening."

They both burst out laughing.

"Three in a row. Not bad," Sid seemed fully freed from his temporary depression. "Last one was sort of a stretch."

"Maybe, but synched with the cigar pretty good, huh?"

Yeah, OK," and they subsided back into their smoking and their contemplation of the moon on the water.

"I got an email from M.D. today. Only a week left. Alison was in D.C. reporting in last week. M.D. and her crew will all be coming in on Wednesday for the March on Saturday."

"I can just see her fingers firing off emails at gatling gun speed," Sid dripped sarcasm.

"OK, OK, yes she's a bit over the top. She's a worrier. She just got done with the Grand Jury."

"Yeah, I wouldn't be the least surprised if she killed that Amerigas guy herself," Sid's lowlife defense lawyer cynicism continued to kick sarcastically in.

"You really don't like her, do you?" Charlie was more charging Sid with bad taste than trying to win him over to M.D.'s side.

"Hey, what's not to like? She's smart. She's tremendously talented. She's deeply involved. She's beautiful in a dark gothic sort of way. But what can I say? She just gives me the creeps. She's like hypertense, never offline. It's like she doesn't have hands. Her arms just end in that computer keyboard. Edward computerhands. That's your M.D."

"Cute."

"Damn Charlie, she's scary."

"Sid, c'mon, she's the leader of a movement. She's the voice of protest. Those kind of people are always scary. Because they're different. They're focused, locked in."

"Oh, she's intense alright," Sid's voice betrayed his boredom with the topic of M.D. Farrow. But Charlie wouldn't let her or him go.

"Like I said, I got an email from her, about the speech I'm supposed to give on the Pier at the end of the March. Sometimes she's got really crazy ideas, but I think this one is a pretty good one. I want to see what you think."

"I'm listening. Shoot."

"She wants me to call for a Revolution, a capital R Revolution. More marches like this Earth Day one. Hundreds of thousands of people in the streets calling for change. Marching against the oil corporations that have taken over the country in every city across America. She wants that to be the theme of my speech on the Pier. Revolution. What do you think?"

Sid chuckled. "Alrighty then," but seeing the frown on Charlie's face in response to this small levity, he turned serious. "Do you feel like a revolutionary?"

"Not really," Charlie stopped to think, to revise his position. "But I'd like to be."

"Yeah, I know. We probably all would," and Sid sank back into smoking contemplation. He realized that Charlie was starting to psych himself up for preaching the revolutionary gospel to a million people gathered for the mother of all camp meetings on the sands of Santa Monica.

"M.D. wants me to give a speech where the whole metaphor is that this March is the start of a Revolution. You see, Sid, it is just such an amazing opportunity. Alison and M.D. think there will be a million people there."

Sid could see that the idea was gaining momentum in Charlie's mind, building like a surfing wave, high and clean and powerful.

"Don't you see, Sid. This March will prove that this is America's movement and we have to revolt against Big Oil. What does everyone in America hate? Who is keeping us all poor? High gas prices. Big Oil. BP and their Gulf Oil leak. Amerigas and their CEO and his prostitutes. That's what they all hate. That's what we need to rebel against and bring down. Is this all crazy?"

"Yes. Absolutely. Wacky. Nuts. You know that this M.D. woman is a fanatic don't you?"

"Yes, I know, but isn't it always fanatics who lead revolutions. If I give this speech they'll label me a fanatic sure as hell. Aren't the people who have the balls to speak out always scary, always called fanatics?"

"Are you sure you want to preach Revolution to a crowd that size?"

"What are they gonna do? They're on the beach for god's sake. It's just such a great opportunity. All those people. All those cameras. It's like M.D. giving me an offer I can't refuse."

"See. There you are. She's like Don Corleone alright." Sid just sat there chuckling to himself, a sort of mad laughter building slowly in his throat.

"What?" Charlie flagged him.

"Oh I was just thinking," Sid puffed in the darkness. "When you start calling for Revolution next week I'm probably gonna have to go into OceanSave full time just to keep you all out of jail. Oh, the Patriot Act people are gonna love you guys. They'll be calling for your heads in every conference room in Washington."

"Yes. Exactly. That's what we want," Charlie was really embracing the whole idea, "and that's why I've got the best lawyer in L.A. for my brother. Right?"

"Yeah right," but Sid made it known by the tone of his voice that he was less than enthralled by the idea, certainly didn't share M.D.'s and Charlie's revolutionary enthusiasm. They sat and smoked for long, silent minutes. It quieted them both down.

"What does Alison think about this?" Sid finally asked. "Have you run M.D.'s whole Revolution scenario past her?"

"No. Not yet. I just got the email from M.D. yesterday. I've been thinking about it."

"You think she's going to like you becoming a Revolutionary leader like Thomas Paine or Patrick Henry or Robespierre or Martin Luther King?"

"Dammit. It's not funny Sid. It's just a metaphor, a patch of rhetoric. Somebody has to say stuff like this. You have to get people's attention. M.D. and Alison both know what my role in this movement is and so do I. I'm the faceman, the orator. So be it!"

The silence ebbed in again as they both smoked deep in thought.

Sid was done. He'd said all he was going to say. He realized that Charlie had already decided he was going to give M.D.'s speech. He was just looking for support, for opposition, no matter which, either would strengthen his resolve. And Sid realized that it probably didn't matter what Alison thought either. Charlie was the voice of the movement. It was his job to put out the party line.

"I think Alison will actually like the idea," Charlie finally broke the silence, continuing to build his case. "In fact, she may even have inadvertently given me my best example for the speech."

"What's that?" Sid asked, though he was totally bored with the whole idea.

"Jerry was driving Alison and I down from Santa Barbara about a week ago through Ventura and the Channel Islands. The whole way we were looking out the window at those oil derricks just pumping away out there in the channel. What if one of them blew up like that one in the gulf in 2010? Alison said it."

"What?"

"She said those oil rigs looked like a whole line of guillotines just hanging over our heads. They could cut off your whole life style with just one accident. Boom! One blows up and the whole south coast is gone."

For a moment Sid could actually feel Charlie's passion. For a moment Sid felt blessed to be the witness to Charlie's Pauline moment, his shock of recognition. Charlie was winding the stem, choosing the words, building his confidence, heating up his revolutionary fervor.

For a fleeting moment Sid felt the power of Charlie's enthusiasm.
But then it passed.

Chapter 16

The March

At sunrise in Los Angeles on the vernal equinox, Sunday, April 22, Earth Day, the streets looked more like the streets of Baghdad or Beirut than the streets of a sunny Southern California beach city. Already by sunrise the path of the March to the ocean in Santa Monica has acquired the tense, guarded look of an armed camp. Soldiers are in the streets, black silhouettes in the gathering dawn, lining the route of the March, automatic rifles held at the ready, battle helmets on their heads, camouflage uniforms and jackboots pressed and polished for action. The Patriot Security Act has invoked its impersonal powers and the National Guard of the Great State of California has responded to its call. All three shifts of the LAPD are also on duty, cruising the March route in their squad cars or loitering on the street corners with their nightsticks. The citizen soldiers and the police are in the streets, but not all of them are happy about the way their government has ordered them to spend their sunny Spring Sunday.

"Buncha hippie tree huggers," one soldier named Joe, stationed on the corner of Olympic Boulevard and Lincoln Boulevard at the entrance ramp to the Santa Monica freeway, complains to his closest comrade in arms as they smoke and wait for the March to begin.

"Yeah," the other soldier, named Pat, agrees grumpily, "I had to get up at two-thirty in the morning to get to my unit and get here for this stupid March."

"They say there's gonna be a million people."

"There's never as many as they say at these things."

"Still, that's a shitload of people marchin'."

"Aw hell, it's all housewives with strollers and fags with their shirts off. We're just here to direct traffic."

"Yeah, but a million people is a lot of traffic."

"Yeah, it's gonna be a long day."

While all the Joes and Pats of the National Guard are yawning and scratching and smoking and fingering their loaded weapons on the empty streetcorners, the first marchers are arriving and marshalling in the streets of L.A.

Pat is partially right. There are housewives with children in strollers lining up in the street, but there are also marchers of every description. By seven AM this morning the sidestreets, the sidewalks, are overflowing with people. At the designated stepping-off point of the March, an elevated stage holds a podium and a microphone. Charlie Castle is scheduled to set the March in motion from the microphone at eight. Protest music from another era half a century in the past croons "where have all the flowers gone?" from a speaker truck behind the stage.

At seven, the March marshals in bright yellow Earth Day tee shirts begin to line the parade route from the microphone stage down the designated parade route all the way to Santa Monica. Charlie will start off the day with a greeting speech from the microphone then will make his way down through the mob to the jumping off point. He will be escorted by an entourage of celebrities, including M.D. Farrow and other music and movie stars, eco-friendly politicians, leaders of the major California conservation and ecology groups who have helped organize the March, and of course Jerry on one side of him and Alison on the other. They asked Sidney to March with them but he declined.

"It's your show," Sidney assured Charlie and Alison, but if things get out of hand, if you all get arrested, you're going to want your lawyer working for you from the outside, not from a cell in L.A. County Jail. But I'll be there. Just call me 'incommunicado,' your Mexican mouthpiece."

"Sid is always thinking," Charlie nudged Alison.

"You just keep thinkin', Butch. That's what you're good at," Charlie kidded Sid in their own familiar language.

Sid worried, as he always did, that he was the only one who thought that something might go wrong when you get four hundred thousand people marching across L.A. to meet another five hundred thousand people gathered on the beach to complain about their unfair treatment by a heavily armed, verging on Fascist, government. *Oh, no potential for trouble there*, Sidney thought sarcastically to himself, but didn't voice his fears because he knew it would do no good with Charlie and Alison.

"Ladies and Gentlemen, welcome, we have a wonderful crowd here. It is exciting that so many of you have turned out to march to save our Earth and our Ocean," Charlie Castle greeted the assembled thousands promptly at eight. He beams out over the huge lake of people, his long blonde hair glinting in the morning sun, his wave taking them all in, welcoming each and every one of them to the battle, to the cause.

"And you are but one fraction of the army of marchers that have gathered today. In mere moments we will strike off toward the ocean but along the way five other assembled groups just like yourselves waiting in five staging areas along the march route will flow into your marching stream like tributaries joining a great river of protest and flowing to the sea."

Charlie is at his inspiration best this sunny morning. The thousands hang on his every word. Their signs and banners bob and float on the waves of people.

"Today is a day of resistance for our nation and we represent all of America today. We are marching for every family that has lost a son or daughter in our government's oil wars. We are marching for everyone in California whose greatest joy is looking out at the vast pure ocean or walking barefoot on clean pure beaches. We are marching to save our world. It's that simple. We are marching to save our world. Let's go. Let's go."

And Charlie steps off down from that stage and struts through that crowd like the proudest, most pumped-up drum major that ever led a marching band, only he is leading a marching mob that before it is finished will number in the hundreds of thousands.

Charlie, with Jerry and Alison flanking him, makes his way through the waiting crowd the two blocks to the head of the March like a triumphant athlete, high-fiving all the way, reaching out to as many people as he can possibly touch. The people love Charlie Castle. He is one of them. He is their leader, their royalty, their voice. He has whipped them into the kind of worshipful frenzy where they will follow him anywhere.

Jerry knows that this moment of mingling with the mob is the moment of Charlie's greatest vulnerability. It is here as the mob surges around Charlie, closes in upon his powerful presence like a whirlpool to its vortex, that Jerry is looking for one person with the deranged eyes and the knife, the one with the mad look and the gun raised to fire, the one full of hate with the bottle of acid raised to fling at Charlie. Jerry's ham-sized hand is already clamped on Charlie's collar. Jerry's forearm is raised to shoulder level to fight off anyone who lunges at his responsibility.

Sidney watches it all from the anonymity of the crowd. He marvels at his younger brother's eloquence, but he worries for his brother's safety. Charlie has put himself out front in this whole protest movement, made himself the prime target for any crazy, radical, hate-filled loon or monster. All Sid can hope is that Jerry is at the top of his game today and that if anything happens (and Sid has a sickening premonition that something bad is going to) he will protect Charlie and Alison, get them through it.

Charlie reaches the head of the huge mob of marchers, cuts a ceremonial ribbon of bright flowers stretched across the street, and strikes off with the mob of thousands falling into step behind him. The protest signs—**"STOP OFFSHORE DRILLING," "IT'S OUR OCEAN NOT YOUR OILFIELD"**—and the streaming banners— **"SIMI VALLEY SOCCER MOMS FOR CLEAN OCEANS**—catch the winds of change and sail off on that river of people like boats in a regatta.

Sidney doesn't join the marching crowd. He has parked his car well off the parade route and will drive to Santa Monica to keep an eye on things from a distance. He plans to be on the pier or close at hand in case anything goes wrong and Charlie needs him. He fully expects Charlie to be arrested before the day is over. Charlie doesn't feel like he's really made his point unless he puts the period on it from a jail cell.

"I love the smell of wino puke in the morning," Charlie had once laughed in Movish when Sid had complained about the frequency of Charlie's ringleader arrests.

"Why can't somebody else from your crew go to jail once in a while?" Sid had groused.

But with his usual beaming smile Charlie had nonchalantly replied: "For the environmental lobby I'm the usual suspect. Believe me, the press would be sorely disappointed if they didn't get a picture of me being carted off to jail."

So Sidney just has to grin and bear it and be prepared to post bail to extricate Charlie from his various Henry David Thoreau impersonations.

The March steps off like some strange mutation of *The Music Man* with Charlie as the radicalized drum major. Sid half expected to hear "Seventy Six Trombones" come blaring out of the sound truck. Almost like magic the March becomes a smoothly flowing river of smiling, optimistic, involved souls flowing past the banks and office buildings and stores and restaurants that enclose it. It is a typical L.A. river, encased in concrete, flowing slowly, smoothly, in a straight line, well contained, toward the sea.

As Charlie walks at the head of this living river, he looks from side to side and can't help but notice the armed presence, the soldiers and police lining the sidewalks all along the route: "Man, L.A.'s getting to be just like *Blade Runner* or *Strange Days*, cops with guns every five feet."

"It proves they're afraid of us," M.D. growls from Charlie's side.

"They don't look very afraid to me," Charlie smiles jokingly. "They look pretty heavily armed and dangerous."

"That's how they always try to look, to intimidate, but it doesn't always work," M.D. said it ominously, as if she knew something they didn't. Later, Charlie would remember how strange he thought it was that Wrig Jones wasn't with M.D. on the March. He was almost always at her side with smoke rising off of him.

As the river of people begins to flow smoothly away from him, Sidney detaches himself from the crowd and makes his way to his car. He can't help but think (suspicion being the stock-in-trade of criminal lawyers) that things have started off too well, are going too smoothly, for reality to tolerate.

The first merge goes smoothly and suddenly the river triples in size. The boulevard, which had only been filled on one side of the divider before now, is now filling up on both sides, all four lanes, as the yellow-shirted marshals lead a whole new stream of marchers in to join the main current. The next merge opens a new floodgate of marchers and feeds them into the main stream which is growing into a coursing torrent.

And the river flows merrily along toward Santa Monica with Charlie and Alison smiling sunnily at its head (and M.D. scowling as usual) as if all really was right with the world.

Chapter 17

Sunrise Soldiers

*I*f you walk the beach in the early morning in your bare feet in the hard sand down by the surf on a regular basis, you can't help but notice how different the beach is every day. Some days the shoreline where the waves ebb is blanketed by kelp, but other days huge globs of soft congealed tar break out on the beach like blackheads on a teenager's face and stick to the bottoms of you feet. Some days seabirds in the hundreds—gulls, pelicans, and those squadrons of tiny toy soldier birds that run in step along the waveline—all congregate in one place in the sand sitting like hatchery hens and staring out to sea as if waiting for some god-bird to arrive and lead them to nirvana. But other days dead gulls or a panting seal lie poisoned on the beach as the red-tide-tainted surf washes over them with its dirty brown foam. On still other days tiny dead hermit crabs and pierced sand dollars litter the waveline, washed up like the bodies of dead sailors after some brutal sea battle. Some days the waves the surfers ride are high and clean and break in cascading tunnels of pure white foam, but other days the waves are jagged and treacherous, stalking, ready to wipe you out at the slightest shift of weight on the board. Oh yes, the beach is different every day, and this day, Earth Day, is going to be more different than any other day on Santa Monica beach.

But if the beach is always different, the Santa Monica Pier has been pretty much the same for the last one hundred years. Built in 1909 and shored up on a regular basis ever since, it has stood its ground against the sea for a century. Its brightly lit ferris wheel and bustling amusement park is its trademark, but it also has its fancy fish restaurant on the end, its Bubba Gump chain restaurant in the middle, and any number of corn dog and ice-blend and shrimp kabob and fish taco and ice cream shops all around. Obscene tee shirts hang everywhere between bike rental garages and fuzzy scarf emporiums. And then there are always the fishermen—Mexican, Asian, Comptonian—warily watching their lines hanging over the rails and plummeting into the hopefully fecund surf below. Oh yes, the Santa Monica Pier has been just such a busy place for years and years and this Earth Day is certainly not going to be any exception to that rule.

But then any sunny April day on the Santa Monica Pier and the beach below is always going to be like a rite of spring. Bikinis in full burst. Tattoos and winter skin in full bloom. Sun and sand and children with buckets dodging the waves. Half-naked teenagers posing and flirting. Unhaltered sunbathers glistening greasily. Surfers watching the waves. Lifeguards in red pickup trucks gazing warily out to sea. On any April day there are hordes of sun worshippers around the Santa Monica Pier, but on this particular April day, Earth Day, there are more than hordes, there are hundreds of thousands. They completely fill the beach for as far as the eye can see on both sides of the pier. The only people with even the slightest bit of breathing room are the surfers sitting on their boards and taking it all in from the waveline. All the others are packed on the sand listening to the bands, camped on blankets, sitting in beach chairs, scoping the sun splashed bodies all around. It is the year's biggest beach day by far thanks to the biggest demonstration ever orchestrated in the city of the Angels.

The people started coming early in the morning, staking out their little piece of sand for the festivities of the day. By ten, the pier was totally enisled by people. The pier itself was being kept clear for the marchers. It is a perfect, sunny California day and the throng is festive. And those who have made it all happen have been more than busy since sunrise.

Since 5AM, M.D. Farrow has been on her laptop and her cell phone sending messages, giving orders, to her minions. She is the epitome of micromanagement as if this whole day must go through her and her laptop. Even earlier than that, Wrig Jones, her chainsmoking weasel of a henchman, has been out and about. The weasel pulls a sleek black stretch limo into the pier parking lot, drives it all the way down to the farthest north exit onto the PCH, and takes up the last two spaces facing out. This is clearly an egress position for making a quick exit onto the coast highway sometime later in the day. He doesn't stay with the car, but walks back up the incline to rejoin M.D. in their hotel.

Red Adams and Debbie Longo are also up and moving early this morning. They are carrying long tubes up to the rooftop of *The Ari-*

zona Hotel and stowing them under a blue tarp behind the stairwell structure that sits like a square pillbox on the flat roof. Two trips. Four tubes. Blue tarp. Could be anything being stored. One more trip down and back and Red and Debbie are setting up camera tripods facing the pier. It looks as if the objective for the day is to film or photograph the event from an unobstructed panoramic vantage point. At least if anyone ventured up to the roof on Earth Day that would be their first impression, although Red has made keys that lock the door to the roof.

Maud Gunn and two more of her *Dykes on Bikes* have rolled their Harley's up against a wall in an alley just south of the pier. They too seem to be stationing their bikes for some kind of quick getaway. Each of the riders wears a backpack. Leaving the bikes, they move down onto the beach and across the sand almost to the water's edge. Ducking under the pier, they hang the backpacks on already waiting nails and retreat back onto the sand. That done, Maud adjusts the doo-rag on her head and leads her cycle-sisters up to a vantage point immediately below the microphone stage on the pier. Then they just settle in to wait like everyone else for the marchers to arrive.

Black Jack Daniels is nowhere near the Santa Monica Pier, but he is up early and quite busy as well. In his makeshift aircraft hangar in Carson, he is running all the final mechanical checks on the two helicopters. They sit inside the hanger painted all black like terrorists' hoods or evil birds of prey also waiting for something to happen, for some order to lift off on a mission. For Daniels it is like it was in the Gulf War twenty years ago. Ironically, these birds are of a much older generation of chopper American soldiers flew their missions in during that earlier failed war over the Black Virgin Mountain, the Michelin plantation, the delta, the Cambodian trail, all those nostalgic places in Vietnam whose lessons just weren't learned. But these birds are much better armed with specially rigged rocket launchers bolted to their side walls.

But M.D. Farrow is the focal point of all this activity, the commander in charge of these sunrise soldiers preparing for action. She has greeted the sun on this Earth Day like some ancient Inca priestess atop Ixtacoatl gathering her troops, issuing their assignments, handing out all of the marching orders.

Charlie and Alison aren't up quite that early. In fact, they made lovely morning love before they even pulled back the covers.

But a darker brand of passion burned in M.D. Farrow's eyes and

heart that Earth Day morning, the fire of readinesss, the fire of confidence, the fiery certainty that her time has finally arrived.

Chapter 18

A Change of Direction

*T*he March drags its cumbersome length along, new tributaries joining the main stream of the river of committed people as if flows, swelling and deepening until the river threatens to become a flood and burst its banks.

"They've all turned out," Alison exults as they march. "They all showed up and it's going to be the biggest march America has ever seen."

As the marchers move closer to the ocean, a marine layer of thin, wispy fog begins to drift in over them, meeting the encouraging sunshine and dropping an eerie and haunted mist over the surging river.

All during the march Charlie has wondered where M.D.'s everpresent weasel has gotten to. He has been markedly conspicuous in his absence from the very beginning, but suddenly M.D.'s weasel appears out of the mist and joins them at the head of the living river. He attaches himself immediately to M.D., leaning in to her like Polonius and delivering some important report that is for her ears only. As Charlie watches the two of them, he is most surprised by the absence of a cigarette in the weasel's hand or mouth. *Probably afraid the crowd will turn on him* Charlie speculates to himself almost wishing that Wrig Jones would light up just so he could see what happens.

Sid, in his car, has beaten them to Santa Monica by an hour. He stations himself at the corner of Olympic and Lincoln and watches the National Guardsmen smoking their last cigarettes on the curbstones and the LAPD cops leaning against their cars finishing their coffee before the huge march materializes out of the fog to the east.

As the river of marchers approaches the 20th Street ramp to the 10, the Santa Monica Freeway, what seems like a small army of yellow tee-shirted march marshals suddenly materializes out of the mist and directs, herds, arms windmilling, motions the head of the river of marchers to make a slight jog left down onto the freeway ramp.

"What the...?" Charlie turns to first Alison then M.D. for some explanation of this change of direction.

"I thought we decided against doing this," Alison shouts at M.D. even as it is being done.

"No. It is a good idea. There are hundreds of thousands of us. We can go wherever we want."

Behind them, at the top of the ramp, fighting has broken out between the marshal's in the yellow tee shirts and the soldiers and police. Nightsticks are flailing and rifles are raised. Yellow-shirted marshals are gun-butted to the ground as they try to block the security forces from moving into and turning back the torrent of people. But the marchers come to the yellow-shirted marshals' aid and the soldiers and police are easily driven back by the sheer force of numbers.

"You said it was too dangerous. That we weren't going to do it," Alison accuses M.D. at the top of her voice.

"Too late. It's done. Our point is made," M.D. glares at them.

"Damn, we're gonna take over the whole freeway." Charlie comes suddenly to the realization with the same feeling of awe that Moses surely felt when the sea actually parted before his raised staff.

"There's going to be hell to pay for this," Alison's voice is both angry and hurt simultaneously. She can't understand why she wasn't told, why M.D. didn't trust her with this major strategy shift.

"There's nothing they can do. We're sending our message of resistance. We are a force they can't contain."

Except for Charlie, Alison, M.D. and Jerry, the celebrity marchers at the head of the relentless flood don't seem to even notice this small change of direction. Traffic on the freeway, light because most motorists have for days been warned off of driving into Santa Monica this day, comes to a screeching halt as the great river of bodies streams down off the ramp and within seconds fills all of the westbound lanes.

Buzzing like dragonflies above the March, the news helicopters dip down through the fog and circle as the huge mob pours down into the channel of the freeway and fills it like mountain run-off coursing down L.A.'s concrete rivers toward the sea.

"What amazing pictures this is gonna make on the evening news," Charlie's acute P.R. sense kicks in as he spots the gaudy helicopters circling above them.

"Yeah, pure visual proof of every agreement we made with the city being broken," Alison, angry and desperate, accuses both M.D. and Charlie this time. "Did you know about this?" Alison grabs Charlie by the arm.

"No. No I didn't."

"It's OK. Keep going." M.D. pushes them to keep moving, keep leading. "Now it's done. Now the whole world will see how many we really are. How unstoppable our message is. This march will be different, not quiet and peaceful like all the others. This march they'll remember. This march will really change things."

They had no choice but to keep moving, to lead the March down the middle of the freeway now that they were on it.

Charlie is nothing if not an opportunist. He is the one who can already see what this must look like through a TV camera. He is the one who is already rewriting his speech for the pier inside his mind to emphasize the power of these huge numbers of people who can close down a whole freeway, bring a gas-guzzling society to a screeching halt. Charlie is starting to think that what they have just done is actually pretty cool, a way of voting with their feet against all the control that Patriot Security has taken to exercising over everyone. Charlie is revising his speech, but he knows nothing of the violence behind him, of three people trampled as the crowd moved against the amateur soldiers and the taken-by-surprise police. All Charlie can see is the empty freeway waiting for them at the pier where he will present the message of the day.

Sid knows nothing about this change of direction. No one thinks to call him on his cell phone. He is perched on the corner of the bridge over the freeway at Olympic and Lincoln waiting for the march to come into sight. Suddenly sirens are screaming all around him and one, two, three LAPD cruisers wheel the wrong way down the freeway ramp and skid to a stop blocking the westbound lanes. Only then does Sid look out and see the amazing sight materializing up from behind a small rise in the freeway. *My God*, Sid realizes, *they're marching right down the middle of the freeway.* As they rise up seemingly out of the ground, it is a bigger crowd of people than Sid has ever seen anywhere before. The three lone police cars blocking the freeway suddenly look pretty silly, helpless, like three small sandbags in the path of a towering tsunami.

A platoon of National Guardsmen with rifles and two more police cars going the wrong way descend the off ramp and take up positions on the freeway below. To Sidney's surprise, the National Guardsmen deploy behind the police cars and raise their weapons toward the oncoming horde of marchers as if they are actually contemplating firing over their heads as a means of getting them to stop. Sidney can't believe it: *Guns raised to stop an Earth Day March.* The marchers are bearing down on the roadblock. They are no more than a quarter of a mile away, close enough for Sid to make out Charlie and Alison and Jerry leading them toward the makeshift barrier of police cars and weekend soldiers ordering them to stop, to return to their designated parade route.

But this river of protest is not changing its course, not bowing to an authority it has already rejected. Like a huge juggernaut it bears inexorably down on the outmanned contingent of soldiers and policemen crouched behind those cars in its path. At its head, Charlie is revising his speech, Alison's gaze is fixed on the barricade of police cars with the line of rifle muzzles poking out over their fenders like porcupine quills, Jerry's eyes are darting left and right searching desperately for escape routes in case a firefight actually does happen, and silently, inconspicuously, M.D. Farrow and her attendant weasel melt backwards into the crowd and stealthily slip away out of the field of fire.

Chapter 19

The Dam Breaks

The March, with Charlie and Alison at its head, bears relentlessly down on the makeshift barricade of pulsing police cars. Charlie and Alison have not even noticed the defection of M.D. and Wrig Jones. One hundred yards, eighty, sixty. Absolutely no way are they going to stop. Charlie knows that he can't stop this river of humanity and his realization is that he doesn't want to stop himself. They shouldn't have to stop. A hot anger at the police for drawing their guns burns within Charlie, sears his resolve. All Alison can see is the guns resting on the roofs of the police cars, poking out from behind their fenders. But it is only five cars and perhaps a dozen guns trying to stop a relentless river of marchers that across the morning has probably grown to 400,000 people strong, Inconceivable that those weekend soldiers might shoot. *No way*, Alison thinks. *They can't shoot into this big a crowd.*

But the police shotguns rest on the car roofs locked and loaded, aimed right at Charlie and Alison. And other policemen with sidearms drawn crouch behind the cruiser's fenders ready to fire as soon as the order is given. And the National Guardsmen stand locked and loaded.

Fifty yards and the Marchers show no hesitation. Forty. Thirty.

There is a sudden quick movement around the police cars. An order has been given: "Back off. Get out of there. NOW! NOW! DON'T FIRE! DON'T FIRE!" Later the news media would report that the order came down all the way from the Mayor's office. The cops dive into their patrol cars, lights still pulsing, and withdraw in haste. Two cars back in reverse to the safety of the freeway ramp they previously came down going the wrong way. The others flip tight U-turns and flee down the freeway in front of the relentless flowing mob coursing toward the sea.

"Dammit!" M.D. cursed. She and Wrig Jones had watched it all from a vantage point up on the Lincoln Avenue overpass. "Dammit! I wanted them to fire." She and her smoking-again henchman look straight down on the biggest protest march in American history surging beneath them right under the bridge. "It would have been perfect. Just like Kent State. They would have fired the first shot, done our work for us, drawn all the blame."

"What's Kent State?" Wrig asks.

M.D. Farrow just looks at him in amazement and then a dark kind of pity. "Never mind, just get me to the car."

Jones makes an immediate cell phone call. In less than a minute two motorcycles ridden by shiny helmeted women riders in black tee-shirts proudly emblazoned with "*Dykes on Bikes*" across the backs weave their way to the overpass. Their riders beckon to M.D. and Jones to climb up behind and they roar away north toward Colorado Boulevard and the Pier.

Within minutes MD and Wrig Jones are sitting in the black limo at the north end of the Pier parking lot. M.D.'s computer is in her lap and her cell phone is to her face. She has entered Field General mode. She is giving her orders to her troops. But she is not calling either Charlie or Alison.

Sid also crosses the bridge and proceeds down Colorado Boulevard to the Pier to meet the marchers. He knows the route to the grandstand from which Charlie will deliver his speech. He crosses the parking lot below the Pier and works his way across the sand to a vantage point just below the huge speakers that are big enough that Sid guesses they will be able to hear Charlie in Hawaii. But Sid has a bad feeling about all this. So many people crowded around the Pier, so many possible assassins. He knows that Jerry is marching right beside Charlie and Alison and he knows that Jerry would take a bullet for Charlie if it ever came to that, yet he still fervently hopes that Jerry is at the top of his game today of all days.

Chapter 20

At the Pier

*T*he Santa Monica freeway, the 10, basically dead-ends into the Pacific Ocean. It goes under the overpass bridge at Third Street then makes a sweeping downhill curve under the steep Colorado Boulevard downramp to the Santa Monica Pier where it merges with the Pacific Coast Highway, Highway 1, going north. The wide and swollen river of marchers, carrying their signs and pushing their strollers and chanting their protest chants and pumping their fists in the air, surges down the freeway and flows fast on a cordoned-off path lined with OceanSave volunteers in bright yellow tee shirts through the lower parking lot and across the sand to the steps leading up to the Pier. Charlie climbed the steps with Alison and Jerry to the speaker's platform. He still hadn't realized that M.D. Farrow was nowhere in sight.

From the speaker's platform in the shadow of the ferris wheel, Charlie and Alison took it all in. Hundreds of thousands of people filled the beach on both sides of the Pier and completely filled the ramp all the way up to Colorado Boulevard. The park along the cliff on Ocean Boulevard was totally lined with people all the way down to the *California Incline.* The speaker's platform faced inland toward downtown Santa Monica, but Charlie could see all 360 degrees of the crowd including the surfers on their boards out in the water. To the north the huge throng of Earth Day celebrants were packed absolutely solid all the way to Will Rogers State Beach. To the south the pulsating mass of revelers stretched halfway to the boardwalk in Venice. The overwhelming size of this gathering spread out in front of Charlie and Alison like a huge anthill crawling with the masses just waiting to be given direction. *Damn,* Charlie thought, *they're waiting for me to tell them what to do.*

Sid had maneuvered himself to a position just off the steps right below the speaker's platform. He could see Charlie and Alison clearly but he doubted they could see him in the middle of the crowd. *Curious?* Sid thought. *Where's M.D. Farrow and her gang?*

Alison introduced Charlie. She kept it short and sweet. She welcomed them all to Earth Day 2013 and simply said: "Do you all know that you are part of the biggest March, the biggest demonstration, of any kind ever held in America. You are a million strong who came out to save our world as we know it. All of our hats are off to you. You did it and the whole world is watching. Now here is who you all have come out to hear today, the voice of OceanSave, the voice of Earth Day, Mister Charles Castle."

Charlie took the podium in a rush, pulled the microphone off the stand and waved it to the crowd. With his long blonde hair, in his yellow tee shirt and ragged jeans and his unquestioned bravado, he looked very much like a rock star. All that was missing was the guitar. The huge speakers on the platform flanked him. He waited, gathered himself to speak, before he finally stepped up, put the hand-held microphone to his mouth and began.

"Earth people. Earth Dayers. All million of you strong. Way to go! You're here which means you know what is important. You're here in the biggest numbers ever for a protest demonstration. But this isn't just a March, this is the first shot fired in a Revolution, a Revolution against the forces that rule our America today. Big Oil and the impotent, confused, corrupt and divided government that takes their orders from Big Oil."

As Charlie began his speech, began to wind the stem on his call for Eco-Revolution, on the roof of *The Arizona Hotel* Red Adams and Debbie Longo began to gear up. They removed the cameras they had mounted on the two metal tripods they had set up for appearance purposes and replaced them with long tubular grenade launchers. Then they started unpacking their ammunition.

"Eight years ago at this time, on April 20, just two days before Earth Day, the Deepwater Horizon oil rig off the coast of Louisiana and Mississippi and Alabama blew up, set the ocean on fire, and then for two months gushed untold millions of gallons of crude oil into the Gulf. That offshore oil rig was a huge fire hose shooting a hard stream of poison into the ocean off of some of the best beaches in America. Look down at the white sand you are standing on here in California and imagine what those people in Louisiana must have felt when their beaches turned black with a tide of tarballs and filthy brown sludge washing ashore with every wave. You surfers out there on your boards" and Charlie took them in with a sweeping motion of his hand "think what it would be like to surf a wave filled with thick sticky oil."

As Charlie drew these noxious images for the throng, only twelve miles away, on the tarmac outside his makeshift hangar in Carson, Black Jack Daniels was revving up the engines on his two jerry-built attack helicopters. Inside the warehouse that morning Daniels had armed their homemade firing pods with air-to-ground rockets, USMC issue, the ones stolen from the Naval armory in Long Beach in February. He would fly one of the choppers and he had picked as his wingman a wartime *compadre* who had flown choppers in Desert Storm and had never been able to let go of the adrenaline high of the experience.

"Ask all those people along the Louisiana and Mississippi Coast who made their livelihood from the Gulf, all those oyster and clam and deep sea fishermen, all those shrimpers, all the people on shore whose only living has to do with beach tourism. Ask all those people and they'll be the first to stand beside all of us here in California in this Revolution. They'll march with us. They know how much one oil spill can change our whole way of life."

Maud Gunn and two of her biker thugs in bright yellow OceanSave volunteer tee shirts were stationed on the Pier just to the right of the speaker's platform. They stood listening raptly to Charlie's speech just like everyone else, except for one difference. They had their motorcycle helmets on with the visors down.

"But this isn't just about saving the ocean or the beaches."

Sid marveled at how his younger brother could spellbind, completely hold the attention of this huge ocean of humanity. Charlie had them hanging on his every word, nodding their heads up and down in affirmation to what he was saying. *If anyone can talk them into Revolution, he can,* Sid realized.

"It's about taking back our country from the crooks who run the corporations and the corrupt partisan politicians who run the government. Albert Camus wrote that you have 'permanent revolution' when it is 'carried into individual experience.' Well that is why you all are here today. There are a million of us together here on the beach, but we are all individuals. The Revolution has to burn in the hearts of each and every one of us every day."

Alison stood next to Charlie on the podium and she had never been so proud in her life. She looked all around her and in every face she saw the power of Charlie's words taking hold in the consciousness of each person. He had them. They were listening to his message, his call to Revolution, the way that the Greek soldiers must have listened to Odysseus as he led them into the wooden horse or the way Napoleon's or Patton's or Alexander the Great's soldiers must have listened to those great men before he led them into battle.

"It's no longer a time for sitting on fences or even just writing our congressmen. It's no longer a time for symbolic gestures. It's a time to march to save our world. It's a time to act as you have today. We need to march and demonstrate all over the country. In every city we need to turn out in the millions just like today. This Revolution needs to sweep all across the country and show them in Washington that a real Revolution is underway. We need to light up the blogosphere, email and tweet and call everyone we know all over the country and challenge them to join the Revolution."

The side windows were down in the black limo and M.D. Farrow was listening as raptly to Charlie's speech as everyone else. She sat with her watch in one hand and her cell phone in the other. Her everpresent laptop sat uncustomarily dormant on her knees. As Charlie's speech built in passion and began to crescendo, M.D. hit her cell phone's send button three successive times. Each time she growled the same message to her listeners: "Go! Go!"

Chapter 21

Apocalypse Right Now

As soon as M.D. Farrow gave her order, all the relentless wheels that had been put in place began to turn and grind toward the inevitable apocalypse.

On the roof of *The Arizona Hotel*, M.D.'s two sharpshooters ripped the tarp off of their improvised ammo depot and loaded up their firing tubes. Red Adams and Debbie Longo alternated firing. They walked their rocket-propelled grenades right down the middle of the beach on the north side of the pier. As each grenade exploded in the crowd, a high puff of sand garnished with flying bodies would erupt upward and subside to be followed by another explosion fifty feet further on marching relentlessly toward the pier. Red would fire and fall back to reload and Debbie would step forward to aim just left of Red's last shot. They fired in a relentless rhythm and their grenades exploded in a perfect line on the beach like flowers of death bursting into bloom. Fire and fall back, fire and fall back, their deadly dance of death ignited the attack on the Santa Monica Pier, shed the first blood of the million strong gathering of innocent Earth Day Marchers who never saw it coming, never even imagined it.

The ferris wheel, empty, revolves slowly above the throng, the surfers sit calmly on their boards in the water, all the hundreds of thousands of people are caught suspended in the moment when the beach suddenly explodes. One moment they are caught up in the fervor of revolutionary rhetoric and the next moment they are being flung skyward and blown apart.

Charlie Castle is still speaking as Black Jack Daniels' two choppers take off from their secret helipad in Carson. The two black unmarked birds of prey lift off and accelerate straight west toward the ocean. When they hit the shoreline they bank hard right in perfect unison and descend until they are no more than fifty feet above the water. Side by side they thump down the beach, their skids skimming the waves almost like water skis. Like two hunter birds they fly the shoreline toward Santa Monica until they are close above the huge throng of bodies crowding the beach south of the Santa Monica Pier. Below on the beach a waving sea of heads snap up to watch them fly over and probably wonder why they are all black and are flying so low. About four hundred yards out from the pier, Black Jack Daniels fires his first rocket right at the ferris wheel. Only a second later his wingman fires a second at the same huge target.

The sequential explosions light the ferris wheel up like a pinwheel firecracker. Slowly it continues in its revolution, but them comes apart in flames and totters slowly over on its side crushing the whole midway beneath. People on the pier try to escape the toppling mass of metal and flaming wood. They try to run but there is nowhere for them to go. The crowd is packed so tight on the pier that no one can even move to escape. The crush becomes a turgid stampede with bodies losing their balance and being trampled underfoot. The two black helos rocket over the pier just as the ferris wheel is beginning to topple. They fly on down the beach over the exploding crowd, then bank and turn back for another lethal pass.

The last one to trigger her contribution to this burgeoning apocalypse is Maud Gunn. Her first task is a simple one, a no-brainer. Stationed right behind the speaker's platform on the Pier where Charlie Castle is addressing the crowd, Maud presses in sequence the four buttons on her remote triggering device. One by one the satchel charges that she and her two henchwomen had hung beneath the west end of the pier that morning explode upward taking out not only the thick pilings supporting the pier upon which each was hung but also blasting out four huge holes in the floor of the pier itself. With four of its main pilings cut out from under it, a whole section thirty yards square right in the center of the pier just falls away, collapses downward, all the carnival rides, all the food stands, all of the hundreds of people who had come early to get a good place on the pier, plummeting to the sand and surf below. The center section of the pier collapses just as if a huge axe has cut its legs right out from under it. And Maud Gunn had accomplished all that simply by pushing four little buttons. Her second task for the day didn't promise to be that easy however.

On the beach, on the pier, all around, chaos reigns, an unimaginable chaos of torn bodies and bomb craters and twisted metal and trampled corpses and burning buildings and stampeding crowds of people too large to even be numbered. Everyone is trying to run but no one has anywhere to go. On the pier the crowd is pushing and shoving and screaming in panic. Below the pier twisted bodies are crushed and buried beneath the fallen timbers of the pier itself and the walls and roofs of the buildings that collapsed when the pier split apart.

The choppers split for their second pass. Black Jack goes right and fires his second rocket at the restaurant at the far end of the pier out over the water. His wingman goes left and fires his pay load into the crowd on the steep ramp leading down to the pier from Colorado Boulevard. What had been the jewel of Santa Monica, is now, in mere moments, turned into a smoking mass of blood and body parts and screaming people and twisted metal and gaping craters and burning buildings and trampled bodies and utter, inescapable, chaotic horror.

The huge crowd in moments metamorphed from a joyous festival into a boiling whirlpool of gore and frenzy and terror. The crowd was like an angry sea, fierce waves of panic pounded against each other, broke over each other, crashed against each other, bursting in a spray of blood and screams. The brutal sea raged and thundered across the beach, over the pier, running headlong to escape. But how? To where? Utter confusion. Sheer bloody apocalypse. It was the uproar of Babel, the holocaust of Hiroshima, the hopelessness of Hell.

As soon as M.D. Farrow gave the order to strike, her black limo with the weasel at the wheel pulled out of the parking lot by the pier and accelerated north on the coast highway toward Malibu. It pulled into the long beachfront parking lot at Will Rogers State Beach, parked right next to the bike path and sat waiting, engine purring.

After their second pass, the two helos peeled off and headed straight south down the beach, low to the water and thumping the air like two killer birds on the run. At the breakwater of the marina they turned out to sea and flew toward the horizon for a mile. Then they hovered over the water, waiting. In a matter of moments a sleek speedboat drew up. It had been anchored in the lee of one of the oil tankers offloading to the El Segundo power station. The two pilots quickly ditched and descended ropes to their waiting swiftboat. As the cigarette boat picked them up, and pulled away, the two helos suddenly exploded in circles of fire, raining flaming shrapnel down on the water. The long slim powerboat slammed into speed, its nose rising out of the water like a knife stabbing upward, and raced south toward Long Beach or

Newport or perhaps even Mexico.

On the roof of *The Arizona Hotel*, Red Adams and Debbie Longo had expended all of their grenades. They abandoned their firing tubes and ran for the stairwell. Debbie stopped at the top of the stairs down and a 9 millimeter Berretta pistol suddenly materialized in her hand. She called to her partner in crime and he stopped four steps down and looked back up at her. She shot him in the middle of his forehead, stepped over his body, and fled down the steps to her motorcycle. Clearly Adams had been tabbed as the fall guy, the Lee Harvey Oswald in this whole operation.

On the beach all was total chaos, but up on the pier around the speaker's platform there was an oasis of momentary space and calm. The stage for the speaker's podium where Charlie stood, mouth agape, watching the bomb blasts walk their way down the beach toward him, was raised a good eight feet so he was above the crowd and out of the path of the sudden stampede. He was flanked by Alison and Jerry who were equally frozen in shock by all the explosions that had suddenly erupted around them. The speaker's platform sat dead in the middle of the pier and right in front of the Santa Monica Police Station. It had been cordoned off by the two huge speakers, the two sound trucks, and two rows of police cars that formed a narrow walking aisle all the way from the back of the stage across the pier to a stairway down to the beach. Maud Gunn and her two biker accomplices, flashing OceanSave credentials, had stationed themselves at the top of this stairway at the end of the police car aisle to the speaker's platform. It was from there that she triggered the satchel charges under the pier. As soon as the explosions began on the beach, at the ferris wheel, their own under the pier, the three of them took off in a sprint for the speaker's platform. When they reached the steps up onto the stage, Maud made straight for Charlie. The other two moved quickly to Jerry and Alison.

The first thing Jerry felt was a fierce blow to the back of his thighs. A body at full speed had hit him from behind, knocking him full force over the front of the raised stage. If that blow had caught him eight inches lower on his leg it probably would have blown out both of his knees. As it was, that blow caught Jerry completely by surprise and sent him hurtling face forward into the crowd gathered in front and below the stage. The pier had just been rocked by four large explosions and people where swiveling their heads trying to figure out what was going on when this large black man was suddenly catapulted into their midst.

Jerry landed on an obese woman in a muu-muu and a bespectacled man in a tie-dyed tank top who had the bad luck to be camped in his line of flight. When he finally got his feet under him, he clawed his way back through the now panicked and fleeing crowd to the front edge of the stage. He pulled himself up and immediately pulled his piece out of the shoulder holster beneath his black coat. But it was too late. Charlie was gone and the whole world was erupting around him. He wasn't the only one with a drawn gun. At least a dozen police officers had emptied out of their parked patrol cars or out of the police station and all of their guns were drawn too. Jerry quickly holstered up. He was afraid that one of those clueless cops would shoot him if they saw his gun. He looked in all directions for Charlie, but he was nowhere to be seen. Then Jerry saw Alison lying face down on the floor of the stage and he feared the worst.

Alison had happened to glance to her right just as a huge woman was covering Charlie's face with what looked like a white gym towel. Then Jerry went flying off the front of the stage and Alison turned to Charlie in alarm. That was when she was punched full in the face. Alison went down as if she had been struck by a ball bat. She never knew what (or who) hit her.

When Alison came to, Jerry was kneeling over her, holding her head and shouting her name. When he got her sat up, and her eyes began to clear, he was still shouting at her. "Charlie, Charlie, did you see what happened to Charlie?"

She just stared blank-eyed at Jerry, not understanding, wondering where she was, why her face hurt so much and blood was running from her nose in a stream down the front of her lime green top.

"Alison, Alison, did you see them take Charlie? Did you see what happened?"

Jerry's voice was strange, almost begging, really not like Jerry. As her mind began to clear she remembered where she was, then she remembered the last thing she had seen before the lights went out. "It was something big," she said, "taller than Charlie. With a helmet, like Darth Vader, on its head. It was wrapping a towel around Charlie's face. What happened Jerry? Where's Charlie?"

Maud Gunn had made straight for Charlie Castle at the microphone. She had a white rag saturated with chloroform in one hand and an automatic in the other. She came up behind Charlie and looped her gun hand around his neck and pressed the chloroform rag hard over his nose and mouth. He went limp in her arms in a matter of seconds. Maud was taller than Charlie so when he passed out he fell back against her chest and she hooked both her musclebound arms under his armpits and started to drag his dead weight back off the stage. Her two henchwomen quickly joined her, their automatic pistols at the ready, as she scuttled backward down off of the stage. It was not until they were halfway down the aisle of parked police cars that they met with any resistance.

When the explosions had begun, especially the satchel charges that had rocked the pier, some of the police had emptied out of the pier station house and had drawn their sidearms. Utter chaos reigned all around them and within seconds the towering ferris wheel toppled and fell almost right on top of them. These policemen had no idea what was going on. They had drawn their guns, but had no clue as to who or what to shoot at.

Then one police officer spotted Maud Gunn, flanked by her two bodyguards, dragging an unconscious man across the pier. He also spotted the automatic pistols in the hands of the two escorts. He raised his service revolver at them and ordered them to stop. He never had a chance. They mowed him down in a concentrated volley of automatic weapons fire that turned that pier into a war zone in the blink of an eye.

Then Maud, dragging Charlie, was past them and home free. The other cops had hit the deck when the volley of gunfire had cut down their unlucky colleague, but when they looked up, the source of the gunfire was nowhere to be seen. The three women dragging Charlie had already disappeared down the back stairway of the pier to the sand. The cops came up brandishing their guns, but, as had been the case before, they just couldn't find anyone to shoot.

When they hit the sand at the bottom of the steps, Maud's two helpmates slung their automatic pistols over their backs on straps and each picked up one of Charlie's legs. The three of them ran with the crowd across the sand toward Santa Monica. When they reached the concrete beachwalk, almost all of the fleeing crowd took it, running south, away from the pier, blindly. But the three women carrying the unconscious man's body continued straight ahead. They darted across the beach walk, between the buildings, and emerged into a wide alleyway that ran parallel to the beachwalk behind the first row of buildings. Only then did they too turn south away from the pier. Their bikes were parked in the alley up against the back wall of the *The Shutters Hotel.*

Unceremoniously they dump the unconscious Charlie Castle into the sidecar mounted on Maud's bike and kick each of their Harleys into growling life. Flanked by her two armed escorts, Maud rockets out of the hotel alley and straight down Ocean Boulevard past the pier which is on fire. The huge crowd fleeing the pier has started to glut the boulevard in panic but the motorcycles don't hesitate, in fact they accelerate, and pedestrians leap for their lives to get out of their way. The three bikes break free just before the *California Incline,* but they don't take it. They race down Ocean Boulevard to its downward curving walled-in end to where it ultimately comes out on Sunset. Then they take Sunset straight to the Coast Highway.

Surprisingly, the traffic on the Coast Highway is still moving as Maud and her two henchwomen deliver their limp package to M.D. Farrow's waiting black limo. Then, with its motorcycle escort guarding its back, the limo pulls out into traffic and slowly, patiently, makes its way north into Malibu. The motorcycles follow for a short way as the limo glides through traffic then two of the three bikes peel off and disappear up a hilly side road headed inland. Maud Gunn, on her bike with the side car, stays with the black limo. The other two bikes ride to the top of a pass and pull off onto a flat vantage point where they can look back at Santa Monica beach and the Pier.

Smoke rises from the Pier. The ferris wheel is down which makes it not even look like the real Santa Monica Pier. The whole scene looks like a battlefield that has just been bombed from the air. They stand by their idling bikes and look back on their handiwork in a kind of awe until one of Maud's henchwomen breaks the trenchant silence: "Awesome!"

At that very moment another bike roars up the curving incline and, braking into a controlled skid, joins them on their flat vantage point. Its rider dismounts, removes her visored helmet, and joins them.

"Hey, mission accomplished, huh." Debbie Longo laughs

"Damn right," the other two women agree.

"Maud delivered our package OK?" Debbie asks.

"Safe and sound," comes her answer.

In another moment they all saddled up and rode off over the hill.

Chapter 22

Aftermath of Apocalypse

*W*hen it started, Sid Castle couldn't believe his eyes. He had managed to station himself right below the speaker's platform, and he was blithely listening to his eloquent charismatic political star of a brother fomenting ecological revolution when the first rocket hit the Ferris Wheel. Suddenly a quite different, utterly violent, revolution broke out all around him. When Sid would think of it later, he would realize that he had been right in the middle of some sort of 21st-century apocalypse now, a shocking surprise attack, an inexplicable explosion of violence.

Sid Castle simply couldn't believe his eyes, couldn't immediately process what was happening. He looked over his shoulder and tracked a procession of explosions marching right down the beach toward the pier, actually coming right at him. He couldn't really see what was going on up on the pier, but suddenly two helicopters flying unusually low came rocketing over the pier and right over his head. His eyes followed them as they flew down the beach and then banked into a full turn and headed back. *Why? News helicopters?* But then suddenly he saw them fire their rockets from the pads mounted on their undercarriages and he understood. They were attacking the pier from the air. All he could think of was 9/11 and those planes going into those twin towers.

Behind him on the beach people were dying. Sid was close enough to hear the screams of the people blown up in the mortar attack. Then to his right, toward the water, a series of loud explosions ripped through the underside of the pier and a whole large section of it just caved in, its underpinnings blown away. Then just further to his right, he watched as the Pacific Park Ferris Wheel, the signature attraction of the Santa Monica Pier, slowly toppled over, blown off its moorings. The Ferris Wheel crashed down like a huge axe splintering everything in its falling path. Hundreds of people, a wide swath of the packed-in crowd on the pier, were crushed under the twisted metal of the fallen wheel.

Sid Castle was paralyzed for a long moment as he tried to take in and process all of the chaos and carnage that had erupted around him so suddenly. The two helicopters screaming back over his head once again jolted him out of his shock and thrust him back into his own precarious situation. All he could think of was Alison (and Charlie) up there on the pier where the rockets had been fired and the explosions had gone off. Sid was actually carried right to the front of the steps by the natural flow of the panicked crowd. But at the steps as one crowd was coursing one way to escape the beach, another rampaging crowd was pounding down the steps to escape the holocaust of the pier.

Sid clawed his way up the steps from the sand, fighting against the rush of the panicked crowd. He finally made it to the base of the bunting-wrapped stage where Charlie had been speaking only a moment before. He dragged himself up on the stage as the frenzied crowd continued to course by him in a mad rush to escape the attack which seemed to have struck all around them. The first person he saw was Alison. She was sitting on the floor next to the speaker's podium bleeding heavily from the nose. Jerry was down on one knee bending over her, shielding her, his gun in one hand, his head swiveling from side to side, searching for the sources of all this violence and chaos. Alison seemed dazed, her hand was to her face and bright red blood was seeping between her fingers.

"She's OK," Jerry shouted to Sid above the din of the roiling mob. "She got punched in the face, knocked down."

Sid didn't say anything, just nodded, as he went down on his knees next to Jerry to tend to Alison. Charlie was nowhere to be seen. Then Alison's eyes went wide and came back to life like a sleeper suddenly sitting straight up out of a nightmare.

"They took Charlie," were the first words she said to Sid and Jerry. "They took Charlie... that way," she tried to point but she was still disoriented and her upraised arm just described a weak arc in the air and then collapsed to her side. Sid looked helplessly at Jerry. Jerry was up on his feet looking around, trying to catch some sight of Charlie or find some avenue of escape down which they, whoever they were, might have taken him.

"Who took him, Alison?" Sid grasped her gently by the shoulders, looked straight into her face, tried to get her to concentrate. "Who took Charlie? The police? Security?"

"They wrapped a towel around Charlie's head and took him."

"Who Alison? Who?"

"I don't know. A really big woman. And more women. In masks, no in helmets. I couldn't really see them. They attacked us from behind. They knocked Jerry down off the stage and then took Charlie with them."

"I never saw 'em" Jerry cut in, still swiveling his head, his eyes, and his handgun on matching planes, looking for some sign of Charlie, of the attackers, searching desperately for their exit route. "By the time I got back on the stage they were gone."

Suddenly Jerry took off running, down through an aisle of parked police cars toward the south side of the pier.

Chapter 23

Chase

*I*t's the only way off the pier, Jerry realized, and he took off running, his .38 police revolver still in his hand but wrapped under his coat out of sight. All of his military training and bounty hunter experience kicked in automatically as if suddenly a key had been turned and ignition had fired all his senses.

His headlong run down the aisle of parked cruisers was unobstructed. Cops were there, but they were bending over a fallen comrade.

At the end of the aisle was a stairway down to the sand. Jerry grabbed the rail and leapt down the steps three at a time. Landing in the sand he stopped and searched. He vectored the beach, facing inland toward the beachwalk and the buildings. One/fourth, then another fourth, then just entering his third quadrant he spotted them, the three big women dragging Charlie like dead weight. The only way he caught sight of them was because the biggest women, who had one arm in Charlie's armpit dragging him, was waving a large handgun, probably a Mag, in front of her in her other hand to menacingly clear their way. Her tactic was working perfectly. The panicked, fleeing crowd opened up before her, jumped out of her way, as if she was unzipping it.

As Jerry spotted them, they were a good fifty yards away but moving sluggishly as they dragged Charlie. He didn't really think of anything. He just took off at a dead run toward them. As he ran after them, the three women carting the unconscious Charlie crossed the beachwalk and disappeared with him into an alley between two buildings, one low and seedy, the other a six-storey fancy beachfront hotel. The crowd zipped closed behind them.

When he reached the beach walk he had to fight his way across it. *I don't have time for this shit*! Jerry realized, and he fired one shot into the air and screamed "Get out of the way!" twice. That caught the attention of the immediate crowd and they fell off and let him by.

At the head of the alley he slowed and set his pistol straight out in front of his face with his off-hand steadying his wrist. Its barrel served as a sighting point as he traversed the alley with urgent caution, moving the barrel from left to right in quick horizontal sweeps looking for bogeys to show up on his screen and be identified. Nobody challenged him in the first alley which dead-ended into a second wider alley littered with dumpsters and trash cans and a few parked cars and golf carts. As he stepped out of this first alley into the bisecting wider driveway, suddenly three large motorcycles roared to life, leapt out from their parking space up against the building wall on the other side, and rocketed straight for him. He tried to raise his piece to fire but they were on him in an instant. He had to dive out of the way to keep from being run over.

He tucked and rolled against a flimsy metal garage door as the bikes roared past, pushed off with one hand and came up firing, but the bikes were moving too fast, withdrawing out of range, and he hit nothing. He did note, in a blink of an eye, that the far right bike had a sidecar with a passenger slumped in it that he was sure was Charlie.

Then they were gone.

Jerry's mind raced. His failure bared its teeth and bit at him for one brief second, but he immediately kicked it away like an annoying dog. *This ain't over yet*, he snarled to himself.

Chapter 24

Tracking the Chip

*T*ears and blood were still running down Alison's face.

"Here, hold this to your nose," Sid gave her his white silk monogrammed handkerchief, a useful tool that defense lawyers always carry in their suitcoat breast pocket handy for giving to sympathetic female witnesses when they break down into well-rehearsed tears on the stand.

"When Jerry went over the front of the stage I turned and she hit me right in the face." Tears were running down Alison's cheeks. "I grabbed my nose with both hands when I felt the blood gush. Then through my fingers I saw the big woman put the towel over Charlie's face and drag him away."

Chloroform, or something like it, to knock him out, Sid thought. *But Why? It sounds like some kind of commando operation. Man*!

"Why would they take Charlie? Who are they, Sid? Why did they do this?"

"I don't know. It was all like some kind of military operation."

Jerry suddenly materialized beside them like a hulking phantom. The crowds had moved on. The stage was actually a small haven of quiet in the midst of the devastation of the gutted pier. "You guys OK?" he asked.

Jerry was looking around. His eyes darting.

"Just stay right here, both of you, don't move." Jerry was giving orders, not asking. "I need to be able to find you right away when I get back."

He moved away from them into the lee of the nearest building which happened to be the Santa Monica Police Station. He was rapidly hitting keys on his cell phone accessing his GPS app and punching in the user ID number of Charlie's tracking chip. And there it was. The street map of downtown Santa Monica had leapt up followed immediately by the pulsing of a small red blip across the face of the map.

Got 'em, Jerry expanded the image, zooming in, with his thumb and forefinger. The blip was just entering the curving incline at the end of Ocean Boulevard where it feeds into Sunset toward the PCH and the beach.

Why are they doing that? Jerry thought. *They're coming back into traffic not trying to get out and away.*

The blip stopped at Sunset and the Coast Highway. *They're crossing it,* Jerry realized. *They're going off road. They're on the beachwalk. That's one way to beat traffic.* Then, in the parking lot of Will Rogers Beach the blip came to a halt, stopped dead.

Jerry knew that he had to get moving, *but how?* Traffic was in gridlock. He had no vehicle. He couldn't have chased them in a car anyway. His eyes scanned left and right, searching.

Abandoned against the wall of the police station no more than ten feet from his position was a police bike patrol bike. *Whatever!* Jerry thought as he grabbed the bike.

Chapter 25

Pursuit

*J*erry walked the bike to the edge of the stage. It looked like
Alison's nose had stopped bleeding. She and Sid were just sitting there in silence. They had subsided into a kind of shock
as they looked around them and saw all of the devastation, the fallen
ferris wheel, the collapsed section of the pier, the buildings on fire, the
huge "Pacific Park" arch sheared right in half, and the people, the poor
people, screaming in pain, wailing in despair as they held dead loved
ones in their arms, blood everywhere. It looked like a small city had
been bombed, a holocaust tragically complete.

"What the hell?" Sid jolted out of his stupor when he saw Jerry
pushing the bicycle.

"I think it's the fastest way to try to catch up with them. Nobody's
goin' anywhere in a car. They're on motorcycles on the beachwalk but
that only goes to Will Rogers State Park, then they have to get back
into traffic. Maybe I can catch them this way."

"Real hi-tech, eh?" Sid shook his head in disbelief.

"Yeah, right," Jerry saw the irony of it. "Look, Sid, take Alison to
the beach house when you can get clear of this mess and wait for my
call. Even if I can't catch up with them, we'll know where he is from
the chip. Okay?"

"Yeah, I'll take care of her. Go! Go!"

Jerry ran the bike down the steps to the sand and across the beach
to where the bike path came out from under the pier. He couldn't even
mount the bike for the first two hundred yards down the path due to
the remains of the fleeing crowd. But then, his GPS still pulsing on his
phone in his head, he climbed on and started pedaling. He took off
north toward Malibu. It wasn't a bad bike, a 15-speed mountain bike
with thick tires and a heavy duty yoke, not nearly as good as his bike,
not fast but durable, good for city streets. But it was well tuned and ran

smooth. He flipped it into a low gear and pedaled hard but it was slow going at first. He had to weave his way through what looked like a line of refugees from a war zone.

As he worked his way north, he suddenly realized that all around him was human carnage and death. If he thought the scene on the pier was chaotic and horrible, that was nothing compared to what he was pedaling through.

It was the sounds of agony and loss and hopelessness that struck him first and most powerfully. Shrill screams, guttural moans, death rattles and wails of mourning vibrated all around like some roiling atonal bedlam. They were the sounds of the damned, the dying, the suffering and the hopeless.

Oh no.

Oh God no.

Oh God no.

As if imploring some merciful God to intercede, to turn back time, to return everyone to that carefree day at the beach, to Earth Day, to the time before their world exploded, to the time before the terrorists attacked and rained death down on all of them.

And no help in sight. No paramedics or ambulances or doctors or anyone had made it to this part of the beach to help any of these poor lost people who were just wandering around like ghosts. All that was what Jerry Creogan weaved his way through on the track of Charlie's electronic blip.

It was slow going for Jerry at first as he pedaled north, but once he got past the scene of the attack there was no one to block his way and he stood up on the pedals and flew. Out on the PCH nothing was moving and Jerry saw clearly that he had made the right decision, chosen the right mode of transportation for this chase. He was an experienced, even accomplished, cyclist. He had two triathlons under his belt. Conditioning was not even a consideration as he powered north on the bike. The blip was still there on his phone's GPS. The Will Rogers State Beach seemed to be the immediate destination of the blip.

When he hit the State Beach, he stopped in the parking lot of a refreshment stand to check his phone. The blip was still on the move but no longer moving north. In fact it seemed almost to be moving in a circle or hovering and it wasn't far from his location at all. The bike path had dead-ended into a long beach parking lot that paralleled the coast highway for almost a mile. Jerry mounted up and slowly pedaled north up the parking lot. Then he saw the single Harley with the sidecar. It was parked right up against a black limousine. Both vehicles seemed to be abandoned. No limo driver. No occupants in the limo. No Amazon woman biker. Nothing. Where the hell could they have gone? He looked to the highway. Gridlock. He looked all around in the parking lot. Not a sign. No one. As a last resort he looked out toward the ocean.

A good two hundred yards away, all the way across the beach, four figures were climbing up on the rocks of a groin that reached out into the waves.

A powerboat was coming in toward them through the surf.

The huge, tall biker woman was pulling Charley across the rocks. The other two figures on the rocks were smaller, muffled, and Jerry couldn't make them out. In a mere second as he watched, he suddenly realized what was going down. The boat was coming in to pick them up. *They're getting out of this mess by sea*, he thought. *If they get into that boat I'll never catch up with them.* He took off running hard across the sand.

The boat coasted in and maneuvered around until it was faced back out to sea. A rope was tossed to the towering biker woman who caught it and pulled the stern of the boat in close against the rocks.

Jerry watched it all happen as he ran toward them. He knew that in another minute they would have Charley aboard that boat and be off. He had to do something. He was still out of range but he pulled his gun anyway and fired off a shot at them. It caught their attention. They hadn't seen him before as they had been watching the boat come in and they had no idea whatsoever that they had been followed from the pier.

Jerry kept running but he knew it was too late. He was just too far away to stop them or drop them. He went down on one knee and fired off two shots but he was still out of range.

The two smaller, hooded figures, one in a baseball cap, the other in what looked like a scarf, maybe a birka, were stepping down into the boat. Charley was unceremoniously pushed down into the back of the boat by the hulking woman who no sooner than she got rid of his dead weight drew her gun and looked for the shooter who had interrupted their little boarding party.

She found Jerry on the beach right away, running straight toward her, about thirty yards out. Without hesitation she went to one knee and squeezed off a volley in his direction.

As soon as he saw her gun start up, Jerry yanked himself into a left-ward dive and roll into the sand and came up firing back, but nothing happened. His gun was completely jammed, probably from the sand. Everything seemed to go into slow motion. The huge woman with the gun jumped up and dropped over the back side of the groin and disappeared. The boat pulled away from the rocks and headed out to sea. They were gone and they had Charlie and he was left holding a useless gun and watching their boat recede into the distance out to sea.

He didn't watch for long, two maybe three seconds. He realized how exposed and helpless he was so he jumped to his feet and ran, keeping low, to the cover of the rocks. As he ran he just waited for that tall biker woman to rise up from behind the rocks and commence firing at him again. But she never did and he made it to the cover of the rocks safely. Still, he knew he wasn't out of the woods. If that woman stayed to fight and came after him, he was pretty much defenseless unless she was stupid enough to let it go to hand-to-hand.

He crouched in the shelter of the rocks, waiting. He looked out to sea and the boat with his charge, Charlie Castle, the voice of the ecology movement in America, was pulling away, growing smaller and smaller in the distance as it chugged toward the horizon. He poked his head up over the nearest rock, wary that it might get blown off, and the big woman with the gun was disappearing in the distance. At a full run she was almost all the way across the beach headed for her Harley in the parking lot. Jerry stood up, tucked his useless gun into his belt, took one last hopeless look out to sea where the boat had turned north and was almost out of sight, and started the long trudge toward the beach. As he walked he could hear the Harley fire up and roar away. *Terrific*, he thought, *some bodyguard you are.*

He sat down on the parking lot curb, apped his phone to the GPS tracker and watched the blip, Charlie, progress steadily out from the land into the indeterminate void that represented the ocean. All that the small screen on his phone showed was a line of demarcation between the land and the sea. Charley was just a blip that had crossed that line and was disappearing into that light blue emptiness that was the Pacific Ocean.

Where the hell are they going out there? he wondered. *Where are they going to put ashore?* As he sat there on the curb a feeling of helplessness took hold. *Stop feeling sorry for yourself,* he scolded himself inside his head. *Get on it. This isn't over yet.*

PART THREE

Circuses and Prisons

Chapter 1

American Circus

*I*t was the very best of times for the national media in the days immediately following the attack on the pier. The legitimate newspapers, the TV news shows, the tabloids, the social media, the blogosphere, the twitters, went wild. The national media, of course, descended on L.A. and the Santa Monica Pier like maggots to a rotting corpse. But the L.A. media certainly held their own in the feeding frenzy. After all, media, every conceivable form of media, is L.A.'s business just as money is New York's and politics is Washington's. Helicopters hovered over the gutted Santa Monica Pier like vultures circling. It was a mad dash for every branch of the media to be the first to fully capture the event from every angle and then to try to understand it, figure out just what happened, what it meant, who did it and why.

Like the Zapruder film of the Kennedy Assassination, cell phone shot stills and videos kept popping up like hand-held nightmares on every news show and *faux* news show. Only the comedy news shows had the good sense to leave it alone because there was just nothing funny about it. It was all about death. It was a massacre of innocents.

Predictably it took on a media life of its own just as 9/11 did and Katrina and the Deepwater Horizon and the Arab Spring did. The newspapers and the tabloids and TV news hours rapidly reached a consensus and named it the Earth Day Massacre. The speculation ran rampant. Almost everyone figured it for a terrorist attack like 9/11 or the hotels in Mumbai, but in the days immediately following the attack no one claimed responsibility. No Al-Qaeda or ISIS video wound up on Al-Jazeera's doorstep. Almost everyone in the media figured it for another instance of some underground cell of terrorists seizing the opportunity to take out large numbers of innocent Americans on a symbolic occasion in a symbolic place. Endlessly into the nights the media speculated and discussed and dissected the event and its potential meanings. Who did it? And why? And, especially, what did it mean?

And then the conspiracy theory buzz kicked in. Not everyone in the media or in the political punditry business subscribed to the terrorist scenario. At least two tabloid pseudo-news shows brought out the "usual suspects" of conspiracy theorists as so-called "experts." These sinister speculators cast off in all directions and floated their deep-cover plots in whatever direction the prevailing winds blew. They speculated that the oil cartels or the drug cartels or the CIA or the anti-global warming forces had staged the Earth Day Massacre. As with all conspiracy theories, there had to be someone or something big behind it— Big Business, Big Oil, Big Brother, who? There had to be some Mister Big, like Osama Bin Laden or Moammar Khadaffi, pulling the strings and dispatching his minions to wreak havoc.

Charlie Castle's kidnapping was never more than a sidebar to this media circus, at least at the beginning. But he was a celebrity and, after all, this was L.A. where celebrity is an actual occupation, news genre and hunting season. So it didn't take overlong for Charlie's fair face and flowing locks to become familiar images on tabloid television and in the tabloid magazines and newspapers, so familiar in fact that by the second day after the attack on the Pier even the mainstream news outlets were beginning to notice.

A young reporter for the glossy magazine *Daily Celebrity* just happened to be on the pier at the time of the attack stalking celebrities in the crowd of marchers and snapping cell phone pictures when Charlie got snatched. She just happened to snap a picture of Maud Gunn wrapping Charlie's head in a chloroform-soaked towel. She didn't even know what she had photographed until she sought safety from the explosions and clicked through the digital snaps she had taken. *What is that huge woman doing to the featured speaker?* this cub reporter wondered.

It took almost a full day for that reporter's glossy gossip magazine to publish her photo on its cover of the kidnapping actually happening. When it hit the newsstands Charlie became the new load of chum for the media sharks. Within hours his face was splattered all over the media beneath headlines like "Where's Charlie?" and "Charlie Snatched." TV and the websites were all asking "Charlie Castle, darling of the ecological movement, kidnapped in midst of terrorist attack. Why? And who?" or "Who snatched Charlie Castle, the golden boy of the eco-movement?" or "Castle Kidnapped. America's Eco-Conscience

Silenced." That woman reporter's snap of Charlie being chloroformed was shown so many times that it became almost indelibly etched on the "American Consciousness." It was that kind of photo and the woman reporter sold it over and over to anyone who asked (and paid handsomely).

As for the police, they had their hands full. It took hours just to assess the damage. There were bodies on the beach and on the pier. The police had to call in help for the wounded (the dead would have to wait). Traffic shut down the whole city all the way to the 405 Freeway. When the traffic stopped and the freeways clogged and became gridlocked parking lots, the drivers abandoned their cars and cowered under bridges fearing that the terrorists might return. It fell to the police to try to untangle the biggest traffic jam in the history of Los Angeles. The beach became a roadway, the only way in and out of the attack site. The emergency vehicles all had to enter the beach at the Venice Pier off Washington Street and drive the length of the sand all the way to the Santa Monica Pier in order to bring aid to the wounded. Then there were the looters who preyed on the abandoned stores and cars vulnerable in the utter confusion. Plate glass windows in the Third Street Mall were shattered. Abandoned cars on the 10 Freeway was stripped. Shops in the area of Santa Monica up close to the pier were rifled and plundered. The police didn't have a chance. Nobody did.

Chapter Two

The Quiet After the Storm

*Y*es, for the American media it was the very best of times. But Charlie Castle wasn't watching the TV news or reading *The Los Angeles Times*. He never saw his famous picture on the cover of *Daily Celebrity* magazine. He was sitting in a rusty metal room handcuffed to some sort of thick sturdy pipe alone and waiting. He knew he was on the water because the room was moving ever so gently as if being rocked by the waves. He spent a whole night there on the floor of that metal cell trying to understand what had happened. He had awakened in a boat speeding steadily across the surface of what he presumed to be Santa Monica Bay. It was broad daylight so they quickly blindfolded him when he stirred, but he saw that it was M.D. Farrow and Wrig Jones in the boat with him. Vaguely he remembered things from before he lost consciousness. Explosions out in the sand in front of him, helicopters thumping very low overhead, loud explosions on the pier, Jerry falling down, Alison screaming, then everything had gone black.

Then he woke up in the boat and they pulled the bag over his head—*M.D. and Wrig Jones, his colleagues at OceanSave, his allies in the movement, his friends. What was going on? What had they done? What were they doing?*

The boat had delivered them to this place that seemed to be floating on the water, creaking like a ship at sea. *Why was he handcuffed? Why had they blindfolded him?* His mind raced. *Alison? Was she OK? How had their wonderful Earth Day gone so bad?* Alison was his first thought. He was desperate for news of her. The last thing he had heard before he blacked out was her scream.

Then he began to put it together. For some reason M.D. and Jones were taking him out of the public eye, putting him on ice. He realized that he had been drugged and abducted, by supposed friends no less, *but why? What kind of a game were they playing?* He had trusted M.D. They shared the same principles, same vision for the world, for humanity. *Was it possible that she had betrayed them and him?* But then he remembered Sid's warning. *You're the front man. You're the face and voice of this whole movement. You're the one who goes to jail for the cause a couple of times a year. You're their recurring fall guy,* Sid had cautioned him more than once after bailing him out of jail. *They are taking advantage of your good nature, your fervor for the cause, your celebrity and your good looks,* Sid had shaken his head time and again at Charlie's naiveté. *They're going to screw you, Charlie. Mark my words, it's going to happen sometime.*

And now it has, Charlie realized as he sat alone in his rusty cell for long hours, *they're holding me for some reason, for the right time.*

He couldn't understand what had happened at the Pier. Everything had been fine. He had been giving his "Revolution" speech as he had come to think of it. The speakers were working great. That huge crowd of people on the beach could all hear and they were really listening and liking what he was saying. But then all hell broke loose. *Where had the explosions come from? Who had attacked them from behind on the stage? How did M.D. and Wrig Jones fit into it?* Charlie asked himself these questions for hours but he never could make any sense of it. *Why would M.D. attack her own people? Or was it the government that was finally cracking down? Had M.D. just snatched him to protect him? To insure no harm came to the most visible member of the OceanSave movement, of the Earth Day Coalition?* Charlie tried to convince himself that in fact this more optimistic view of the proceedings was the case but somewhere deep inside his mind his brother Sid's cynicism kept prodding at him. Sid was his guardian angel, his big brother, all the things that Charlie knew Sid would just scoff at, probably through a hangover. *They're using you Charlie,* Sid had warned.

But if they're using me, why did they snatch me off that stage? Charlie asked himself over and over. *If they want to make me a martyr for the cause, why didn't they just let me die back there at the pier when everything started blowing up. Damn! They're all questions that can't be answered,* Charlie realized. *I don't have a clue what's going on and I'm in prison.* He buried his head in his hands and just gave up on all of it. *Screw it,* he thought, *they've got me.* But as he bent over with his head between his knees staring at the floor he spotted the tiny chip that Jerry had attached to his shoe lace and he realized that maybe he wasn't really alone.

But if Charlie was alone, in prison, and not reading the newspapers or seeing his own image on TV, Jerry and Sid and Alison at the beach house in Malibu certainly were. They had the first day's *L.A. Times* and the TV coverage was non-stop. Jerry hadn't left his computer screen since he'd arrived at the beach house. All of them were glued to the TV as the first videos of the attack on the pier came in. All three listened as all the talking heads tried to analyze the event and came up with nothing but the babel of confusion. Jerry and Sidney and Alison read the paper and watched all the TV reports, but not for long.

Jerry's computer screen demanded their attention. Jerry had tracked Charlie's computer chip to somewhere in the middle of the Santa Barbara Channel, but then the steady pulsing of the blip had become intermittent. At times it would be strong, then it would fade completely, then it would gradually come back only to go away again. What Jerry did know though was that the blip was standing still, emanating from one position, meaning that Charlie had come to ground (or water) somewhere at sea.

"Where the hell is he out there?" Alison's voice shook with her fear for Charlie.

"I don't know," Jerry's eyes were locked on the blue expanse of the computer screen with its tiny yellow blip fading in and out spasmodically. "It could be an island or a boat. All I know is that he is out there and he's standing still."

Now Alison was right over Jerry's shoulder as they both pored over the computer screen. "Why is the signal so weak?" she asked.

"Maybe they're holding him underground, in a cave or a room with stone walls. Or maybe there's something around him, a microwave transmitter or some wireless setup that blocks his signal temporarily. I just don't know."

"But what's out there?" Alison's desperation rasped in her voice. "He's in the middle of the ocean for god's sake!"

"Here's what's out there," Sid waved a page of *The L.A. Times* at them. "There's ten, twelve, maybe twenty of them out there, big ones, little ones, working ones, abandoned ones, the Santa Barbara Channel is mined with them." Sid was holding up a picture of a Persian Gulf oil platform. The headline over the picture read: "SAILORS GUARD OIL IN GULF." It was a story about how the U.S. Navy was protecting the oil platforms and terminals in the Persian Gulf from terrorists who had repeatedly tried to blow them up via kamikaze raids in small, fast explosive-laden boats. "As soon as I saw this picture it made me think of them," Sid pushed it at Jerry. "They could have him out there on one of those oil rigs in the Channel. Hell, you can see some of them from the shore in Oxnard and Ventura."

Jerry stared at Sid, then grabbed the paper and stared at it, then just stared through the window out to sea for a long moment. "You could be right Sid. There's a bunch of 'em out there. One way to find out." Instantly, he was on his cell phone: "Yeah, Marty, Jerry Creogan, yeah, I need a favor big time like right now. Are you gassed up?"

Jerry listened to the man on the other end for a short moment.

"Good. Pick me up on the beach about a half mile north of the little Malibu fishing pier. I'll be out there flagging you."

Jerry listened, then laughed.

"No, no gunfire this time. I've just gotta take some pictures. Okay. Soon as you can," and he turned back to them to explain.

"Bounty hunter buddy of mine. He's got his own helo. You guys sit tight. There's only room for me. We're gonna do a little recon flyover."

Chapter Three

Dragonfly

Like a dragonfly, its rotors tracing a gauzy buzzing circle in the air, the chopper floated over the water, swooped left then left again, circling, riding the zephyrs above even as the waves below crested and broke and then crested again across the ocean's illimitable expanse. The wave-ribbed surface of the channel stretched out blue-green beneath them to the horizon as the helicopter searched and doubled back then searched some more. Jerry Creogan had a pair of high-powered binoculars imbedded in his eye sockets scanning the surface of the sea for he knew not what exactly.

"Stay up high for now," Jerry instructed his chopper pilot/bounty hunter *compadre* Marty Hughes who for some inexplicable reason went by the professional name of Frank Buck. Jerry had asked him once about that.

"Frank Buck. You know, 'Bring 'em back alive,' that Frank Buck."

Utterly in the dark, Jerry replied, "What?"

Exasperated, Marty answered: "You know, Frank Buck, the great white hunter, you know."

"Who?" Jerry didn't have a clue.

"Man, you're ignorant," Marty finally concluded throwing up his hands in frustration. "Go Google it, you moron!"

Marty even had bounty hunter business cards printed up under his Frank Buck alias bearing the logo "I bring 'em back alive."

"Stay high for now," Jerry instructed Marty or Frank or whomever.

Jerry wasn't completely sure what he was looking for, but he knew Charlie was being held out there somewhere and he meant to find him or burn all of Marty Hughes's gas trying. Up over the water it was pretty serene, the first peaceful place Jerry had been all day. The chopper was a new one, not one of the old thumper models, so the sound didn't much disturb their tranquility. The sun was moving toward setting out on the horizon and Jerry knew they'd only have an hour of daylight left at best and they'd need ten minutes of that to fly back to the coastline. The ocean seemed limitless, silent, repeatedly patterned in long wavy lines as it stretched out beneath them. If Jerry hadn't been so determinably intent on finding Charlie out in the vast emptiness, it would have been a spell of Zen-like meditative beauty, of peace, of the confluence of sky and sea, of the gods of the air and the waters of life. But for Jerry it was no such thing. Charlie had been taken on his watch and he had to get him back safe and sound. "This is one we really do have to bring back alive" he impressed on his bounty hunter friend Frank Buck.

The good news was that as they banked out over Oxnard and flew out to sea the signal from Charlie's GPS chip became much stronger, pulsing steadily on Jerry's GPS screen. The only problem was that the whole rest of the screen was functionally empty, just a bluish-greenish background signifying "ocean." What Jerry didn't know was that the signal got stronger because Charlie was out being walked by his captor Wrig Jones on the deck of his temporary prison.

"Ok, slow down and fly a little tighter circle. But stay up high. This thing's really pulsing now. He's gotta be down there somewhere." It was Jerry pretty much talking to himself. Marty was quite content to just fly the helo and follow Jerry's orders. They'd been through hunts together before and completely trusted each other. "Yeah, stay up high. I don't want to set off any alarms for those pricks who've got my man."

"You know you're payin' me good for all these orders I'm takin' from you, don't you?"

"Don't worry," Jerry laughed. "I'll give you gas money."

"Screw that! I want a new automatic rifle and a new high-powered Taser and some new night goggles and at least one night in a Las Vegas hotel with two totally expensive hookers."

"Sure, no problem. Whoa! Watch out for that pig flying by at three o'clock."

That cracked Frank Buck up.

"I'll tell you what I'll do," Jerry became conciliatory. "Besides gas money, I'll buy you a new tattoo," and he pressed the binoculars back into his eye sockets.

Frank Buck just grunted.

"There, over there," Jerry barked almost immediately and pointed out the north east quadrant of the helicopter's windscreen.

Out over the water, well below the horizon, almost invisible against the solid blue-green background was an oil rig, one of the small old ones, a platform for just one pump. But it looked like it was abandoned. There was no movement aboard it, no machinery on the platform, no flags on the cross braces of its tower, and no workers in evidence. But it was the boat tied up to its base that had caught Jerry's eye.

"That's them. We've got 'em. That's the boat," Jerry's voice betrayed his excitement. "Stay up here high. Turn and fly away. I don't want 'em to see us."

Marty banked and climbed at Jerry's prompting.

Jerry had already mounted the fat, long telephoto lens on his camera and started clicking off pictures of the oil rig before the helo even started to turn away. He probably got fifteen shots of it before they flew out of range.

"The coordinates. Give me the coordinates. Where exactly the hell are we?" Jerry barked, half laughing, as he clapped Marty on the back. "We found 'em. Hey, we found 'em."

"Give me a beer," Marty pointed to the cooler behind their seats. "My work here today is done."

"And not a shot fired," Jerry popped the caps off two beers and handed his pilot one.

Chapter Four

The Track of the Storm

When Jerry got back to the beach house from his flyover, it was almost ten. Sid and Alison were up drinking, waiting, watching the TV which had turned into what seemed like a repeating roll, the same images—the explosions in the sand, the panicked stampeding crowd, the ferris wheel slowly toppling, the dead—being shown over and over again, the same speculation spouting over and over from the talking heads.

"I know where they've got him," Jerry said coming through the door. "We found him. Not we've gotta go get him."

"Where? Where is he?" Sid and Alison jumped to their feet as if they had been sitting on tightly wound springs just waiting for Jerry to return with some real news.

Jerry got right to it: "They're holding him on an old abandoned oil platform out in the Santa Barbara Channel off of Oxnard. Here, see for yourself.

He took the digital photo card out of his camera, and with a patch cord attached it to Alison's I'Pad.

"There it is. See. It's pretty much stripped. Their boat is tied up at the base below. It looks like there's maybe five or six rooms in that superstructure that hangs beneath the platform where the pump tower is mounted. I didn't want to spook them so we didn't go in close. I didn't see any signs of life and there are no signs of people in any of my pictures, but they're there. They're holding Charlie there. And I'm gonna go out and get him."

Jerry's rather long speech (certainly for him) had rather matter-of-factly rolled out of him leading inexorably to that final declaration of war which didn't surprise Sid or Alison at all.

"And how do you propose we do that?" Alison broke the silence.

"I don't know. I'm gonna have to take Sid's boat. It'll be just like a bounty hunting job."

"Jerry, Alison said 'we.' I'm going with you," Sid interrupted him.

"I am too," Alison spoke before Sid had even finished. "He's my husband."

"No way," Jerry glared at them. "They snatched him on my watch. I'm gonna go get him and I'm gonna do it alone."

"He's my brother, and I'm going," Sid's voice was hard and set.

"He's my husband," Alison repeated as if she was sort of fixed on that thought.

"This is no job for amateurs," Jetty tried to argue them out of it.

"I can drive Sid's boat. I've done it before when Charlie and I went fishing," Alison countered.

"You know I can handle a gun," Sid chuckled. "You taught me yourself."

"On a range, not for real. C'mon Sid," Jerry's voice was close to desperate. "I don't want to get you and Alison killed. It's too dangerous. Just stay here. I'll go get him and everything will be back to normal." Sid was his boss and didn't seem to really give a shit about things like death anymore. And he could see in Alison's face, her undaunted eyes, the stubborn set of her jaw, just how determined she was to see this whole thing through. *Great. Now I'm gonna have to get three people home safe instead of just one*, Jerry thought. *Terrific!*

"Look. Lets sleep on it. We can't do anything more tonight. I've got to study these pictures more, get a diagram of that platform done. You two go to bed. Get a good night's sleep. Tomorrow's gonna be a long and dangerous day."

Only after they had gone to bed was Jerry able to fully focus upon the problems at hand. And there were real problems. But planning and tactics were Jerry's specialty and he stayed up until three in the morning doing what he did best.

Over coffee and orange juice on the deck the next morning Jerry laid out his plan to Sid and Alison. He had drawn a rough diagram of the abandoned platform using his photos and his memory of what he saw in the flyover. He laid it out between them on the table and pointed out the crucial points on the landscape.

"We're going to come in super quiet from the seaward side not the landward side. I'm going to get some special mufflers for your boat's engine that I'll install this afternoon. You two's job today is to go get the boat, run it up the coast to Channel Islands Harbor, find a place to dock it so I can work on it this afternoon, gas it all the way up to the top and buy an auxiliary gas tank and fill that too. I just don't know how far or how fast we're gonna have to run tonight and I sure as hell don't wanna run out of gas. Plus, coming in silent from the seaward side is gonna mean a big circle out to sea before we turn back."

Sid and Alison listened silently. Jerry, by the tone of his voice and the worried look in his eye, was making it abundantly clear that this was totally his operation, that he was the boss now, not Sid , and that their job was to do exactly what he told them to do.

"After dark we'll head out from Channel Islands Harbor. I want you both in totally black clothes. If I had my way you'd be invisible. We'll wear night goggles. I've got two sets and I can get another one from a friend. They take some getting used to so we'll put them on when we leave the harbor and wear them all the way out to the target. Alison, you're gonna drive the boat and stay at the wheel through this whole operation. You got that."

Alison nodded, submitting to Jerry's harsh brook-no-opposition tone. "How are we going to find that thing out there at night?" she finally asked.

"I've got compass coordinates," Jerry answered. "I plotted them on a chart last night. I'll find it. The secret for you is to concentrate on the driving, to position the boat for us getting out of it and back into it and our escape."

Jerry wanted to make it sound like he was piling heavy responsibility upon her, and he was, but his main concern was for her to stay with the boat out of harm's way, or at least the greater threat of it. He wished he could find some way to keep Sid on the boat too. Some job for him to do but he knew that wasn't going to happen unless he knocked him unconscious and hogtied him before they boarded the oil platform. No, he realized that he was going to have to babysit Sid all through their little commando operation.

"We'll pull up slow and silent to the base of the platform. Their boat is tied up on the landward side at the foot of the only ladder that goes up to the deck of the platform. I don't know how many of them are out there. There's M.D. Farrow and that little weasel who smokes all the time..."

"Wrig Jones," Alison supplied.

"...Yeah him, and probably at least one other guy who was driving the boat when they snatched Charlie in Santa Monica."

"But we've got the element of surprise on our side, right?" Sid offered.

"I sure hope so," Jerry was still deadly grim. "Look, you're right, they don't know we're coming. They don't know that we even know where they are. But that still doesn't mean that they're not gonna to be on the lookout. That's why we're not gonna use that ladder to board the platform."

"So how else?" Sid asked the logical lawyerly question except that he didn't already know the answer. He and Alison were fully settled into their co-conspirator roles and were totally intent on Jerry's every word.

"If they have posted a sentry or someone is patrolling the deck of the platform, they'll be right at the top of that ladder since it is the only way up there, or so they think."

"It's not?" Sid continued his questioning of the witness.

"I'm going straight up the far opposite side of the structure with a grappling rope and suction cups. If we got caught trying to go up that ladder they'd pick us off from above. Our worst nightmare is getting found out before we get onto the deck of the platform. If they catch us in midair, we might as well be ducks in a shooting gallery."

"Do you really think they are that well-armed?" Sid questioned.

"Gotta be. Look at the firepower they brought to bear on the pier. If I can get us up on the deck, then I can handle them."

"What about me?" Sid was actually pretty nonchalant about this inquiry. "I can see you making it up there, but what about me?"

"I'm gonna need you up there with me for backup," Jerry said it like he actually believed it. "For you, the secret is going to be patience and, above all, silence. When I get up to the deck of the platform I'm going to lower a rope ladder for you. Sid, listen to me, you will climb that ladder slowly, carefully and completely silently. In fact, all of us, when we get within two hundred yards of that platform we're going to complete silence."

Sid and Alison both nodded, silently, as if Jerry's grim focus had already put them into silent running mode.

Jerry turned their attention to his diagram. "It looks like there's a number of rooms on the platform. A big box is mounted right on the deck of the platform. See, there," and he tapped the diagram. "We'll board up the side behind it, see, here, use it for cover," and he tapped the drawing again.

"It was probably the control room for the oil rig," Sid was totally focused.

"Yeah," Jerry nodded. "The other two rooms are hung underneath the deck. Here and here. That's where I'm betting they're holding Charlie. Sid, if we get up there, and they get on to us, I'm gonna take 'em on and you're gonna go find Charlie. Your job is just to keep yourself and him from getting shot. You two have gotta stay out of the line of fire or this will all just be a waste. Got it? Keep your head down!"

"Head down, got it, head down."

For the first time in this whole colloquy a shadow of a grin passed over Jerry's face as Sid gulped out those words. "Yeah," Jerry grinned at the two of them, "I expect a firefight. You two still want to do this."

Chastened, they both nonetheless weren't shaken in their resolve.

"When I find Charlie, and get back to you on the deck..." Sid began.

"I may be with you when we go looking for Charlie," Jerry interrupted. "It just depends on what happens when we get up there. Personally, I'm hopin' they're all asleep."

"Wouldn't that be nice," Alison wished.

"When we get Charlie, we go back down the ladder, or if he's hurt we'll lower him first on the grappling rope, and as soon as all three of us hit the boat, you" and he nodded to Alison, "are gonna put the hammer down so hard out to sea that we'll be like a bullet out of a gun getting out of there."

"What if they come after us?"

We'll have the night goggles and will be running without lights. They shouldn't be able to find us. But it they do I'm gonna mount a fifty caliber machine gun in front of Sid's fishing chair and we'll just blow their ass out of the water."

Awkward moment. They all just sat around that sundeck table looking at each other as first the plan and then all the dangers to be encountered in the plan sunk in.

"That's it," Jerry finally said. "That's the best we can do now."

"Yeah, sounds good," Alison's voice sounded like she had just been condemned to be thrown into a volcano. Now that it was all laid out for them it suddenly seemed like an impossible task, like traversing a minefield at night or pushing a huge boulder up the side of a mountain.

"OK, here's what you've got to understand," he said as if lecturing small children. "When we get out there, when we start doing this, it's not going to be the same. It won't be like we just went through it. It never is. These things never go like they're supposed to no matter how well you plan. Believe me, if it can get all screwed up, it will get all screwed up. When we're doing it we're going to have to deal with whatever happens. You must make good decisions. Dammit, you need to not get yourselves shot!" And he smiled a stupid little smile at them and shrugged out his hands: "Hey, you heard it here first."

Chapter Five

In the Tomb

*C*harlie spent long hours, a whole dark night, on the floor of that cell handcuffed to that pipe. He had awakened from his drugged sleep there like that. The last thing he remembered, the only things he remembered, were the explosions on the beach in front of him and Jerry flying forward off the front of the speaker's platform. He vaguely remembered the severed heads of M.D. and Wrig Jones floating detached in what seemed like wispy dreams. How he got there? Who was holding him prisoner like this? What had happened at the rally at the pier? He hadn't a clue. After he woke up, all he could do is sit there and imagine things, bad things, alone in the pitch blackness.

When the door to his little room opened, brilliant white light streamed in piercing his eyeballs. Two black figures came through the door, faceless, nothing but silhouettes against the blinding light behind them. It took long moments for his eyes to come around and start seeing again. He realized that it was M.D. and her toady Jones standing over him, waiting.

"M.D., what's going on? Why have you got me locked in like this?" Charlie's voice modulated between confused and angry. But above all, when he spoke he was utterly open. He had no idea what was going on. Not a clue.

"Charlie, Charlie, calm down. It's OK. We just have to keep you out of sight for a while."

"Out of sight? What the hell, M.D., what happened back there at the pier? I saw explosions in the sand."

"There was an attack on the pier. Hundreds, maybe thousands, were killed. A terrorist attack, like 9/11."

For some reason Wrig Jones chucked softly through his cigarette smoke as if this was all some kind of a joke.

"An attack?" Charlie still wasn't able to process what they were saying.

"Yes," M.D. seemed warming to her subject. "The biggest crowd for a protest rally in the history of the United States, over a million people, and you had them Charlie. They were listening to you. And then the attack began. Mortars firing on the beach. Rockets firing on the pier from helicopters. Explosions on the pier itself. Charlie, it was perfect. It caught the attention of the whole world, the whole world."

"Perfect? Attention of the whole world? What do you mean? Thousands killed?" Charlie's voice was just stunned. He wasn't really talking to M.D. He was just repeating her words, trying to sort them out.

M.D. and Jones listened silently as he mumbled his way through it. Twice they glanced at each other, exchanging *how-much-should-we-tell-him* looks.

Finally Charlie looked up, his face still all questions: "An attack on the pier, on our rally, with rockets and mortars and bombs. Who did that? Why attack our Earth Day Rally?"

"Because it was so big. Because there were so many people in one place interested in one thing, stopping this lust for oil, ending the oil wars." M.D. answered in a quiet level voice, matter-of-fact really, not at all outraged or shocked or sorrowful.

"But who attacked us?" Charlie persisted. His mind was so wrapped around this stunning news that he hadn't even questioned yet why he was still on the floor, still handcuffed to a pipe.

"Who the fuck knows?" This time Wrig Jones answered and his voice was openly impatient with this whole charade. M.D. immediately raised her hand and touched his puny bicep, silencing him.

She leaned over Charlie, took him by the shoulders with both of her hands, looked into his face: "Don't you see, Charlie? That attack on the Pier was our Kent State, our 9/11. Who did it doesn't matter. Terrorists. Patriot Security. The CIA. Whoever did it, it works perfect for us."

As she spoke he could see the fervor, the fanaticism, in her face, hear it in her voice. He realized that he had never seen her like this before. He had thought he knew her. But as he looked into her eyes he realized that she was completely different than she had seemed. He realized that she was crazy.

"Perfect? How can this be perfect? You said that thousands of people died."

She stepped back from him. Took a moment to think. "It works in our favor in so many ways" she finally went on. "You were talking about revolution back there on the pier, Charlie, and you had them. The whole world was listening. And now, with this, they'll never forget your words. It's a real revolution. Blood has been shed. It was our Bastille. It wasn't just another Earth Day for a bunch of tree huggers. Innocent blood is smeared all over Santa Monica beach. Don't you see, Charlie? We've got 'em."

Listening to her, seeing the mad fervor in her face, realizing that they hadn't undone his handcuffs, it suddenly all dawned on Charlie Castle, came clear to him. "Oh my god, you did it, didn't you?"

He could immediately tell by her face, by the look that darted between her and Jones, that he had struck home. Of course she did it, he thought. *Omigod, she attacked her own people. She and I and Alison, we got them all together, then she murdered them.*

He felt like some poor fooled *film noir* detective, like Jake in *Chinatown* or Marlow in *The Big Sleep*. He felt stupid, betrayed, unbelieving that he had never seen it the way it really was, had never seen it coming until the bombs literally started exploding all around him.

As all these thoughts raced through his mind, he just stared up at M.D. Farrow as if reading a book or watching an actress on the screen. But now he knew that it was all too real, that she was no *film noir femme fatale* but rather a monomaniac, an eco-terrorist, who for some reason was holding him prisoner.

"What we've done is sewn confusion," M.D. actually sat down on the floor across from him and lit a cigarette as if they were plotting together around some campfire. "They don't have a clue what's going on out there. They're looking under rocks for terrorists. The media is blaming everyone from Al-Qaeda to the CIA to Exxon and BP for the attack. They're doing all our work for us. They're bringing our story to all the people in the world. We've got their attention and now all we have to do is exploit it, turn it against the crooked politicians in Washington and the oil companies who own them."

"Why? For god's sake, why?" Charlie's voice was begging for some sanity, some reason, but he couldn't avoid that fierce look of relentless fanaticism in M.D.'s face. "We'd just put together the biggest protest march in history, wasn't that enough?"

"Why did we attack the pier? Our own people? To get the attention of the government first and the rest of the world too. We had to do it. Don't you see?"

"Innocent people, M.D., innocents! You turned a quiet beach into a war zone."

"Oh don't be so naïve Charlie. In every uprising, every revolution, there is always collateral damage. Americans sell weapons to terrorists who turn around and shoot us with them. Look at the Mexican drug wars, all fueled with American guns. It's just like the offshore drilling. We refuse to make laws that protect us from ourselves. That's why, Charlie, that's why. The imperial powers of Big Oil have never been more in control than now and we need to throw them over any way we can."

There was a brilliant sort of twisted logic about it all Charlie had to admit. He wanted to kick himself for not having seen it coming, for actually having helped put it all together. He felt like he was the rallying voice that had led all of those poor lambs to the slaughter.

"Dammit Charlie, you of all people should understand this," she actually seemed trying to coax him over to her side, to argue away his horror. "It's all about symbolism, Charlie. You know that. It's all designed to send a message. Symbolic acts like the attack on the Earth Day Rally make people mad, make people stupid, make governments go to war over stupid things or over things that don't exist at all. This time, in the twenty-first century, it's just all about oil, Charlie. We needed to catch the attention of the powers that run Big Oil. Sew confusion in their minds. Expose them."

She was trying to win him over to the rightness of her terrorist cause. "Think about it, Charlie, thing about it awhile. We'll be back. We'll talk some more."

And she and her smoking henchman were gone, and the silent blackness closed back in on Charlie Castle.

They've got me locked up here because they don't trust me. They don't know where I stand on their choice for bloody revolution rather than bloodless. They don't know if I'll go along, how I will react to their wonderful staged massacre. Charlie's mind raced. He remembered the chip on his shoe and hoped that Jerry and Sid were on their way to get him out of this mess, to set him free of this nightmare. *I've got to get out of here alive to tell the world what happened and who did it* was the one thought that kept echoing in his consciousness.

It must have been four or five hours before they came back, those same two sinister black silhouettes pouring brutal light into his black hole. That whole time, sitting there in the dark, Charlie worked to figure it out, but he still came up empty.

Why am I here and just what do they have in mind for me? he kept asking himself.

He couldn't figure it out, visualize what they might do with him, but he knew he had to stall them, keep them talking, give Jerry time to get to him. The one thing he was pretty sure about though was that they had a use for him, were still intent on using him just as they had been using him all along. Sid had warned him about them. He should have listened. But this time when they came back, he was ready for them. He didn't wait for them to speak. He just lashed out at them as soon as they came through the door.

"What the hell is going on M.D.? Why am I down here? Are you just gonna leave me here cuffed to this pipe?"

"Just for now, Charlie, for now," she tried to placate him. "I knew you'd be upset about the incident at the pier. I just wanted to give you some time alone to see the 21st-century logic of it."

"Logic? Incident?" he was dumbfounded. "There's no logic to murdering a thousand people!"

"Oh but there is, Charlie, there is," and her voice had taken on a kind of faraway dreamer's softness, "and it's going to bring down an incredibly corrupt government and it's going to change our whole way of life in America." She came to him like some priestess of a new religion, sat down crosslegged on the floor before him, a slight feminine buddha, cupped hands outstretched to him. "Don't you see, Charlie? It was the only way to really get their attention. There has to be blood, death, apocalypse, before you can ever build a new world. Now OceanSave is in the middle of a real revolution. And you can be an important part of it, Charlie." She was coaxing him now, playing him, trying to seduce him, pull him back in.

"Me?" he exploded. "What do I have to do with it? Why am I in a cellar handcuffed to a pipe?"

"Charlie. Charlie. You are one of OceanSave's most valuable assets," she spoke to him like a protective mother trying to calm an upset recalcitrant child. "We had to take care of you, protect you, make sure you came out of that mess at the pier in one piece."

"Mess? A mess? That's what you call it. It was a massacre."

"The whole world says it was the government that attacked the Earth Day demonstration. That it was the big oil people in Washington that called in that strike as far away from their little circle of beltway hell as they could get it. The global press is invoking CIA, Black Ops, Blackwater, hell they'll probably have the grandchildren of the Kennedy assassins and the children of the Watergate burglars in the mix pretty soon. It's beautiful."

Charlie looked right at her in silence. He couldn't believe what he was hearing, the twisted unreal logic of her ecstatic words.

"Don't you see, Charlie. We've opened the Pandora's box of conspiracy theory and all the demons have come rushing out right on cue." She was in a kind of holy trance as she spoke as if she was channeling some ancient voice of revolution.

A strange silence settled over the windowless room when she stopped speaking. Wrig Jones smoked sullenly by the door. The two revolutionaries sat facing each other on the floor.

"Cry havoc and let loose the dogs of war," M.D. finally whispered in her best imitation of some ancient Amazon warrior priestess. "And you can be a part of it."

"Me? How? Why?"

"Do you remember Patty Hearst, Charlie?" M.D. was no longer the visionary mystic of before. Now she had come back to the hard pragmatic planner/manipulator/plotter that Charlie knew so well. Once again she was the dark lady of the laptop, the wireless avenger.

"Vaguely. A bit before my time. Way before my time." She was serious, he realized. Serious and totally insane, fanatically insane, bomb vest, going postal, Oklahoma City and Phoenix parking lot insane, yet so calm, so cold.

"You ought to pay more attention to history, Charlie."

"What do you mean? What do I have to do with Patty Hearst."

"Don't you see? You could be our Patty Hearst. You're every bit as much of a public figure as she was, even more so. You've always been our spokesperson, the voice of the OceanSave movement. On the pier you were the voice of the new revolution. When you rise from the grave the whole world will listen to you. Don't you see, you'll be like a 21st-century Christ risen from the dead to spread the word. They'll eat it up."

"Why couldn't you just stick with the process, M.D.?" he took one last stab at reasoning with her. "Things were starting to go our way. Why couldn't you stick with peaceful protest. My god, it was the biggest demonstration ever in America."

"What are you, some kind of Pollyanna?" she hissed at him. "Damn the process! They were getting ready to vote to open up the whole country to drilling—offshore, the Pacific Northwest, even Yellowstone and Yosemite and Zion and Bryce and the Arches. Every single national park will have oil wells pumping right in the middle of all the beautiful natural things that people drive all across the country to see. Imagine an oil well right next to Old Faithful. Imagine riding the rapids on the Colorado down through the Grand Canyon with oil rigs pumping away on both banks. Hey, they're already out here in the Santa Barbara channel. How about filling up Santa Monica bay with them too? How about putting oil wells right in the middle of your favorite surfing spots? How about pipelines criss-crossing the country like superhighways?" She just stopped as if she'd run out of gas.

Charlie had known for long minutes as she unfurled her fanatical screed that he had to humor her, play along, or she wouldn't hesitate to kill him.

"But M.D., all those people died on that beach, on the pier. That wasn't in our plan. How could it have ever gone that far?"

Now her voice was as patient as a kindergarten teacher: "In real revolutions people die."

"But we killed a whole lot of innocent people."

"I know. But it has to be that way. The only chance for real revolution is breaking the control that the government exerts, shaking things up, doing the unexpected, screwing them the way they have been screwing us all along in this devil's partnership with big oil."

"But how do you know they will blame the government."

"They already have. It's just like Prague Spring was so long ago and like Arab Summer was in 2011. When innocent protestors get shot at like in Egypt and Libya and Syria, suddenly the whole world is on the peoples' side. The cameras catch it all and the blame goes straight to the government that the fired-upon crowds were protesting."

"How do you know they'll blame the government?"

"Because you are going to tell them to."

"Tomorrow, or the next day, you are going to resurface and the media is going to descend on you like you're Elvis or Marilyn Monroe come back to life. The timing will be everything. We just have to wait until the main story of the attack on the pier starts to lose its legs, until all the speculation starts to die down, then we bring you in and it all heats up again. Yours is a voice they listen to Charlie. You can drop the blame on them like an anchor that can take this government and all the oil money that owns it straight to the bottom."

Charlie Castle, the voice of OceanSave, the inciter of the eco-revolution, was speechless. He almost believed her. She was so calm yet fervid as she laid it all out for him. She was totally insane. He was certain of that. But everything she said seemed so reasonable, so do-able, so possible. *She really does want to change the world*, Charlie thought, and for a short moment he was attracted to the idea, to the daring and the potential for change of it. But then he remembered all of those dead bodies back there on the beach, those holy innocents, and he knew he could never go along with this, throw in with these murderers. *I've just got to stay alive, stall them, until Jerry gets here*, Charlie knew. *Then I can expose the whole hoax. Place the blame for all those deaths where it belongs. It'll set the poor ecology movement back years.* But he knew that was what had to be done. It was M.D. and her violent bloody revolution that had betrayed the movement.

Abruptly M.D. arose out of her yoga-like position opposite him on the floor and moved toward the door that Wrig Jones was simultaneously moving to open for her. "Think about all this, Charlie. You can speak for all of us, millions of us. We've created a wonderful opportunity. Seize it. Lead a revolution."

Chapter Six

To the Lodestone Rock

*J*erry wasted no time marshaling his troops the next morning. He had them up and ready to go by seven. The beach house kitchen over coffee was their briefing room. Jerry's maps and diagrams were spread out on the island. His orders were short and not be questioned.

"Go to the marina, get the boat and run it up to Channel Islands Harbor. Find a temporary dock for it where I can work undisturbed and gas it all the way up to the top. Buy the biggest auxiliary tank you can find and fill that with gas too. I should be up there by about one or two. Then I've got to work on the boat." He didn't ask for any questions.

Sid Castle owned a forty foot Larson powerboat that could sleep six comfortably. It was more than a fishing boat though not quite a luxury yacht. But it was a good ocean boat and it was pretty fast, not cigarette boat fast, but fast enough. It was a gorgeous morning on the water. Sid and Alison would have had a really nice boat ride up the coast if they didn't have Charlie's captivity and their impending commando operation hanging over them. The sky was baby blue and cloudless. The sun was warm and bright and the air clean like the first day after a big storm has passed through. The sunlight glinted on the waves.

They coasted out of Marina Del Rey at 9:30, sped up and headed straight north. Almost the first landmark they passed was the bombed-out Santa Monica Pier. The ferris wheel was still lying on its side atop all of the debris of the shattered buildings it had crushed. Construction vehicles, large front-end loaders and shovels and dump trucks, were the only signs of life on the pier now, all working to clear away the devastation, probably still searching for bodies. Running past the pier, seeing its skeletal remains, only deepened the darkness of their anxiety.

How ironic, Sid thought. Alison sat silently on the bow sofas as he drove from the cockpit. He knew she was thinking only of Charlie, of finding him, of rescuing him. More than once Sid had secretly fantasized of being alone on the boat with Alison, just the two of them sailing off, her sunbathing naked on the front couches, him driving the boat toward some secluded anchorage, some special harbor, then the two of them making love in the big triangular bed in the bow below decks. It was a dream idyll that Sidney knew could never be. *How damn ironic*, he thought. *We're alone in the boat and the whole world is coming down around us.* They hardly talked at all as they cruised the whole length of Malibu and the cliffs of Point Dume. Two dolphins escorted them for about fifteen minutes as they passed the naval base. They were in the Channel Islands Harbor by noon. They gassed up the boat on the way into the harbor and then went looking for an empty berth. They found a vacant one off the far end of a float pier and tied up to wait. No one approached them to charge them for their mooring or complain about them trespassing on someone else's space so they just did their shopping in the marina store, filled the auxiliary tank with gas, then got out of sight below decks and waited. Jerry rang Sid's cell at just about 1:30.

Jerry's morning had not been nearly as leisurely. After he left the beach house, he made a number of stops. The first was to his private armorer in San Pedro for weapons and ammo. He rented two .50 caliber machine guns and two different sets of mounts, and bought automatic pistols for both Sid and Alison. His next stop was to the custom boat dealer in Marina Del Rey for specialized parts. His third stop was his communications guy in Venice Beach next to the tattoo parlor where he picked up four powerful hand-held walkie-talkies. Jerry made two more stops before he finally hit the coast highway going north to meet Sid and Alison.

When Jerry got to Channel Islands Harbor, Sid described to him where they were moored and he drove around until he sighted them. He found a parking place as close as he could to their float dock, picked the lock on the gate in the chain link fence and propped the door ajar with a rock from a nearby flower bed. Then the three of them unloaded his tools and equipment from the car to the boat. It was just a lazy afternoon in the marina and nobody bothered them, no one saw them as anything out of the ordinary. Jerry worked on the boat's engine the better part of the afternoon while Alison and Sid loitered around him, occasionally handing him a tool when he called for it, but mostly just trying to kill time. By five, they were all starved and headed to a fish house on the promenade for dinner. They left the harbor right at sunset. It had been a long and tense afternoon of waiting for Sid and Alison and they were both really keyed up. Jerry saw how nervous they were and had the perfect cure for all their tension.

About a mile out, he told Alison, who he had ordered to drive from the very beginning of the operation, to cut the engine and let then float. Then he broke out their automatic pistols. He made them both fire a full clip out over the water just so they could get the feel of the weapon in their hand. He didn't really expect them to hit anything with them when they got to their target, but the autos put out a lot of covering fire and, who knows, they might come in handy.

Jerry had envisioned this as a totally stealth operation which explained the afternoon's installation of the special engine mufflers and the black turtle-necks and knit hats that he had made them all wear. Even Mother Nature seemed to be cooperating with his plan as she delivered up an exceptionally dark moonless night on the water.

"We got lucky with the moon tonight," Jerry said looking up at the black sky as Alison restarted the engine. "How often do we have cloudy nights in southern California?"

The interlude of shooting and the movement of the boat over the glassy surface of the sea had calmed them all down. Jerry could sense their readiness. He briefed them again on every move they were to make when they reached the oil platform. He quietly took his readings off of his compass and told Alison which directions to steer. He was also monitoring the pulsing of Charlie's shoe chip on his laptop screen. They were getting close.

They had put on the night goggles right after their little weapons practice interlude and were quite used to the hazy greenish world of filtered darkness by the time they saw the first skeletal outline of the oil platform in the distance. Jerry instructed Alison to circle wide to the right out to sea and then to throttle down and bring them in very slowly on the seaward side of the platform.

"Don't go in yet," Jerry waved Alison off in a whisper. "There's at least two men moving up on that deck," he explained. "I want to see what they're doing." They stood well off to the west for almost fifteen minutes while Jerry first studied the deck of the platform then went below to talk to someone on the walkie-talkies that he had distributed to them when he'd handed out the guns. He was talking in a low voice to someone but they couldn't make out what he was saying.

When Jerry came back up from the cabin, both Sid and Alison knew just by looking at him—the set of his jaw, the steady movement of his hands as he checked his weapons, the two handguns in his belt, the sawed-off shotgun slung across his back—that it was time.

"OK," Jerry took a deep breath and glanced at his watch, "in another four minutes we're going in. Their guard is down. They're just sitting around the top of the ladder over there on the front side of the rig. If we're lucky, we'll be up on the deck before they even know we're here. We've got that building between us and them. Alison, go in slow, pull us up to that south-most leg of it."

Alison carefully slipped the powerboat out of idle and eased it almost silently in on the oil platform. Sid stabilized it as well as he could with one mooring line around the steel leg of the platform. Jerry had his grapple hook rope wrapped around his right shoulder and his plastic rope ladder hanging on a hook at his hip. He couldn't throw the grapple from the boat because the platform was just too high and the boat too unsteady. So he began to climb the steel pylon using suction cups to create handholds, pulling himself up to cross beams where he could stand on one foot, then pulling himself up again.

In the boat Sid and Alison marveled at Jerry's strength and skill. He was a big man and yet he was doing this incredible Spiderman imitation up the side of that drilling platform.

When Jerry reached about twenty feet from the floor of the platform deck, he stopped and slipped his climbing rope with its grapple hook on the end off of his shoulder and swung it out over the water twice before looping it up onto the deck. The grapple hook was padded with Styrofoam so it made no sound when it landed on the metal floor of the deck and was dragged back across. It took Jerry two tries before he got the grapple hook to catch. He pulled it tight, tested it, and went up it like some high school athlete in gym class. It seemed as if he was up on the deck in a blink of an eye and almost instantly the rope ladder for Sid came snaking down out of the darkness to hang right next to the boat.

"Wish me luck," Sid squeezed Alison's hand and climbed gingerly onto the bottom rung of the rope ladder. He didn't ascend to the platform nearly as quickly as Jerry had, but he struggled up the swaying ladder and made it to the top with more exertion than he had probably put on his arms and shoulders in years. He was already breathing hard when he joined Jerry on the platform deck. It was dark, but he knew exactly where Jerry would be waiting from the diagrams. And there he was, crouched against the low building in the deep shadows of its roofline with his gun drawn.

"Damn, I thought that would be the easy part," Sid whispered when he crouched behind Jerry.

Jerry glared at him, put a finger to his lips demanding silence, and pointed to his gun and then Sid's.

Sid figured out that Jerry wanted him to draw his gun too. *Looks like it's all hand signals from here on in*, Sid thought, and did what he was told.

Together they moved along the wall to the front corner of the small building. Back at the beach house, Jerry had speculated that it must have been some sort of control room for the machinery on the platform deck when the oil rig was in operation. From the corner Jerry could see ninety percent of the deck of the platform. There were two what looked like portable gas or oil lanterns sitting on the floor of the deck on the far side where the two sentries were stationed at the top of the ladder. The two men had automatic rifles slung over their backs. They crouched next to the lanterns, smoking and talking. Outside the halo of light from the lanterns, the rest of the deck subsided into deeper and deeper darkness. Jerry and Sid were lucky that there were no lights mounted on the front of the control room building. The front of that building was all deep in shadow. There was no way the sentries all the way across the platform could see them in the darkness.

Jerry motioned for Sid to follow and moved around the corner of the building, keeping to the wall where the shadows were deepest. The front of this building seemed to be one large window as far as Sid could tell by touching its frame as they crept across to the only door. The big window was dark, the door was closed, no signs of life at all.

They've gotta be down below, Jerry realized. *That's where they're keeping Charlie.*

But even as he was figuring that out, he heard heavy footsteps, combat boots coming up a stairwell somewhere near. It was too dark to see anything nearby, but he could hear the footsteps ascending and he coiled for action.

The man came out from behind the other corner of the building, big, blocky, striding purposefully toward the two sentries on the far side.

The stairs down must be right around that corner. Where did all these guys come from? There was no sign of them yesterday. Jerry's mind was racing. *No plan ever goes right,* he knew. *We've got to get down those stairs and find Charlie,* he decided. *But what about these three,* he knew he'd have to deal with them sooner or later. *Better now,* he decided. And he stood straight up and shot the man walking away from them right in the back between the shoulder blades.

The shot and their comrade falling face forward brought the other two to their feet, grabbing for their rifles, looking around for the source. Jerry had subsided back into the deep shadow of the building. The two gunmen were still too far away to shoot at so he waited to see what they would do. They must have been military at one time, trained in firefights, because the first thing they did was split up, flanking the dead body of their fallen comrade, moving out of the lantern light into the darkness on the edges of the platform.

Jerry didn't like it.

Chapter Seven

Dragon's Breath

Sid watched as Jerry extracted his walkie-talkie from his vest. His eyes darted out across the deck looking for the two sentries but they were nowhere to be seen. He knew they were out there in the darkness around the edges of the oil platform. He knew they were converging on them from two sides. Both his hands tightened on the automatic pistol, raised it to ready position.

"Marty. Come on in. Light it up. I've got two bogies flanking me. I'm up against the building. Light them up and take them out."

What the... Sid thought, then he realized what Jerry was doing. He was calling in an airstrike. *I should have known he wouldn't bring us out here without back-up*, Sid's mind raced.

They waited crouched in the shadows, a long minute, two. Jerry was up on one knee, his auto raised to eye-level, darting it back and forth, looking for his targets, waiting for them to attack out of the darkness on both sides. Then Sid heard the low throbbing hum descending down on them out of the black sky. And suddenly the whole night, the whole deck of the oil platform was lit up by a searing white light and the hovering chopper opened fire raking the deck like an angry dragon breathing bullets.

"Alright Zammo!" Jerry exalted. "Take them out. Pin them down," he barked into his walkie-talkie. "Keep them off me. I've got to get below and find my man."

Jerry turned to Sid. No more hand signals now. The whole world of the oil platform had exploded into a free-fire zone. "Let's go Sid, They sure know we're here now. Get behind me. Down that gangway. Be sure you safety's off. Be ready to fire. We've got to find Charlie now. Stay behind me. There may be more down below."

Then Jerry was up and running in a crouch toward that dark stairwell down. Sid followed instinctively now, not even thinking, thrust headlong into the frenzy of the moment, bullets raining down all across the deck behind them out of that burning white dragon's eye.

Jerry literally dove into that gangway it seemed to Sid who followed him at a run but more carefully, tentatively. *Now is no time to hesitate*, Sid's first cognate thought in a long minute prodded him and he took one hand off of the butt of his automatic pistol, grabbed the railing and followed Jerry down the metal steps going so fast that it was all he could do to keep himself from tumbling headlong.

They found themselves on a narrow catwalk open to the understructure of the platform above. To the left it was all eyebeams and metal cross-braces and other catwalks branching off. To the right were two corridors leading to doorways into rooms that were probably once the sleeping quarters and storage rooms of the working oil platform. Jerry was already into the first corridor, his sidearm raised in front of his face, a flashlight blazing forward held atop the barrel, locked and loaded. Sid followed blindly.

The light beam settled on the knob of the first doorway then raised up to firing level. Jerry tried the knob and the door opened without resistance as he stepped to the side out of the line of fire. He flashed the light into the room, then moved catlike to the side through the doorway and swept the other half of the room behind the door. Sid waited carefully as Jerry moved the light across the walls of the small square room, nothing but empty bunks, no signs of anyone there or having been there. In a short second Jerry was back in the corridor motioning for Sid to follow, trying the second door. The same. Empty. More abandoned sleeping quarters.

The door to the third room at the very edge of the short hallway was ajar and light seeped out through the crack. Low lamplight. This one was live.

Then Jerry did a crazy thing (at least to Sid's way of thinking).

"Screw this!" Jerry growled and went through that door like a human battering ram, shoulder down, gun up.

But this room was empty too. People had been here, and very recently. There was a bed with two blankets and a desk and two chairs and a butt-filled ashtray with a cigarette still burning in it as if its smoker had abandoned it in a hurry.

"They've been here," Jerry muttered. "This is taking too damn long" and he ran out of the room and down the corridor, dove right and ran into the second corridor along the catwalk. Sid followed as fast as he could but when he got to the second hallway Jerry was already going through the first door which seemed to be wide open.

When Sid got to the open doorway and looked in, Jerry was standing in the middle of a completely empty room staring at the wall. A pair of handcuffs on the floor attached to a pipe seemed to have mesmerized him for a short moment. Sid's coming through the door snapped him out of it.

"They're gone, Sid," Jerry's voice was grim.

Chapter Eight

The Avenue of Escape

"We spooked them too soon," Jerry said. He stood there for a long moment just looking at the handcuffs on the pipe, trying to parse it out. Then he was moving again.

"C'mon, they can't be too far," Jerry shouted over his shoulder as he shot past Sid and out of the room. When Sid caught up with him, he was standing on the catwalk at the end of the corridor shining his flashlight beam out into the darkness of the undercarriage of the oil rig.

The gunfire from the chopper still rattled overhead on the deck. It came in spurts and the light from the chopper kept moving around and switching on and off. That meant that Jerry's buddies were still in a firefight taking evasive action to keep from getting shot down even as they continued to lay down their covering fire.

"No way they went up there," Jerry was really only talking to himself, not to Sid. "They've gotta be down here somewhere."

"Where?" Sid swiveled his head looking for them or at least for some avenue of escape they might have taken. Jerry kept shining his flashlight in wide arcs across the underside of the oil rig platform. The whole structure was probably about seventy yards across and the flashlight started losing illumination about forty yards out. All the rest was just dim shadow.

"There," Jerry pointed, "there! There's a light."

Sid squinted hard in the direction Jerry was pointing. Just down from them was the opening to a long narrow catwalk hung beneath the deck that ran from these rooms all the way across the underside of the platform. Sid couldn't see the end of this catwalk in the darkness but Jerry seemed to think it was the escape route Charlie's captors had taken.

"Damn!" Jerry cursed himself, "I shoulda thought of this." He knew there was no way he could have seen this maze of cat walks on his flyover, no way he could have predicted this escape route beforehand, but there it was and they had used it to get away. "Damn!" he spat again in frustration and launched himself through the opening and on to the catwalk. He took off running in a low, bent-over shambling sort of way to keep from knocking himself out against the underside of the oil rig deck. Without even thinking Sid followed. *Maybe there's still a chance,* he hoped without much conviction.

When they had worked their way about halfway across this catwalk Jerry stopped and focused his flashlight again. The beam swooped and traveled and finally settled. Suddenly the whole situation came dimly clear.

The catwalk where Jerry and he stood ran all the way to the edge of the platform where it ended at a steel ladder down to the water. Two figures struggling with a third who seemed to be dead weight were most of the way down that ladder toward a sleek powerboat moored at the bottom.

"C'mon Sid. Our only chance is if their boat won't start. They've got Charlie. C'mon."

Even as they ran bent over across the catwalk to the top of the ladder, they could see those two dim figures below without ceremony drop Charlie's inert body the last six feet down into the boat and clamor down after it themselves.

Jerry was already hurling himself desperately hand over hand down the narrow rungs of the ladder. Sid followed more slowly, afraid to look down. Jerry was almost halfway down when the powerboat's engine caught and rumbled into life. All he and Sid could do, looking straight down at it, was watch helplessly as it pulled away. They couldn't fire at it, try to disable it, because Charlie was there right in the middle of it and they might hit him or blow him up. In mere seconds the boat and Charlie disappeared into the blackness of the night ocean. As if mocking them, the moon came out from behind a cloud and sent a laser beam of light across the surface of the sea. But the boat was gone and with it their hopes for rescuing Charlie.

"Marty. Zammo. Disengage. Cease fire," Jerry screamed into the walkie-talkie." They got away in a boat. See if you can find them heading toward shore with the light. If you find them, put the light on them and track them. We'll be right behind you in our boat."

"Roger, but I'm getting low on gas. I don't know how long I can last before I have to head in."

"OK. See if you can find them on your way in. We'll try to catch up with them."

"Man, it's a big dark ocean out there. I don't know."

"Yeah, I read ya. Give it your best shot."

It took Jerry and Sid long minutes to recross the catwalk at the far side and then find the rope ladder down to the boat.

"Towards shore Alison, that way," Jerry ordered almost before his feet hit the deck of Sid's boat. "Open her up. Maybe we can intercept them."

Sid half descended, half fell off the rope ladder and collapsed exhausted onto the cushions. All that climbing and running and trying to keep up with Jerry had sapped all his strength and drained every ounce of his adrenaline.

Alison tried, first trying to catch up with the swooping light from the helicopter out over the water, then when that light suddenly went off zigzagging across the waves hoping to spot the other boat. But it was hopeless in the dark.

They were gone and Charlie with them.

Chapter Nine

The Trail Goes Cold

"Alison, take it back to Channel Islands Harbor. I've got to get on land and get a signal, see if Charlie's chip is still in operation. Marty's headed in, running low on gas."

As they enter the harbor mouth, Jerry shouts a jubilant "YES" and starts clicking animatedly on his thumbpad. Long seconds passed and then, "I've got him!"

Jerry watched as the faint blip pulsed weakly over the map grid on the computer screen. Sid moved to look over Jerry's shoulder at the screen.

"The chip's still working but its dying out," Jerry reported to the others. "It's solar fueled and it probably hasn't been in sunlight since they snatched him on the pier."

As Alison docked the boat, Jerry and Sid watched as the blip moved inland from the water.

"They landed right in the middle of Malibu, see, there," Jerry pointed to the screen that left a faint track where the blip had been, "probably just beached their boat and got off, abandoned it. Now they're in a car heading up into the Malibu hills. They're on Kanan Road."

They're heading right up where Beth lived (and died), the two very disparate thoughts (one engaged, one suddenly sad) ignited in Sid's mind. *A good place to hide out,* he thought. *I know that area.*

But as all three of them watched the computer screen, suddenly the fading blip went out.

"They've probably gone into that tunnel about halfway up Kanan," Jerry speculated.

"We're going to lose him soon, aren't we?" Alison's trembling voice expressed all of their growing hopelessness.

"We may have already," Jerry's voice was grim, angry with failure, "the tracker's not coming out of that tunnel. I think we've lost the signal."

"No," Alison cried, "no." She knew that the tracking chip might be their one last hope for saving Charlie. She threw herself away from the computer screen and buried her tear-stained face in Sid's shoulder. "Oh Sid, Sid, they're gonna kill him, aren't they? We've lost him."

Sid held her close, guilty in the joy he felt as he clasped her warm body close to his, felt her wet tears and her warm breath against his neck. But he could only savor that beatific moment for a short second. He knew it wasn't at all about him. She had only turned to him out of her love and concern for Charlie.

"No Alison, not at all, we haven't lost him, not yet. They've kept him alive all this time. They took him with them when they ran from the oil rig. No, they've got plans for Charlie. They've kept him alive for a reason. They're gonna bring him back, resurrect him like some prophet of the movement come back from the dead. Un-uhh, they're not done with Charlie yet." As he talked, Sid's head had been down, thinking it out, but now his head came up and he looked first at Alison and then at Jerry. "And that means we're not done yet either."

PART FOUR

Brothers

Chapter One

A Call to Arms

The second day and the third day out from the attack on the Pier, the so-called Earth Day Massacre, a funny thing started to happen in America. Crowds carrying "Green Power" signs started forming up outside courthouses and Federal Buildings and police stations and city halls in big cities and small towns all across the country. They were protestors, but they were also sympathizers. They were mourning the dead in California, but they were also sending the message that the movement to save the environment couldn't be silenced by gunfire. It was hard to call it a movement. It didn't really have any leaders or agendas. It was started by some computer hackers who, appropriately, signed themselves *Anonymous*. It spread across the country via Twitter and Facebook and U-Tube. Probably the biggest crowd of all formed outside the Capital in Washington. They carried signs that pleaded things like **EARTH DAY LIVES** and **REMEMBER THE ECO-INNOCENTS** and they shouted things like **LISTEN TO THE DEAD, STOP BIG OIL** and **HOW MANY DEATHS DOES IT TAKE FOR CONGRESS TO LISTEN?** In L.A. shock turned to fear turned to anger turned to protest. The whole city was screaming for some kind of resolution. As the days unfolded, and no answers materialized, more and more of the people all across America were blaming the government. And the media did exactly what they do best. They fueled the fire. They gave the most strident voices a soapbox. They stuck microphones in the faces of the men in the street and let them say whatever they wanted. On TV tears flowed and charges flew like arrows raining down on the powers that be, all screaming for answers. The talking heads on the radio and television blamed Middle East terrorists, Right Wing American terrorists, government terrorists, everybody from the Neo-Nazis to the Drug Cartels to the CIA. Conspiracy theorists came out of the woodwork on TV and radio talk shows. The media circus was just warming to this latest attack on America.

The kidnapping and disappearance of Charlie Castle became one of the main sidebar stories of the whole Big Event circus, but it took on a sameness to all of the other groundless speculations. No one knew anything in the press. No one knew who the attackers were. No one or no group had yet claimed responsibility. None of the usual suspects—Al-Qaeda, ISIS, the Taliban, the militia crazies—had crowed over their triumph. No one knew where Charlie was or why he had been taken. No one seemed to know anything.

Except for Sid, Jerry and Alison.

Then the video surfaced.

It showed up in a manila envelope at all four of the L.A. network TV stations an hour before the evening news on the second day while Sid, Jerry and Alison were mounting their own rescue operation on the abandoned oil rig in the Santa Barbara Channel. They saw it on the news the next morning. Sid immediately copied it to his smart-phone and took it straight to Matt Morris for analysis. It was all Charlie Castle fomenting revolution, exhorting the eco-movement to rise and bring the country and the Congress and all the President's men to their senses. It painted Charlie as a true prophet of doom, a rabble-rouser for the environment, a Paul Revere of the 21st-century spreading the word from village to town to city to the steps of the Capital that the day of apocalypse was coming if something wasn't done.

"It's all cooked," Morris said immediately after plugging the phone into his huge flat-screen and playing the video only twice. "It's all video excerpts from Charlie's speeches all pieced together by a really good editor. See there, it starts with a long shot of Charlie's speech at the pier so the viewer can see where he's supposedly giving the speech but—there, see—each time they cut to a close-up of Charlie or to a tighter shot, they're editing in words and sentences from other speeches. They've got a good sound guy to. He's almost got Charlie's voice modulated perfectly when they cut something in. It's professional work," turning to Sid, "but they're setting your brother up for something. I don't know what because this is all stuff people have heard before, stuff he's said in public, but I don't like it. They distributed it for maximum media dispersal, perfect timing, the major outlets. They want everyone thinking of Charlie."

Chapter Two

Underground Man

For the second time in three days, Charlie Castle woke up from a drugged sleep in a prison room. This time it was in a locked room in a barn somewhere. Handcuffs again, to a four-by-four wooden post in a storage room in what looked like a horse barn. Straw all over the floor. Hay bales stacked against the walls. Bridles and saddles hanging on nails. A mattress on the floor for him with a plastic pitcher of water within his reach. Sunlight filtered through cracks in the walls and as the day went on he heard motors coming and going outside. Motorcycles also came in and out. In what he thought might be mid-afternoon from the angle of the shafts of sunlight coming in, M.D. and her pull-toy Jones unlocked the door.

"Charlie, are you OK? Food is coming. I'm sorry we have to keep you under wraps like this, but it's for your own protection. People have tried to kill you once already."

Charlie didn't believe a word she said: "What the hell is going on? What's with the handcuffs? Bull shit my own good! You're holding me prisoner."

"No. It's not like that. This is only temporary. We're going to release you soon. This is just a place to camp until all the furor dies down. Until it's the right moment for you to reappear. The whole world is waiting for you to resurface."

"Release me? Resurface? What happened at the pier? Why are you holding me?"

"Calm down. Calm down. We're just waiting for the moment of maximum media impact. One more day, that's all. One more day."

"Just let me go."

"Not yet."

Wrig Jones lit a cigarette.

"Put that out," M.D. barked at him, "you could burn this whole place down, you idiot."

Charlie almost laughed at that as the weasel scrambled to extinguish his smoke.

"Here's the deal, Charlie. It's a new kind of war we're fighting. A war to save the world not rule it. Now we've got their attention and you are the voice of the whole revolution. You can turn the tide Charlie. We're right and you can make them see that we're right."

She's insane, Charlie refreshed his certainty. *She's gone over to the dark side completely.* He had to pause momentarily to laugh at himself and his choice of movie metaphors inside his mind. *It's a new kind of war alright* he thought *and she's some kind of whacked out eco-terrorist.* Now he was even more convinced that he had to go along with them if he ever hoped to get out of this alive.

"Jeez M.D., what have you done? This is a disaster."

"Not at all, Charlie. It's a new beginning. We've sown total confusion out there. Their old world ruled by Big Oil and special influence and to hell with the cost to the environment is over, Charlie. You can point the finger right at the villains in this revolution, You Charlie. You."

"They'll crucify me."

"No way. You'll be a hero. He who speaks the truth. You're the one they trust. They all know that Congress can't be trusted anymore. You'll drive that home. We've already released a video to the press of your speech at the pier."

"Speaks the truth. I don't even know the truth. What happened back there at the pier? Why did you drug me? Why have you held me prisoner the last two days?"

"None of that is important now," she dismissed all of his questions with a grim face and a hand on his knee. "Now it's your turn to bring the whole country together against this corrupt government and their oil wars and their off-shore drilling and their rape of America. Here's what we're going to do. Here's what you're going to say."

For the next five minutes she laid it all out for him. He listened to it all and when she was done he realized he'd actually have to do it, say those things, that he'd have a gun at his back the whole time, that it was the only way he was going to get out of this alive.

With that she left him there to think about it, to stew over it.

She's gone, totally gone, was all he could think. He couldn't believe that he'd never seen it, her fanaticism, her insanity, her cold murderous hate.

Chapter Three

The Trail

*A*ll the time since they had lost that blip on the computer screen, Sid had been thinking. Like Butch Cassidy, that's what he did best. After talking the video over with Matt Morris, it all started coming together for him. All of his lawyerly instincts kicked in and he started building his case, putting together his arguments.

First he sat Alison down at his computer.

"You've got the OceanSave passwords. Go to their financials. We'll probably need to search at least the last year. Real estate transaction in the L.A. area, leases, rentals. They're holding him someplace up there. There's got to be a paper trail."

He produced a map of northwest L.A. that included all of Malibu. He took a protractor out of his desk, stabbed its point into the Kanan Road tunnel, stretched its pencil leg, and drew a large circle

"He's in there somewhere" he tapped the circle on the map with his forefinger. "Can you find me any property on the OceanSave books in that area?" He felt like Dustin Hoffman in *All the President's Men* setting out to "Follow the Money."

It took Alison almost an hour of clicking and scanning before she found something: "This is strange."

Sid, sitting behind her, stood up and bent over her shoulder to see the screen.

"There," Alison pointed, "the B-Bar-Q Horse Ranch off Topanga Canyon. OceanSave rented it about 8 months ago. What would they want with a horse ranch?"

"I don't know," Sid was thinking so fast that the thoughts were tumbling over each other. "Where is it?" they both turned to their map and Alison ran her fingers over the marked roads.

"Should be somewhere right in there," she pointed.

Sid took the pen and put another much smaller circle inside the one they had drawn before.

"Is that where they've got Charlie?" her voice was eager with re-newed hope.

"Maybe. We'll see. When Jerry gets back we'll talk about it." Sid picked up the map and studied it more closely. "This is near where my ex-wife lived before she died," he said, not really talking to Alison, more as if he was thinking out something, trying to decide.

I've got to get out of here before Jerry gets back. His approach didn't work the last time. He'll want to go in there with all guns blazing. Another assault like that could get Charlie killed. I've got to do this myself. He's my brother. All the time he was thinking he was folding the map. He pock-eted it and went into his bedroom. He was sort of like a man sleep-walking and it kind of creeped Alison out. He changed into jeans and a pair of hiking boots, took his opera glasses off of his bookcase and put them in his pocket with the map, then stopped and thought a second. He went to his nightstand and picked up his smaller cellphone. In the bathroom, using white athletic tape, he taped it to his abdomen just inside the top of his boxer shorts. When he came out of the bathroom, Alison was waiting for him, her face a clear question mark.

"I've got to get out of here for a little while. Clear my head. Think this all out. I'm going for a walk. I'll be back. My cell's on. Call me if you need me." And he left before she even thought of protesting.

But a minute later she knew he wasn't walking as she watched him pull out of the garage in his Jeep.

Chapter Four

The Hiker

Sid pulled the Jeep off into the brush on a side road and walked back to a trail entrance he knew well. He and Beth had hiked these hills many times in the old days before it all went bad.

As he hiked, he kept turning it all over in his mind. The bright California sunlight filtered down through the overhanging trees in thin shafts. *But what do they want Charlie for? Why that video?* Then he remembered what Matt Morris had said. *Why are they so intent on keeping him on ice? What are they waiting for?* As he walked through the sunlight and the shade, those questions kept nagging at him. Then it hit Sid right between the eyes. "Omigod, they're going to assassinate him on TV." He actually said it aloud to himself, then quickly looked around to see if anyone had heard, but only the brush and rocks were listening. *They're going to make him the movement's martyr. They're going to bring him out of three days in the underground and then sacrifice him right in front of the whole world on TV.* Sid took the Malibu map out of his pocket, consulted it, and kept climbing up into the hills.

Half an hour later Sid was standing on a hilltop peering through his opera glasses down on a ramshackle ranch that he was pretty sure was the one he wanted. He'd had little trouble finding it. He had hiked these canyons many times before. He was taking inventory. A broken down farmhouse, two rotting outbuildings—*probably old horse barns*, he suspected—and a corral with most of its rails in disrepair from neglect. In front of the house two cars and three motorcycles were parked. A really large woman and a skinny man of average height lounged in rocking chairs on the front porch smoking. *That's M.D.'s bass player*, Sid identified the man. The big woman just looked scary. *Those two, M.D., probably at least three more from the motorcycles*, Sid lowered the glasses and took stock. *At least six of them plus Charlie*, he guessed. The whole scene reminded him of his ex-wife's place a canyon away. He went down into a squat, picked up a couple of small rocks, threw them away, stood up, took a deep breath, and started down the hill.

As he descended, his hiking boots crunching on the loose shale of the path, he felt like the hiker in *The Petrified Forest* dropping in on Bogart and his armed thugs. *Damn, what was Bogart's character's name?* his mind wandered. *Duke, Duke Mantee. That's it. D.M. And she's M.D. That's cool,* he thought, laughing at himself and about how the mind loves to create coincidences. Halfway down the hill he saw movement on the front porch of the ranch house. The huge woman was up and rushing inside. By the time he reached the bottom of the hill and came abreast of the parked motorcycles, a whole line of people was pouring out of the front door and coming down the steps to meet him. Two of them had guns drawn. Sid stopped and faced them with the widest smile on his face that he could muster.

"M.D. Farrow. Fancy meeting you here. I'm looking for my brother."

Chapter Five

Together

M.D., all of them, stood there looking at him as if he was some kind of alien, an E.T. who had just dropped out of the sky into the middle of their armed camp.

After a long moment, with Sid smiling from ear to ear as if it was all just a big joke, M.D. asked the most obvious of questions: "What are you doing here?"

"Where's Charlie?"

"He's here and he's safe. So what?"

"Why I think you know full well, don't you?"

They were sparring like two verbal boxers waiting for an opening.

"What are you doing here?"

M.D. repeated herself, refusing to let down her guard.

"Hey, not only is Charlie my brother, but, as you know full well, I'm also his lawyer. He's going to need a lawyer after all that's happened, don't you think?"

M.D. Farrow just stood there with her hands on her hips glaring at him.

"Search him Maud," she finally said and the tall tattooed biker Amazon leapt to her command. She ran her hands all over him roughly and with little regard for discretion. She emptied all of his pockets, threw his wallet, his reading glasses, his opera glasses, his keys, his cell phone on the ground in front of M.D. She patted high up his inner thighs but she didn't go low on his abdomen and she didn't find his back-up cell phone.

"That's it," she cued M.D.

"OK, take him to his brother. Cuff them together. I've gotta think."

Almost thirty short steps, ushered roughly by the huge biker woman, and Sid was in the barn stall and finally face to face with Charlie.

"Sid, damn, did they grab you too?"

"Not really. I just decided to come looking for you."

"What? Did they catch you snooping around."

"Not really."

Tattoo lady had undone Charlie's cuffs and put one of them around the pole and on Sid's wrist. *Cuffed together like Sidney Poitier and Tony Curtis in The Defiant Ones*, Sid thought. When she was done she just left without a word but with a sour look of contempt.

"That moose is a real sweetheart, isn't she?" Sid tried to laugh the whole thing off.

"Are you crazy?" Charlie was in no mood for joking. "What the hell are you doing here? Are you out of your mind? These people are crazy and dangerous."

"I thought they were your people."

"Yeah, so did I."

"I guess that makes us both look pretty stupid, doesn't it?"

"Sid, why did you come here?"

"I thought you might need some legal advice. At least that's what I told them."

Charlie just shook his head.

"Yeah, they didn't buy that either," Sid responded wryly. For some reason he couldn't stop being a wise guy.

"What the hell is wrong with you? They could have shot you on the spot."

"I just decided you needed company."

"They say they're gonna let me go tomorrow. They just want me to hold one last press conference, at the head of the pier. She said they blew it up. Did they? They knocked me out before I could see what was going on."

"Oh yeah, they blew it up alright. It was like a full scale military attack on the rally and the pier—mortars, helicopters, rockets, explosives. Charlie, hundreds of people died."

"Oh my God!" Charlie just stared at him horrified.

"It was a massacre," Sid saw no reason to sugarcoat the bitter pill.

"Oh my God, what have I done?" Charlie's hands went to his head.

"Look, Charlie, you didn't do anything. They played us from the very beginning. They set us up and now they're setting you up to be their fall guy. Like Oswald."

"What do you mean?"

Now Sid had Charlie's full attention. The hand-wringing over both of their heedless naiveté in the face of M.D. Farrow's whole scam on the eco-movement was over. Both realized that it was time to face up to their situation and try to find some way out.

Sid had his hidden cell phone, but he hesitated to use it. He was afraid that as soon as he made the call Jerry would come storming in with as much firepower as he and his bounty hunter friends could muster. Then there was a good chance that he and Charlie would just get killed outright by M.D.'s people or get caught in the crossfire. So he decided to wait.

"I mean we have to find a way to come out of this not only alive but in the clear when it finally all shakes out. And eventually it will. But not if we're dead. Don't you see, you and me especially, but Alison and Jerry to a lesser degree, are the only ones who know what really happened, how this whole massacre took place."

"OK Einstein, what the hell do we do? In case you haven't noticed, the two of us are handcuffed to a pole in somebody's barn." Sid was glad to see that Charlie was getting his sense of humor back.

"Tell me what they said about this so-called press conference?"

"Man, I feel so stupid."

"I know. She took us all in. But that's over and done. First we've gotta get out of this alive and then we've got to set the record straight. And you're the only one who can do that."

"OK, that's fine, but how do I do it? You're the expert at proving somebody didn't do something. How do I prove I knew nothing about it? Is anyone going to believe that I was completely out of this loop?"

"There have been pictures in the papers of them knocking you out at the pier, taking you. Everybody knows they took you against your will. That's all in your favor."

"But this press conference. They want me to get up there and blame the government and some oil interests black ops when it was really us, Sid, us, my organization, OceanSave, that did the whole thing. They're gonna arrest me on the spot."

"I know. That might happen. Don't worry. If it does I'll take care of that. I'm your lawyer, aren't I? But that's not what I think is going to happen."

"What do you mean?"

Sid could see that Charlie was still too confused to have really put it all together yet.

"What exactly is the deal with this press conference?"

"M.D. and Jones laid it all out for me. My story is supposed to be that I was kidnapped by some nameless militia types, some paramilitary black ops team. They released me and I came to OceanSave. Then they want me to point the finger at the government, maybe the CIA, all bankrolled by the oil companies. I mean, Sid, it's so far out. They want me to say it was all some huge government conspiracy. Like the Kennedy assassination. She told me exactly what I had to say. She typed it all out on that laptop of hers. Look, I've got the statement right here."

"Yeah, but you see Charlie, it's not gonna happen that way at all. They're gonna kill you Charlie. They're not gonna let you get to a microphone. You're their Oswald. They're gonna assassinate you on national TV and sew even more confusion. You're their fall guy, their movement's martyr. It's actually all sort of brilliant in a crazy twisted way. The press will find the statement on your dead body. The message will get out and you'll never get the chance to blow the whistle on them."

They looked at each other in silence for a long, long moment. Sid knew that Charlie was trying to process it all, overcome his disbelief. Sid also knew that Charlie was trying to decide if Sid could possibly be right. Charlie had always been the up brother, the optimist, the sunshine surfer, while Sid had always been the realist, the pragmatist, the distrustful suspicious pessimistic brother. But Charlie knew he could trust him. He'd always been there to bail Charlie out, literally. Finally Charlie smiled: "OK Butch, but I gotta tell you one thing. I can't swim."

"Hell, the fall will probably kill us."

Chapter Six

M.D.'s Private War

About a half hour passed before M.D. Farrow, this time alone, came back into the barn.

"You've told him about the press conference, right?" She addressed Charlie, ignoring Sid.

But it was Sid who put his hand on Charlie's shoulder signaling him not to answer.

"Yes, he told me the whole script. Do you really think anyone is going to believe this?" Sid confronted her without hesitation. In doing it, this strange feeling of strength surged through him. He realized that he was doing what he did best, speaking for his client, standing up for an innocent man (*a somewhat different experience for me*, he thought wryly).

"He is the spokesman for OceanSave," she shot back. "They'll believe him. No one knows who was responsible. He's our voice. He'll have everyone looking at the faceless villains out there, the oil powers. He can convince all of America to oppose them once and for all."

"Terrific. So why did these faceless powers kidnap him and then let him go?"

"Easy answer. They kidnapped him to silence his voice. But he escaped. It will make him even more of a hero. Every talk show and news show and newspaper in America will want him. His message, our message, will spread like wildfire."

"Why didn't they just kill him?"

"What, and make him a martyr of the cause?"

"Didn't you give them enough martyrs out there on the beach and on the pier?" The two of them were throwing questions at each other like two boxers squaring off. Sid had to hand it to M.D. Farrow though. She had her script and she was sticking to it.

"And what's in it for Charlie, besides you setting him free, us free," and he held up the ridiculous handcuffs at her.

"He becomes the leader of a new revolution, the voice of all the people that the government and Big Oil have been screwing all these years." She turned to Charlie, who Sid had not yet allowed to say a word. "Isn't that what we set out to do Charlie? Isn't that what we've wanted from the start? For them to listen to our message."

"But we never talked about violence, about killing innocent people."

"Damn! Haven't you two been paying attention. It is all about oil. Katrina takes out most of New Orleans and what do those pricks do. They raise the price of oil. There are natural disasters everywhere but the price of oil just keeps going up. Hell, they create their own natural disasters. Their oil spill poisons half the Gulf and the shorelines of four states and what happens? The price of oil goes up again. Don't you see? Nobody gives a shit. Until now. Until the Pier Massacre. Charlie's going to brand it 'Oil Terrorism,' coin a whole new term. In Alaska, in Yosemite for god's sake, right here in Santa Monica Bay. Nobody was paying attention. Until now. NOW Charlie. And you can show them the way. Think about it. Do the right thing. They'll listen now."

She was like a firebrand, a hot coal that had suddenly flared up and blazed, then just as suddenly she was done. She was breathing in deeply. Her cheeks were slightly flushed. Without another word she backed out of that stall, turned on her heel and left the barn.

No question that her sudden eruption of emotion had caught Charlie's attention. He thought back on all the speeches he had made for OceanSave, all the protests he had led, all the times he had been arrested. No question that the possibilities in this one last speech had momentarily captured his imagination. Even Sid was impressed. The sheer heat of M.D. Farrow's fanaticism couldn't help but capture one's attention. But almost immediately his lawyerly skepticism kicked in and calmed him down. *How much did she really believe and how much of that was staged purely for Charlie's benefit?* he asked himself, and opted for the easy answer, half and half. Sid realized one thing though, the one thing that M.D. couldn't fake or hide. She needed Charlie. That's why they were going to bring him back and give him a bully pulpit. He was the face and voice of their movement and they needed him. *But what for? And how?* Those were the questions that nagged at Sid Castle's mind as M.D. Farrow stomped away from them.

"What bull shit!" Sid turned to Charlie who had fallen strangely quiet. "She's nuts. Fanatical crazy. She's using you Charlie." Sid, as he looked at his brother, felt he had to deflate M.D.'s influence. He was right.

"She means every word of it," Charlie actually defended her. "She's a true believer. That's one of the things that drew me to her and the movement in the first place."

"Charlie, she's insane."

"Yeah, I realize that now."

Sid wanted to get Charlie rethinking things, get his mind off of the powerful speech M.D. had just delivered. "What is her deal anyway? Where did all of this come from?"

"That's the funny thing," Charlie smiled. "She actually comes from an oil family. Her father worked for Enron."

"Enron? Yeah, I remember, that Texas oil company that went belly up. Insider trading. The executives and the accountants cooked the books so they could sell their stock."

"Yeah, Enron. Her father had a good job with them and was about a couple years from retiring. When Enron folded, he lost everything: his job, his pension, his insurance, his savings, everything. And then he killed himself. M.D. found him hanging in the garage."

"So it's not the environment, it's not really offshore drilling, it's just simple revenge that's made her hate Big Oil so much. So that's why she declared war on them."

"No, it's just not that simple Sid. She was already writing songs about the environment, developing her unique brand of C&W eco-rock. She was a prodigy. When her first album came out *Rolling Stone* said she was like the John Denver of the twenty-first century."

"Charlie, she's totally insane, off the deep end, and she's gonna take you down with her."

"But I've been with her all along. OceanSave was just a tiny store-front environmental lobbying group when M.D. took it over and started raising money, mostly with her music, benefit concerts, protest rallies. Then she brought me on board after my first book went wild."

"Look, Charlie, all that may be true, but I'm telling you..." Sid stopped, trying to marshal the right words to make his brother understand, "she's setting you up to be the fall guy or worse. She's a terrorist, Charlie, a mass murderer, and she wants you to give a speech blaming it all on someone else, on some faceless corporate or government conspiracy, or both. Oh Charlie, she's just using you."

Charlie didn't say anything for a long time. As they sat there in the silence and it began to get dark Sid rifled his memory for the arguments he needed to get Charlie out of this mess. One thing nagged at his mind, something that for some reason he always remembered every time he saw M.D. Farrow or her name came up. When they had been driving across the desert on that cross-country trip what seemed so long ago they had talked on the phone to M.D. in Washington. He remembered it was nighttime on the desert so it must have been the middle of the night in D.C., and M.D. told them that the CEO of Amerigas had been murdered. *They didn't even discover his body until the next morning,* Sid realized now, *and she already knew. She did it. She's murdered before.*

"She's a murderer, Charlie," when Sid finally spoke his voice was measured, under control, not asking at all but telling, decisive, doing what he did best, serving as his brother's lawyer. "She murdered the Amerigas CEO last year and now she's murdered all those people at the pier. And she's trying to drag you into it with her. Here's what we're going to do."

As the night closed in around them and moonlight began to filter in tiny shards through the chinks in the walls of the barn, Sid devised their whole strategy for the next day. It took hours and they talked it all out, tried to account for every possibility.

"We've got to go along with them until we see an opening," Sid argued most strenuously, "then we lower the boom when you get to the mike."

Only when they had thought through every possible scenario did Sid extract the hidden cell phone and call Jerry and Alison. He gave them explicit directions for the next morning.

Chapter Seven

Last Dance

M. D. let them clean up from their long night on the floor of the barn using a basin of water she carried in. She came in flanked by the towering woman with the tattoos who had frisked Sid so ineptly and another, smaller, woman also copiously tattooed. Their handcuffs were removed. They were given bottles of water and M.D. offered them gum before they were hustled into a large black SUV for the trip to the press conference.

Maud Gunn, for that's what they later learned was the Amazon's name, drove the SUV and M.D. sat in the front with her. Sid and Charlie were in the second seat. The other woman, visibly armed with a large hand gun tucked in her belt, sat behind them in the third seat.

Strange, Sid thought as they drove the Coast Highway through Malibu, *where's that little weaselly guy who's always with her smoking the cigarettes?* Wrig Jones was nowhere in evidence and Sid couldn't figure out what M.D. had done with him.

As for Charlie, the brunt of the playacting fell to him. As Sid had prepped him, it was up to him to make M.D. believe that he was really going to go through with this press conference, this publicity stunt. As they drove, he and M.D. went over one more time what Charlie was to say, all that Charlie was to feed the press to fuel their fantasies.

When they pulled to the curb on Ocean Boulevard just at the head of what was left of the Santa Monica Pier, they drove into a very Hollywood scene. In the corner of the park that looked directly down on the burnt-out pier, some competent little press agent had set up a podium on a postage stamp of a raised stage big enough for only one speaker. That clearly was to be Charlie's bully pulpit. Flanking that little stage were two security thugs in black turtlenecks who if they'd only had hoods on their heads could have passed for executioners. The surprising thing though, for nine o'clock in the morning, was the impressive size of the crowd that had turned out to see Charlie Castle make his return from the underworld. The first wave, marshaled tightly right in front of the podium, were the press out in full force.

Ah the press, Sid thought, *how nice of you to come! They're our witnesses*, Sid realized, *the whole world's witnesses. Or are they M.D.'s witnesses?* his lawyer's mind was racing. *They're just like those awful women knitting at the guillotine.*

As their hulking black SUV pulled up at the press conference, it wasn't at all as Sid had envisioned it as he lay awake all night planning for today, not at all as he had pictured it in his mind's eye as he gave Jerry and Alison their whispered stage directions over his secreted cell phone in the middle of the night. The crowd was much bigger, tighter, stretching all the way back down the length of the park, dwarfing the tiny stage and podium. And the large contingent of the press were all fully armed with what seemed like dozens of microphones, at least ten or twelve of them mounted right on the podium in a large bundle. TV cameras, both shoulder mounted and sitting on tripods, completely surrounded the podium. Boom mikes stretched out over the podium like gaunt birds of prey. And then, of course, prowling the fringes of the press gang were the ever-present paparazzi, their long-lensed cameras at the ready like the greedy beaks of circling vultures. Two police cars blocked the down ramp to the pier and other uniformed police officers were visible circulating through the crowd. The cops in the cars eyed the whole affair suspiciously, probably wondering with everyone else just what kind of a freak show Hollywood had come up with today. No, it wasn't how Sid had envisioned it at all, but it was what it was, and Sid knew that whatever happened he would have to deal with it.

Charlie turned to Sid, and, shrugging his two hands out in front of him palms up and breaking out in a huge grin, said "Showtime!"

Roy Schieder in All that Jazz, Sid caught it immediately.

M.D. got out and opened the side door, staring in on them like some dark angel of death.

Sid stepped out of the car first, but held his hand behind his back for Charlie to wait just a second. As soon as Charlie stepped out of the car, Alison, right on cue, burst out of the crowd, through the phalanx of cameramen and photographers, and ran straight to Charlie. One of the black-clad security thugs left his post by the podium and tried to cut her off but he wasn't quick enough. She darted past him and flung her arms around Charlie's neck in a passionate embrace.

Every photographer, every TV camera, every talking head with a microphone, greedily fed on this touching reunion scene between the media darling and his adoring wife.

They're eating it up, Sid thought, *good*. And he scanned the crowd for Jerry.

"It's OK. It's OK. She's my wife," Charlie waved off the security man as he turned away from the crowd and gave Alison another long passionate kiss for the cameras. It was a perfect diversion, exactly what Sid had ordered.

While that touching scene unfolded, Jerry emerged from the crowd and moved straight to the side of the podium. When the other black-clad security guard took a step to challenge him, Jerry immediately raised both hands in front of him in a placating gesture. "It's OK. I'm one of you. I'm her security. I'll stay out of your way. No problem." And he stationed himself right next to the podium in the space the other security guard had vacated.

Alison clung to Charlie as they walked the few short steps across the grass to the make-shift stage.

Sid walked on Charlie's right shoulder close enough that their elbows brushed as they moved. M.D. walked behind them, not happy at Alison's intrusion on her little choreographed scenario.

Jerry, facing the press line in front of the speaker's podium, scanned the crowd, watching faces, searching for anything out of the ordinary. Sid's words from the night before on the phone kept echoing in Jerry's mind: "They're gonna shoot him, Jerry. Before he ever says a word. They're gonna shoot him before he gets to that microphone."

As they got closer to the microphone, Alison broke out in another over-the-top display of affection, throwing her arms around Charlie's neck and kissing him hard on the mouth. When she did it, Sid stepped in front of them right behind Jerry.

The cameras ate it up again. For them this was better than reality TV, the best.

But Jerry never even glanced back at Alison's diversions. Like lasers his eyes were riveted on the crowd and he caught the aberration right away. In the front row of photographers, all kneeling on the grass in front of the podium, when all the cameras went up to catch the Alison-Charlie embrace, one camera went down to the ground, one photographer, skinny with a cigarette in his mouth, came up off his knees, his hand snaking out from under his shirt. Jerry caught the movement and knew instantly what it was. It was what Sid had told him to look for.

"He's got a gun, Sid! He's got a gun!"

For Sid, suddenly everything seemed to slow down. It was as if he knew exactly what to do, because he had replayed this scene over and over in his mind all through that long night of waiting. At the very first rise of Jerry's warning voice, Sid flung himself at his brother and Alison, leapt on the two of them arms outstretched as if he was trying to block a punt in a football game.

One shot boomed out, then another. Then everything went quiet. The fierce sounds of those shots were the last things Sid heard as he collapsed on top of Charlie and Alison on the ground.

Chapter Eight

Tackling Practice

*J*erry got to Wrig Jones, the shooter, just as he was raising his pistol for his second shot, hit him hard and square right in the chest, knocking him straight backward into the phalanx of the cameramen and sending his second shot firing harmlessly straight up in the air. He came down on top of the skinny little weasel and hit him once, hard, right in the middle of the face.

Everyone in the crowd was either hitting the ground or running for cover. The press, the cameramen and paparazzi, who had only moments before been ruthlessly elbowing their way to the forefront were now turning tale and stampeding to the rear, their cameras all but forgotten in their rush to save their skins.

Everyone in the crowd was running away except for the police with their guns drawn who were converging slowly out of the crowd and out from behind their cars parked at the top of the ramp. Jerry rolled off of the unconscious Wrig Jones, his hands raised high in the air, hoping against hope that one of those cops didn't panic, get trigger happy, and shoot him.

As this whole scene unfolded, as Jerry took out the shooter, as the police started to converge, M.D., clutching her laptop to her chest, started slowly backing away toward the waiting black SUV at the curb.

From the ground, Alison caught the movement of M.D. Farrow out of the corner of her eye. Extricating herself from Charlie and the dead weight of Sid, she scrambled to her feet and took off at a dead run toward her former boss.

"Stop you crazy bitch!" Alison heard herself screaming as she went airborne and tackled M.D. from behind a good five yards from the escape car. The laptop went flying off to the side as Alison and M.D. rolled in the grass scratching and tearing at each other.

Alison, the former volleyball player, was surprised at how strong the smaller woman was. As they rolled on the ground, Alison tried to get her in a headlock and roll over her, but M.D. easily extricated herself and tried to roll away. But Alison had the advantage of those long legs. She swung them hard at M.D.'s ankles as M.D. was trying to scramble to her feet and knocked the smaller woman's legs right out from under her. Once she got on top of M.D., straddled her, pinned her arms to the ground, the fight was over. She sat on the subdued M.D. Farrow and took a quick look around. Like her, Jerry was kneeling over a subdued body on the ground in front of the speaker's platform about ten feet away and also looking warily around. Behind her Charlie was kneeling on the ground, shouting something, waving his arms. In front of her the large black SUV that Charlie and Sid had arrived in suddenly coughed into ignition and pulled away.

"Wait. Wait. Stop." M.D. Farrow was screaming at the departing SUV as it pulled out into traffic and moved slowly down Ocean Boulevard. Alison straddled her and had to laugh at the woman's clear frustration. But she quickly realized that none of this was really funny. M.D. Farrow had planned and organized and carried out the terrorist murder of hundreds of people.

"My laptop. Where's my laptop? I need my laptop!" M.D. was screaming.

Alison couldn't stand the sound of M.D.'s mewling voice. The woman had tried to assassinate Charlie. Alison hauled off and punched her hard in the face twice until she shut up. *You monster, you ruthless monster* was all Alison could think of the woman she had worked so hard for at OceanSave. But M.D. Farrow hadn't just betrayed her; she had betrayed everyone in the movement, everyone who had embraced Earth Day, who had protested offshore drilling, who had thrilled to her songs about the ocean and the earth and the sky. Alison had never felt so betrayed and it felt really good to hand M.D. over to the police.

As the police were handcuffing M.D. Farrow and leading her to the squad car to take her away, Alison retrieved the laptop from the ground and delivered it to the arresting officers.

"All the evidence you'll ever need about all this," and Alison's arm swept the whole panorama of the burnt-out pier, "is in that laptop," and she gave M.D. Farrow a triumphant grin as the cops put her into the car.

Chapter Nine

Anesthetic Dreams

*T*he blurred image of the ferris wheel turning and pulsing and cartwheeling over the blue-green surface of the lowering clouds under a blazing sun pounding down on a stampeding crowd to sharp reports of exploding voices moving in tight white-coated circles wielding sharp knives and wearing ghostly masks under color bursts of laser light surrounded by the steady hum of bouncing machines hooked to pop-eyed monsters poking, poking, poking. Then, after how long he didn't know, all the cascading kaliedoscoping images started to settle down, sort themselves out, and all that was left was the darkened room and the green faces of the blipping machines and concerned eyes of the floating heads above looking down at him. It took him awhile but finally he was able to make them out, Charlie, Alison, Jerry, all looking down at him.

"Hi guys," he thought he said to them but he wasn't sure if they (or he) was real.

It made him feel good though, their heads all together like that, as if he'd done something right for a change and they were all there to celebrate with him. That feeling of wellbeing was too much to handle and he decided just to give them all a smile and go back to sleep.

Crazy dreams all populated with flashing lights and falling objects and floating heads and strange crinkling surfaces smoothing then cracking, expanding and contracting, crinkling like aluminum foil when you squeeze it or ball it up to throw away. Every once in a while the pulsing, crinkling dreams would stop and a dark shadow would pass over the dream world that he seemed suspended in, then the shadow would withdraw and the lights would start flashing again and always the ferris wheel in blues and reds and yellows and whites and greens turning and rolling and careening and falling and falling. All of these spinning, darting, shattering images were like that last scene in the

Crazy House from *The Lady from Shanghai* or the abstract sets in that early German horror movie whose title he could never remember or like in *Vertigo* when everything starts spinning. Everything breaking down into shards of reality, life spinning out of control, fragments of truth and trust slipping away. All those dreams like crazy movies pulsing all around him.

It took Sid Castle two days to wake up. He spent the better part of the first day in surgery. He lost a lot of blood and that's what the doctors attributed his lingering in a semi-coma to. At the press conference at the pier Sid had taken a bullet in the upper right side of his back in the fat of his shoulder blade. Luckily, or so the doctors told Charlie and Alison and Jerry when Sid finally came out of surgery, the bullet had missed his lung and had evidently hit a bone and lodged in the shoulder tissue which sort of smothered it. The doctors attributed this lucky ricochet to Sid's rather out-of-shape plumpness that served to cushion the blow and saved him from more severe damage if the bullet had broken up into fragments. It had taken them three and a half hours to remove the bullet, stop the bleeding, and sew him back together, but he had lost a great deal of blood and that is why it took him so long to wake up. Sid found out later, when he asked, that the anesthesia probably provided the hallucigenic dreams. When he described those dreams to Charlie later, he said: "You remember that time in high school when we dropped acid? It was like that. Not really fun."

In the days that followed in that hospital room as Sid recovered, Jerry never left his bedside. Charlie and Alison were periodically pulled away to give statements to the police, the FBI, every investigative entity that the Earth Day attack on the pier had drawn into its conspiratorial web. Sid started eating his third day in the hospital but nothing tasted good to him except the peaches (and it was hospital food after all). His curiosity didn't come back until the fourth day when he actually managed to stay awake for more than a half hour at a time. He knew he had been passing in and out of dozes ever since he woke up and he was getting sick of the crazy painkiller dreams made up of those color bursts and lightning slashes and splintering shards of reality and always that damn ferris wheel tumbling.

They were all there when his curiosity finally sparked and he started asking questions.

"What happened out there?"

"You called it, Sid," Jerry jumped on his question. "You called it all just like some kind of psychic or something."

"Called what?"

"When you called me on your cell phone in the middle of the night and told me and Alison what to do. You called it all."

"Sid, it happened just like you said it would," Charlie took his turn at trying to make Sid understand. "They wanted to shoot me before I ever got to the microphone, assassinate me on TV."

"She wanted to make a martyr out of you, her own martyr, OceanSave's martyr, like the Kennedys or Martin Luther King."

"Yes, but you had it all figured out," Alison had reached over the rail and taken his hand. "You saved us all Sid."

As they talked, it all started floating back into his drug-addled mind. He remembered how worried he had been because the press conference, the size of the crowd, all the cameras, hadn't been exactly how he had envisioned them in his mind. But Alison and Jerry had played their parts well, he remembered. It had all been like he was directing a movie, not real at all, just actors on a set, playing roles.

"But what happened? How did I get here? What's wrong with me?"

"You got shot, Sid. Don't you remember?" Charlie said with a strange catch in his throat.

"But weren't you the one who was supposed to get shot?"

They all laughed at that one and Sid laughed with them though he didn't really know why. So he just went back to sleep.

When Sid woke up the next time he found himself feeling curiouser and curiouser like the Cheshire cat in the *Alice in Wonderland* movie, all smile.

"Who shot me?" He felt like apologizing for asking such simple questions, but he didn't really remember it at all. It was all a blur after they got out of the car and started walking toward the crowd.

"Jones. M.D.'s little Headhunter."

"Some Headhunter," Sid joked. "Feels like he shot me in the back."

"Sid," Alison, deadly serious, pressed her hand around his wrist, "Sid, you jumped on Charlie and me and the bullet hit you in the back."

Sid just looked up at her in wonder for a long moment as if he was trying to sort it all out, sort himself out. *Damn, I actually did it,* he was actually thinking, pretty surprised at himself, but the thought made him break out in his old mischievous grin: "From the feel of it I'm not thinking that catching that bullet is the best thing that's happened to me lately, but it sure is a far better thing than all of us being dead."

And that cracked them all up.